Yeshua: The Gospel of St. Thomas

Yeshua:

THE

GOSPEL

OF

ST. THOMAS

A NOVEL BY

ALAN DECKER MCNARIE

PUSHCART

Distributed by W. W. Norton & Co
500 Fifth Ave., New York, NY 10110

Acknowledgments

A 2000-year-old mind is a place no author can enter alone. My own journey required ample assistance from both books and people.

The most obvious of my fellow travelers were those who read the manuscript in its formative stages. Prof. Speer Morgan gave a risky project its first official encouragement; Bill Henderson finally gave it a home. In between them, Isabelle Sowmu, Barbara Thiede, Adam Davis, Father J. Robert Barth, and Sandy MacDonald all played some of the roles of the novel better than I could myself; their comments and encouragement sharpened Yeshua's authority and generated new details.

Other people supplied real experiences. I owe particular thanks to Shmariel Gutman and the other workers on the 1981 archaeological dig at Gamla, where I learned the proper way to move large rocks; and to a gang of children in Old Delhi, who taught me the consequences of generosity in a desperate society.

Among some 90 books and articles surveyed in writing Yeshua, *a few deserve particular mention. J. N.*

Farquhar's "The Apostle Thomas in North India" and "The Apostle Thomas in South India" provided a demythologized itinerary for Teoma's later travels, while P. Thomas's Christians and Christianity in India and Pakistan recounted Indian traditions of the disciple's final years. Grollenburg's Penguin Shorter Atlas of the Bible saw heavy use in planning routes and scenarios; William S. McBirnie's well-researched but horribly written The Search for the Twelve Apostles passed on some traditions that fleshed out Yeshua's other disciples. Josephus contributed authentic 1st century biases, and an account of the Gamla massacre; Scheemelcher and the Higher Critics supplied ideas for sorting out what I was reading. Decades of vividly illustrated National Geographic articles proved invaluable in picturing Teoma's world. So, surprisingly, did a volume called Great People of the Bible and How They Lived, published by Reader's Digest Books.

I owe special debts to three people—two living and one long dead. Dr. Bonnie Devet supplied a sympathetic ear at the very beginning of the project. Susan Decker McNarie patiently shared my attention with an ancient Hebrew during our courtship, and later lost much sleep to the noise of husband and word processor battling in the next room. And finally, there is an anonymous 3rd- or 4th-Century Syrian Gnostic. His apocryphal Acts of St. Thomas is probably neither reliable history nor great theology. But it is full of drama, spectacle and a strange, wry humor; without the kernel of its narrative, Yeshua would probably never have grown.

Alan Decker McNarie

Yeshua: The Gospel of St. Thomas

I.

Anand has brought me a gift. It is a lacquered writing case, with reed pens and black ink—not the vile mixture of soot and boiled horse-urine that Tamil scribes prefer, but good ink-cakes such as I once used in Galilaia. He also brought pounded palm leaves for writing, and a frame for ruling lines, and more lamp-oil. He can't read this, but he is a good youth; my first words record his kindness.

My name is Yehuda. That is my oldest name, at least. I've also been called Teoma, which is Aramaic for "twin"—or Didymus, which is the same in Greek—for like my ancestor Ya'akob, who tricked his brother Esau out of their father's blessing, I also came into the world's light with my hand clutching on another's heel. The Romans, when they put my name as a slave on my masters' tax rolls, wrote of me as Judas Thomas; the Hinds and Tamils here in Mylapore call me Mar Toma, and other, less complimentary things.

I have also been called the Doubter. This was my strangest name, but perhaps the most true, for doubt shaped me as a stoked fire shapes the wood it burns: almost without notice at first, but building quietly to consume my brightest moment.

As I write this in my prison cell, that moment is long past. And the name has outlived its truth: I no longer doubt.

Instead, I remember.

The memories come clearly now. Outside this cell, when I was younger, the present made the past into pale shadows. But now, with my visitors few and work gone to other hands, there is little to keep me from memories. They come each day, and especially each night, in visions too hard-edged to be dreams: sometimes full of bright colors and subtle motions; sometimes hardly seen at all, only voices addressing each other with terrible clarity in the darkness. My master Yeshua often looked forward in time to prophesy; I think, in my last days, that he has given me the gift of looking back, for sometimes I even see memories of things that I was not there to see. I don't know if such experiences are true or false. I only know that I see them nightly, so they truly exist as visions, at least.

I've decided to write all these things down. I don't know if anyone will ever read them. I know of script only Aramaic, a little Hebrew, and this poor Greek; Aramaic is unknown here, and even Greek is little used. Even so, I will write. If you would understand how I no longer doubt, consider this act of writing.

This is what I remembered tonight:

Mid-morning: a hot, dirty desert morning, smeared with the dust that the pilgrim caravans have stirred up on the road from Yericho. Beyond the dirt-caked shoulder

10

of Yeshua's cloak, I see the first mud walls of the village of Bet Aniya, where Eleazar, who calls himself Lazaros, has his house. We've traveled all night, to avoid attention; we're too close to Yerushalayim and the Romans. But now Yeshua has forgotten all caution and led us on into the hot sunlight. I'm still trudging close after him, in an unaccustomed position of leadership; behind me, I hear Shimon the Rock swear softly, as he trips over one of his namesakes. Yeshua pauses and stares back at us; his eyes look wide and slightly feverish. Then he starts on, into the town.

We're too late. Even before we enter the square, we hear the professional mourners, chanting a psalm in long sobbing tones while the customary two flutes shriek and trill. There are only three singers; Lazaros was prosperous, but not rich. Three are enough, though. Yeshua sits down on the rim of the village well. He stares across the dusty square at the mourners in their carefully torn black robes, their faces white with hearth-ash. He stares at his lap. He weeps.

I sit, exhausted and cross, at his feet. I feel his hurt too strongly, and armor myself with spite. "Well, Master," I say, "You've led us here?"

"You didn't have to come with me," he says.

"You waited too long to come, yourself," I retort savagely. "They sent two messengers for you. Even if he weren't dead, what did he suffer, waiting for you? Don't tell me you haven't sinned."

The rabbi sobs once more, and then looks back at me from behind puffy eyelids. "I'm tired," he says.

"What good have you done, if you can't deal with *this*?" I ask, relentlessly.

11

Yeshua stares at the ground. Then he touches his hand to the skin above his beard, and stares at the dampness left on his fingers. His face goes almost blank.

"I can do something," he says, and starts toward the house.

He pauses a few feet from the threshold. "Where is Lazaros?" he asks the mourners.

"Are you his friend, or his relative, or do you have business?" asks the leader of the mourners. She takes advantage of the break to throw a handful of dust over herself, adroitly dodging most of it.

"I have to choose?" Yeshua asks.

Then Miryam appears at the door. She sees Yeshua, and runs to him, weeping. He leads her back into the house. We crowd in after them.

Inside, her sister Martha is directing a crew of relatives and neighbors, who are preparing unguents and grinding spices. The odors of frankincense and sweat mingle with the aromas of cooking from the little courtyard in back.

"Where's Lazaros?" Yeshua repeats.

"Where do you think?" says Martha, bitterly. "You're too late. He died three days ago."

"But we only heard he was sick three days ago!" protests Shimon the Rock. It is a lame lie. But Martha seizes on it eagerly.

"May those two messengers rot in the sixth depth of Sheol," she curses matter-of-factly. "Sarah, stir this cedar potion for a bit." She comes over and hugs Yeshua.

"He's not dead," the young healer tells her.

Martha stares up at him, and for a moment something flickers in her face. Then it dies. "Don't do that to me again," she says. "He's dead. I couldn't believe it. I felt his chest and his stomach three times. I held his face next to mine, and half-screamed for joy when I thought I felt his breath on my cheek. But it was my own breath, not his. Then I hugged both him and Miryam to me at once, but he was already so much colder than her. . . . " Then gruff, ugly, imperturbable Martha shudders, and her breath catches.

"He's not dead," Yeshua repeats. "He's just sleeping."

"Yes, he's sleeping. Until Judgment," Martha retorts. "In the meantime, what do *we* do?"

"Where is he?" Yeshua asks.

"In the tomb! Where do you think?" She rushes off to the near courtyard, and starts shouting orders to the cooks.

One of the older women stands up from her grinding and approaches Yeshua. "Please, Rabbi," she asks, "could you calm Martha down for us? She's been frantic ever since it happened. She wants to pack the body with spices again, when it's already decomposing. She's going to spread the Cave Fever, if she keeps reopening the tomb."

"Of course we'll reopen the tomb," says Yeshua. "How else can we get Lazaros out?" He starts out the door.

"Adonai preserve us!" exclaims the old woman. "Not the Rabbi, too!"

We crowd aside to let Yeshua through the door, and then follow him across the square. A couple of dozen relatives and neighbors trail after us. By the time we reach the necropolis, there is the usual crowd.

"He says the man's just sleeping! Haw!"

"He healed that sore on my mother's arm. Maybe. . . . "

"Who is he? What's going on?"

13

"Hurry up, Miryam!"

"Don't open that thing up again! It stinks!"

Yeshua sets his shoulder to the round disk of stone at the tomb's entrance. After a moment's hesitation, Shimon the Rock and Shimon the Zealot rush to help him.

The big stone shudders and rolls aside.

The stench rolls over us like a rock slide.

"It's too late, Master!" I plead. "Close it up!"

"Lazaros!" Yeshua bellows like a slave foreman. "Come out of there!"

"Lazaros!"

II.

A vision of the time in Galilaia, when I was still a slave:

"Alhouri, you stupid donkey!"

The stones are huge; they have to be. They will bear the weight of the entire wall, as well as the soil and trees behind it. And they must fit precisely; if they are close and tight, they will hold each other together. But if not, if a gap of two sheets of papyrus in thickness is left, then the treacherous soil of upland Galilaia will pull them a little further apart, and the weeds will do the rest.

The last stone of the line is slightly out of place—and tilted at that. Alhouri the Nabataean is stooped over it, in the wrong position himself, frantically trying to lift the thing. His partner Nuba is not helping. Nuba merely claws at the stone and screams. His foot and ankle are underneath it.

Alhouri manages to shift the stone sideways. Nuba screams more loudly. "You ass's pelvis!" I yell, and shove

15

Alhouri out of the way. This is the first time I have lifted a stone since I became a supervisor. Instead of stooping, I squat carefully, and feel the stone for a safe grip. I find one, and cry to empty my lungs.

"*Helli!*"

The stone rolls smoothly over—now completely out of line, I think sadly. Nuba shrieks one last time and then lurches away, gurgling. I follow him, and get Alhouri to hold him down while I examine the foot.

Nuba is a dead man. Perhaps he knows it, for he faints. The foot is smashed. Three small bones stick out through the skin; bits of soil cling to them. A demon almost certainly will enter, and rot the flesh up Nuba's leg to his heart. His only hope is if we take him to my master's barber, and have the entire foot cut away at the ankle, and the stump singed with fire. And of what use will he be to my master, then? I don't know what will be done with him; this is the first such case I have dealt with here. But I do know that, as the overseer, I will be whipped.

The workmen have gathered around, muttering. If I were a halfway decent overseer, they wouldn't behave this way; a whole wall would fall, and the ones not under it would still stay at their tasks for fear of me. But I'm too absent-minded, too afraid to use the whip. And I'm a slave, too. A foreman should be free, to have his workers' respect.

"Alhouri, give me your headdress," I order. "And Alexandros, go find Yoav the Barber." I wrap the head-scarf, redolent of stale olive oil, around Nuba's foot, and say a small prayer to keep the scarf free of demons. The scarf may have been a good choice: it's no dirtier than anything

16

else here, and its oily fabric will hold the blood back better than a dry cloth might. The pain of my wrapping, though, draws Nuba back from his dreams. He shrieks again. Another workman grabs his arms to keep him from striking or biting. Still, I receive a knee in the face before the job is done.

"Sir!" It's Alexandros again.

"You're back already?"

"I didn't have to go back all the way. I met a runner. The master wants you at the house, right away."

"Yoel!" I shout. "You're responsible. Put the men back to work. And oh, Alhouri, you and Themba find an old robe, one of the ones we've been carrying rocks with, and snake a sling between two pry poles. Carry Nuba back to the house, as soon as permission comes."

I stay long enough to see that they've at least started to do what they were told. Then I start toward the house, and take Alexandros with me to bear messages. "How did he find out so fast?" I ask him.

"Find out what? Who found out?"

"*Him.* Our owner. About Nuba."

"I don't think he has."

"Did the runner tell you anything?"

"Yes. It was Aristides. He said there was a holy man come to visit."

"A scribe?"

"No. A rabbi, a healer."

It takes a moment for this to sink in. Then I break into a fast jog.

"Did he bring his herbs?" I pant to Alexandros.

"I don't know," the boy says, between gasps. He is still winded from his first run.

17

"But this is backwards!" I explode. "If the master didn't know there was an accident, why would he send for me?"

"Aristides says he looks like you. The healer does, that is."

Something inside my chest seems to twist suddenly. I stop in my tracks. Then I start off again, at a run.

My master's house is on a hillside overlooking a village near Sepphoris. It is a sprawling, tile-roofed, brick-and-plaster building, designed in the Roman style: a big square around a small central courtyard. On the road before the front gate, a crowd has gathered: the curious and those who prey on them, mostly, but also others on more pressing business: cripples and paralytics, a demoniac child tied to his parents' wrists, a white-eyed blind man, a woman with no eyes at all. Amazingly, these beggars aren't circling on the fringes of the crowd; they've jammed themselves into a knot just outside the gate. And except for an occasional hand stuck out from habit, they aren't plying their own trade.

One of the houseboys meets me at the door. "Go wash up," he says. "They're in the atrium."

"But . . . " I start to say that there's no time, that I must see the healer—then I realize the futility of *that* approach. The beggars, meanwhile, have closed in like a wall behind me.

"Please go find Yoav the barber," I tell the houseboy. "Make certain he knows that there's a crushed foot down at the end of the new terrace. Say to him that he should sharpen his knives. Is this holy man a good healer?"

18

"I don't know," says the boy. "But he looks enough like you to be your brother."

My heart is thudding—from the excitement over Nuba, from the jog here, I tell myself. I wash myself at the kitchen water-jar, then go to my quarters and get out the good woolen tunic that Archimedes, my first foreman, had given to me when I was sold by my first master. I pull the tunic on over my workman's kilt, and then go to the atrium.

Alexandros meets me at the entrance. His eyes sparkle under the beads of water in his eyebrows.

"The barber is stropping his knives," he says. "But we won't need him."

"Did Nuba die?" I ask.

"No. But it's a very good healer. Yeshua bar Yosef, of Kafer Nahum."

"You've heard of him?"

"You haven't?"

The master is in the atrium, speaking with a young Hebrew man. They look up as I enter.

"Ah. This is the workman I told you about," says my master. The visitor is a rather plain fellow, with high, heavy cheekbones and thick eyebrows, a wide mouth, and large, deep-socketed eyes. His hair, worn long like a Nazirite's, is a deep red-brown. In short, he might have been my twin brother.

But he isn't. My brother's hair had been black.

"Doesn't he look like you, Rabbi?" gushes my master, with his usual false inanity.

"A little," says Yeshua, politely. But he holds his hands stiffly clasped, as if not quite at ease.

19

Chew bitter herbs quickly, I think. "Master," I say, with the proper groveling bow, "I must report something unfortunate. One of your slaves has been hurt." Without meeting his eyes, I watch him with all my senses.

But Alexandros is making a scene. Instead of bowing to our owner, he has bowed to the healer.

Yeshua saves us both. "Who's the second young man?" he says quickly.

"Another slave," our master says, looking poison at both of us. "His name's Alexandros—Hellenist family."

"He seems a respectful enough Jew, himself," says Yeshua, mildly. My master forces a polite smile.

"Master," I repeat, doggedly, "I understand your honored guest is a wise healer. Perhaps. . . . "

My owner stops me with a glance. But the healer suddenly bends, and tears a small piece of cloth from the ragged edge of his tunic. He spits on the cloth, then dips it in the lowest basin of the atrium fountain.

"Alexandros." The healer motions to the boy. Alexandros gets up shakily; his eyes are wide in their sockets.

Yeshua hands him the bit of cloth. "Go put this on the man's foot," he says.

"Yes, Rabbi," the boy says, and rushes off. The master and I both frown: the master, because the boy hadn't asked him leave to go, and myself, because I'm beginning to suspect the healing methods of this man, who is too young to be a real rabbi, anyway.

But my owner's frown holds something else—a sudden concentration. Watching him with the furtive glances that a slave must master, I note his own eye rapidly traveling up and down the young healer's body, as if taking a mental measurement. Then my owner smiles. "Rabbi," he says, in his most gracious voice. "I'm worried about these crowds. Do they ever leave you in peace?"

The healer chuckles—a nervous, high tenor sound. He cuts it off quickly. "Not when they know who I am," he says. "But if I need to sleep, I can always go to a village where I haven't been before."

It's my master's turn to chuckle. I sense one of his improvised schemes developing. "I think, Rabbi, that you'll soon run out of villages," he says. "Maybe I can give you a better solution. Yoachim!" My master's eunuch instantly appears—he always waits just out of sight and within earshot—and the master gives him a curt set of instructions in their native Edomite tongue. My owner, like old King Herod, only pretends to be a Jew.

"There are a couple of hundred people out there now," he observes, after Yoachim has gone. "If you leave by the front gate, there's liable to be a riot."

"Aren't they more likely to riot, if I don't go out?" the young healer asks, smiling tentatively.

"Oh, I think I can get them to behave themselves," says my master. "Ah, Yoahchim!"

Yoachim has reappeared. Hung over his massive pale arm are thick folds of cloth, banded purple and white.

"Good! Your new robes. I had them made for myself, as a spare," the master gushes. "The mantle is the finest Tyrian lamb's wool, murex-dyed. The crowd is waiting at the front gate for a young man in ragged cloth, not someone in a fresh white tunic and fine coat."

The young rabbi keeps up his act, just as I'd expected him to. "My *ephod* isn't as ragged as those beggars' clothes," he says altruistically.

21

"Of course not," retorts the master. "They're beggars. Do you think they'd get one copper coin out of anyone if they didn't look shabby? No, you take the clothes. You can leave your old tunic behind for the beggars; they'll find it more useful. I'll give them some other clothes, as well." He hastily gathers the cloak off Yoachim's arm and presents it, with both hands, to Yeshua.

The young charlatan eyes it thoughtfully. Then he smiles. "Thank you," he says.

Still hanging from Yoachim's arm, and exposed now by the removal of the cloak, is the white tunic. "And a new *ephod*, too," my master chuckles, handing it to Yeshua. "Now, just to be sure, when you leave in the morning, you can slip out the back gate if you wish. I'll send your new servant," he adds, eyeing me sweetly, "out the front."

"My new servant?" repeats Yeshua, looking as stunned as I do.

"Of course. Yehuda here is an utter failure as a master builder," the master says, with a forgiving smile. "But surely this remarkable resemblance is a sign from Adonai. The robes will perhaps fool the crowd outside, tomorrow morning. After that, though, Yehuda will be a more effective diversion. I'm sure he'll be worth much more to you than he is to me."

Yeshua stares at him for a moment, considering. "Thank you very much," he says, finally. "You're a very generous man. However, I think I should leave this afternoon, instead of tomorrow morning."

"Then surely you'll at least stay for supper, and honor us with a blessing?" the master protests.

"No need," Yeshua replies, with a gracious smile. "Your generous acts are a far better blessing than my lips could speak."

"Very well," says the master, a bit sullenly. "If you'd like to change to your new garments, Yoachim will show you to a room. Just leave your old tunic on the floor."

"Thank you," the young rabbi says, and follows the smiling servant into the guest quarters. I am still standing, stunned. I'd expected punishment—but to be made the handservant to a wandering quack? I'm not a healer, or even a good Jew, but even I know that spittle is unclean and apt to attract demons. And I have just washed Nuba's blood from my hands, have felt the crushed bones grating as I bound up the wound. For a moment after that stone fell, the whole accident had seemed unreal— as if anything that could happen so suddenly could surely be undone as quickly. But that wound had grown more terribly real with each passing moment; beside the vision of such mangled flesh, now, the rabbi's little piece of damp cloth is so horribly, obviously ridiculous. . . .

I consider, briefly, trying to persuade Yeshua to take his old tunic along, spoiling my master's—my former master's—intended profit. Instead, I say, "I'll go get my things."

"You don't have things. I have things," my former master growls. "I'll need clothing and tools for my new foreman."

Then he goes to the white Grecian marble fountain, and dangles his fingers in it, ignoring me. Behind my slave's mask, I seethe. How can this man coldly seize on the worth of a used robe one moment, and give away a skilled slave the next? Does he value me that little?

23

The thin stream of water runs over my master's hairy white hand, into the lower basin that is already turning green with algae again. Last month, I supervised the laying of new lead pipes from Italy. But the little hillside spring that feeds the fountain still produces only a trickle.

Another failure. . . .

Yeshua re-emerges, wearing the new tunic and dangling the cloak over his arm. He has left his old tunic behind.

"Well," says my old master to my new, "If you're sure you won't stay longer, I'll be glad to show you the way to the back gate, myself."

Why should I care what my owner—my *former* owner, thinks of me? I hate him anyway.

"That's all right," responds Yeshua. "I think I'll go out the front." Then he turns to me. "Here, *teoma*," he says, handing me the cloak. "You should wear this. I'd hate to get it torn."

"Yes, master," I reply, trying to sound sardonic. But my voice cracks, and spoils the effect.

III.

This day should have been a productive one. My usual guard should have come by and chatted, while he cleaned away my meal and my slop. He has given me a jar to use, and usually empties it each day; I've heard that most prisoners must use a corner. Anand or Gund should have visited me, with messages from the brethren and with fresh cotton paper or prepared leaves for writing. But there was a different jailor today, who must have heard the stories about what an evil wizard I am; he wouldn't even look directly at me. And the others didn't come; I don't know why. Perhaps they won't come again. There's always that uncertainty. To a man in a small space, everything becomes significant: tiny changes become portents of life and death. They would become torture, if I let them.

I have a few leaves left. I will write down what came back to me last night:

We call the place "Eden." It is unlike the larger falls upstream, where most of the boys go to swim. That is a big gloomy place, with high basalt walls and deep cold water, where the sun only shines at noon. But Eden is a chuckly clear pool, rimmed with willows and pink rhododendrons, and only hip-deep at its center. It is fed by a waterfall that is little more than a white chute, lined with green pads of fleshy algae. You can sit at the top of the chute and stay put, held there by your own weight— but if you lie down, the water will heave with all its strength, and just manage to carry you, bumping and sliding, down to the pool. It is a beautiful, friendly, quiet place, well protected by the screens of willows and the thistly slopes around it. So of course, when we are in Eden, we do not wear clothes.

But on this particular day, the cascade's chuckle has a mocking tone to it. And the rhododendrons, heavy with blooms, are so mockingly beautiful I hate them.

"What do you mean? How would you know?" I challenge my brother.

"Because I got home from the yeshiva early. I heard them talking."

"What did you do to make the old man send you home early?"

My brother shifts uncomfortably. I notice, for the first time, the cane stripes across his knuckles. "Nothing too bad, anyway," he says. "When I got home, I sneaked in on the roof, and heard Mother talking to the tax-collector—you know, that Greek-lover, Philetos. He told her he was sure they could make a good bargain down in Kafer Nahum."

"How do you know it's me they're talking about?"

"Shemuel's too young, and so are the girls. It has to be you."

26

"What about *you*?"

He smiles smugly. "I'm too sickly. Besides, I'm the first-born. I'm dedicated to Adonai."

"I know," I remark bitterly. For the first time, I realize clearly why I resent my brother. . . . I sit in the cold water that should have been invigorating, and feel its chill.

"Look, they have to," says my brother. "Father still hasn't recovered, but the tax people don't care. I just thought I should let you know." He stands up suddenly, and pulls on his tunic. "Hurry up. We've got to help Amoz with those sheep, or he'll tell on us."

He starts up the slope. I stand up slowly, and ponder. Slavery. Surely they wouldn't. One of my brother's bizarre jokes. . . . I could run away—sneak in on the roof, get my things, and slip out again before the gate closed for the night. And then. . . join the Zealots in the hills? Where in the hills? Join a caravan to Parthia or Syria, perhaps. . . .

What would caravaneers do with an eleven-year-old boy, besides sell him to the Parthians?

I stand knee-deep in the cold water, and watch the afternoon shadows slip up the eastern side of the ravine, until the black stone cliffs of Gamla stand bathing in the glow of a sun that I can no longer see. Then I shrug on my tunic, and start up the cliff toward our house.

IV.

How do you deal with hate? The way the Romans do, building it into walls with fear and brave words, with sword and *pax* and *aequalitas*? Do you subvert it the way the Greeks do, hiding it too deep to stink, growing art and culture from it, until they swallow up the thing you hate, and even your enemies speak Greek? Or do you burn it, as the Zealots do, feeding it arguments and families and Romans, until it blazes out and burns you up, too?

This last, I think, is easiest. Pure hate is very like a fire: a blind, destructive, self-centered thing. It draws your eyes and makes you want to feed it, even as your skin reddens with its presence. *The wrath of Adonai burns against them.* What a silly, trite, horribly apt phrase.

In those first few months as a slave, I nurtured hate carefully; it made wonderful illusions of my own self-importance, of myself at the center of all the unjust forces of the world. I preferred hate to sleep, and lay awake with visions of my heroic vengeances on my father and mother

28

who sold me, and on my master who bought me, and the Sadducees and rich Temple priests in Yerushalayim who had not sent poor Levites such as my father their shares of the Temple revenues, and on the Romans and their tax-gatherers who had taken what little my family had. Like the *Meshiha,* the savior-to-be of our people's prophecies, I would begin alone, unknown, not understood at first. . . . When our grape-picking foreman would beat me the next day for doing something stupid in my fatigue, I would simply heap that little injustice into my hidden fire with all the others, and my face and hands would glow with new energy.

I'd been a slave for ten months when I met Archimedes. It was olive-picking season, by then. My fore-man had just given me a beating again, for staring into space instead of picking up the olives that the older men had knocked down. A vision of that day:

"Get up," a voice says.

I mistake it for my master's voice, and don't even open my eyes. "Finish me. I don't care," I try to say bravely, but the pain in my back and side changes my voice into a mumbled sob.

"You care," says the voice. A sandaled toe prods me in the buttocks, piercing my pain-stupor. "Sit up, at least."

It isn't the foreman's voice. It has the same pitch and resonance, but with a different accent. . . . I sit up. Pain stabs up my right side. I squeal at the shock of it, and collapse on my side, which sends out another shock of pain, which lays me out on my back again.

"Shimeah!" The stranger bellows out my foreman's name.

Shimeah starts trotting up the hillside.

"What did you do?" the stranger asks, squatting beside me as he waits for the foreman.

"I don't know," I tell him. "I didn't pick fast enough."

My persecutor arrives, panting. "Shimeah, you damned idiot," the stranger growls, "don't you know how to use a whip? You've broken his ribs."

The big foreman actually cringes. But his words are brave. "This little swatch of camel's spit," he begins, "argues with every order I give him. I'm sick of his arguing."

"Jews argue a lot," says the stranger, and stares Shimeah the Jew into a small dung-ball. "Come to my house tonight," he adds, finally, "and I'll show you how to *properly* beat a Jew."

"Yes, sir," says Shimeah, looking like an angry dog who knows better than to growl.

"And in the meantime, get two workers and a spare robe over here. Use those olive-beating poles to make a litter. Take the boy to my wife."

"Yes, sir."

Shimeah begins barking orders, and the stranger starts down the hill. I clench my teeth, and scramble to my feet, and try to take a couple of steps, but Shimeah gives me a gentle tap on the ribs that buckles me over. "The overseer said to take the litter," he says. "No more arguing."

When the litter is ready, I am rolled onto it like a big stone to be removed from a field, and two teen-aged slaves are assigned to carry me, none too gently, to the house. "Stupid whiner," says the one in the rear, as he picks the litter up with a jerk. "So now you can lie around, eh, Yehuda? Let's go, Yoav. If we hurry, we can stop for a drink before we go back."

Every jolt of the litter is a fresh agony. I gasp and clench my teeth and make little squeaks of pain, and feel the wet tears dribbling abstractedly down my cheeks, and then I pass out.

I awake inside a house. It is a small house, but clean and well-furnished, its walls and ceiling made cheery by whitewashed plaster. A lamp, in the niche above my sleeping mat, burns cheap scented oil. The light of it is blocked suddenly, as a plump woman bends over me, uncomfortably close. Her odor overpowers the sandalwood fragrance of the lamp; she smells of olive oil and pork and strong herbs.

Then I realize that my tunic has been pulled up to my shoulders. I gasp and try to yank it down, then gasp again at the pain of the sudden movement.

She grabs my wrists. "Stop that," she says. "I'm putting on a poultice. You stupid Jews and your clothes. How do you treat a body, when you can't *see* it?" Her accent is thicker than the man's had been. She is obviously Greek.

"A man's body is the sacred temple of Adonai," I declare.

"So how do you fix it up, if you don't let the carpenters in?" She retorts. I look thorns and hemlock at her, but I leave my tunic up while she applies her herbs.

Her name is Hermione, she says, chattering as she works. She's also a slave. The master gave her to Archimedes years ago, but didn't free her when he freed Archimedes. She's borne the freeman two sons, both dead now—one by accident, one of disease. She is afraid that Archimedes will leave her and marry a freewoman, now that they have no children left. She tells me all this and too much else, while I lie examining my pain. It grows

31

and shrinks with each breath; spreads clear across my chest and pulls back into a fist-sized knot. The weals on my back stick to the straw sleeping mat and pull away as I breathe. She asks me about my family.

"They're all dead," I tell her.

After a while, I pretend to drift off to sleep, so that Hermione will be quiet. A warm numbness begins to seep out of the poultice; it doesn't destroy the pain, but spreads over it like a soft thick blanket. After a while, sleep is no longer a pretense. . . .

I jerk at the sound of a lash striking flesh. Pain sears up my right side. I swallow and choke to keep from crying out, and find myself on my mat in Hermione's house. Dusk-light forms a long faint block on the floor by the doorway. The pain had come from my own sudden motion, I realize. The lash cracks again, outside the doorway. Archimedes must be teaching Shimeah his lesson.

When Archimedes comes in, Hermione has a supper of bread, fish, and olives already set out for him. There is also a pomegranate, which they share, picking the fresh-blood-colored seeds out for each other. I pretend to sleep, as he complains about everything that has happened during the day. His Greek is not quite the Greek of Palestine; the angry, strange-sounding words wash half-noticed across me and my pain.

"This is too much for one man to do," Hermione clucks sympathetically. Oddly, she speaks in Aramaic. "When is he going to buy you a scribe?"

"He wouldn't pay enough money for a good one," grumbles Archimedes, matching her language. "And if he did, he'd probably just keep me until the new slave knew the routine, and then kick *me* out."

"But you're an architect!" she objects. "He's just misusing you, making you do all this accounting work." She gives a little calculated pause, and just as he is about to say something, she breaks in again. "Well, if you're afraid of his buying a scribe, maybe you should train one yourself. Then you could just teach him enough to help, not enough to replace you."

"Hmm. . . . " He scratches his hairy stomach thoughtfully. I realize, now, that Hermione has been talking Aramaic to be sure *I* understood. I shift a little and pretend to moan in my sleep.

"How's the Hebrew boy?" says Archimedes.

"He'll get better." She sighs. "But it will be weeks before he'll be able to lift anything."

"He wasn't much good as a field hand, anyway," says Archimedes. "Too smart and jumpy. He got beaten for arguing too much." He lets her pop another pomegranate seed in his mouth, and sucks the pulp off it. "Well, make up a better pallet for him. If he's going to lie around anyway, we might as well see what he can learn."

So I became an apprentice scribe and architect, for the convenience of a woman slave. But I didn't help Hermione much. She never got me to eat her pork, and after I began walking, she never saw my nakedness again, although she paraded around the house in her bare breasts constantly.

Three harvests later, a demon began to grow in her womb, where none of her herbs could exorcise it. She died shrieking the next winter. By that time, I had become a good apprentice, but I never became her son.

I added her death, though, to my list of quarrels with Adonai.

V.

A vision of the events in Bet Aniya:

"But what happened, happened!" repeats Yohan.

Yeshua is normally a strong man, and a good drinker: wine makes his cheeks rosy, but seems to affect his brain hardly at all. Still, the recent days would have been a strain on any man, and wine on this day has flowed more richly than usual. Yeshua, therefore, has retired early. He is sleeping in the house with Lazaros' family. But with all the relatives gathered for the holiday and the mourning, there is little room left inside for others. So Shimon the Rock has decided to sleep in the courtyard in back, and several of us, including Yohan and myself, have joined him. The family has allowed us to build a small dung-fire, as it is a cool night.

Of all Yeshua's followers, no two could present a greater contrast than Shimon and Yohan. Yohan is among the youngest of us: a skinny mystic who loves to worry at ideas until he's torn off their clothes, poked at their naked meanings, and then redressed them to suit his fancy. Shimon, the big, genial fisherman, has never known quite how to handle him. I had anticipated an interesting night.

For a while, though, it had looked as if we were simply doomed to drowse off. We'd lain around the smoky little fire, silently passing a jar of wine laced with spices and myrrh left from Martha's funeral preparations—each man losing his mind in fumes of the wine and the tremors of the small flame, each afraid to begin thinking. Then Yohan had started it, with his exclamation. This is the fourth time he's repeated it. I'm already sick of it.

"He might have been in a swoon," I interject. "The cold air and the noise may have revived him."

"Then why didn't he come out immediately? Why didn't he cry out, or something? Why did he wait until Yeshua called him, and then just walk out as if nothing had happened?" argues Yohan, his voice rising.

"And how do you explain that stench?" interjects Nathan'el.

"*I* don't think he looked as if nothing had happened," comments Andreas. "Did you see his face?"

"I think he looked guilty," adds Nathan'el, "as if he'd been caught with a girl." He smirks at the idea, and someone titters, but the sound dies quickly.

"He was dead," states Yohan, and the flatness of his voice tells us not to argue that point any further. "Do you realize what this *means*?"

"No," says Shimon the Rock. "You're going to tell us?"

"Immortality!" Yohan beams. "No more disease. No more death. He'll teach us, and then we can teach others. We'll make sure the healers make no more mistakes!"

I expect the Rock to make some retort, or else to join in with one of his unpredictable bursts of enthusiasm. But he simply stares back into the fire. "Maybe," I fill the void, "but I think the Rabbi's been *trying* to teach us. We just don't seem to have learned very well."

"We'll learn!"

But the Rock has had a rare, uncomfortable thought. "If he could revive Lazaros, why didn't he revive his cousin the Baptist?" he suddenly asks the fire.

I shudder inwardly. "Perhaps it's better Johan the Baptist stays dead."

Nathan'el catches part of my thought, and is boggled by it. "Imagine the Baptist's head crying out against Herodias from that jar she keeps it in! It would bring down Herod Antipas in a day!"

"Imagine what it would be like to be inside that head," I point out.

"If we can bring the dead to life, then surely we can put bodies and heads back together, as well," snorts our Yohan. "And put flesh on bones. If we can raise Lazaros, why not Abraham and Yosef and Moshe? The Judgement is here for certain!"

"Not if Herod can prevent it," I remark. "How many dead do you think he'll allow raised to accuse him?"

"What can he do?" smirks Yohan. "Kill them again?"

Nathan'el answers him with something. But I lose track of the conversation. I'm thinking of the hole that Yeshua has torn in reality, if he has really done what he seems to have done. The physicians—will they appreciate all our healed patients? And the landowners—how will they take their losses, if a barrel of well-water is worth a skin of wine, and a handful of wheat flour can feed a thousand? What can money be worth, under such circumstances? What will tax-gatherers and bankers do, if little bits of metal no longer give them any power? And soldiers? And court politicians?

I think of Archimedes. "I can count," he once told me. "That's my life. That's my armor. I'm worthless, except I know how many jars of oil are in the master's warehouse here, and how much that merchant in Tiberias owes him. So long as I can count, I know that I may get beaten across the shoulders, but no one is going to hit me in the head. But more than that, it's the counting, the silly job, that keeps my head filled up. So long as I've got one jar of olive oil to put after another in my brain, I don't have to look at Eternity."

Now Archimedes may have to look at Eternity, if he is still alive—perhaps even if he isn't alive, depending on whether or not Adonai will allow us to raise Greeks. Archimedes, though, might understand what he would gain in return for his job. How many other people have given their whole lives to one trivial little task, to some small niche of power or security? How many will snap like dry tinder, if that niche is destroyed?

How many will see only the threat, and not the promise?

"But that's just it!" Yohan is saying. "We're immortal already! How can we die? Yeshua. . ."—he stops to cough, as the smoke from the fire drifts across his face. ". . .Yeshua will just raise us again! The Kingdom's already here!"

Shimon the Rock picks up an old piece of a clay jar, and wordlessly uses it to shovel a little more dried sheep-dung into the fire; he doesn't want to touch even dried dung with his hands, when no one is sure that we won't be advancing to the Temple tomorrow. I re-enter the fray. "Suppose this isn't a fluke. And suppose that this has nothing to do with what the Scribes say, about the soul staying near the body for the first three days; suppose Yeshua can raise anyone he wants, and he can teach us to do the same. Abraham, we can do. Everyone knows about Abraham. Your grandfather, we can do. And the tribe of Yehuda, who have all their records and genealogies. But what about your Great Aunt I-Forget-Her-Name, who died childless, and whom nobody ever thinks of? What about the Ten Lost Tribes?"

"Maybe they stay lost." Yohan shrugs. "But *we* don't. We're Yeshua's own men. We'll never be forgotten!"

"Yes, we will," I tell him. " 'Never' is too long a word. A thousand years, two, three. . . . Eventually, you're going to be on the road somewhere, having just said good-bye to friends, and not knowing anyone in the next town, and something will happen, and no one will think to raise you. All that this ensures is that sooner or later, we'll all die alone."

"And what if we can't learn?" adds Shimon suddenly. He leans back from the fire, staring through the after-images of flame that must still cling to his eyes, looking through them at the night beyond. A clod of dung, not quite dry at the center, breaks open with a muffled *poff!*, shooting up a little cloud of sparks that spiral like angels in the dark air, and wink out one by one.

"What if we can't learn in time?" says Shimon the Rock. "What if something happens to Yeshua first?"

VI.

"It's not the name I was born with," says Archimedes.

In front of us the slaves of the Romans sprawl, motionless, taking advantage of the coolness of the freshly scraped earth. Sweat gleams in beads and rivulets on their skin, or spreads in dark stains over their ragged tunics.

"It's a little free thing I did for myself," the foreman explains to me as we eat lunch, while sitting against a stone roller on the low, hot hillside. "I didn't like my old name, so when the Romans took my city and I got enslaved, I just stole myself a new title."

He expects me to ask "Why?" or "How?" I don't. He clears his throat and explains anyway.

"My first master was a stupid soldier who couldn't write. So he had me write down the names of all the new slaves, and I listed myself as Archimedes, after a good dead man."

He pauses again, waiting. I decide not to bait him too far. "Who was the old Archimedes? A friend?"

"A great man of our people," he answers. "He invented the screw, among other things."

Archimedes' employer, my master, is a rich Sadducee who sided with the right people when the Romans came. He is not a harsh man, I hear, as masters go. But to keep the Romans and the Herods away from his lands, he sometimes pays them off with other men's lives. Thus Archimedes and I have found ourselves, today, working under a nervous young tribune on an aqueduct to Caesaraea. All morning, Archimedes has directed the leveling of a road for hauling the stone. The slave gang has been using the basalt roller to compact the disturbed soil, the way housewives use a smaller version to pack earthen floors; the heavy coastal air has become clogged with the odors of torn earth and crushed green wheat and laboring unbathed bodies. It has been hot, exacting work, even for the supervisor's apprentice, and I don't appreciate Archimedes filling our short break with his Greek ramblings.

"Archimedes was a great man in many ways," the architect continues, then casually lowers his voice. "He nearly defeated the Romans themselves, once."

I perk up my ears. If a Greek could nearly defeat them. . . .

"How did he do that?"

Archimedes grins. "He called on Apollo."

I sink back sullenly, careful of my sore buttocks. "Really? Why not Zeus?"

"He brought fire out of the sun to burn their ships."

"For an engineer," I remark, "he must have said good prayers."

To my relief, the foreman ignores my sarcasm. "He didn't have to pray. Hold out your hand; feel that." He stretches one hairy paw out under blazing sun. "My

40

namesake polished bronze shields into mirrors, and had dozens of them to reflect sunlight against a single point on each ship's sails."

"Interesting. So the sails caught fire from the sun's heat?"

"Yes. You catch on quickly."

"And the ships burned?"

"Yes."

"So why didn't he win?"

"Too many ships."

"So the Romans crucified him anyway." I tear off a hunk of stale bread, disappointed.

"No. The new procurator spared him. He was too valuable to waste like that." The Greek's smile twists sardonically. "He was killed later, by a drunken soldier."

"They can't do good things even when they mean to," I remark, bitterly. "They've turned loose too much hate and corruption to handle it all."

At my words, a couple of the laborers roll over to watch in our direction. Archimedes deliberately chews a piece of bread, but his glance travels up the slope, to where the two Roman guards recline. Beside them, within easy grasp, are their javelins: tempered barbed heads and soft iron shafts, designed to plunge deep and bend and then tear flesh and organs as they're pulled out. The guards give no outward sign that they've heard me. But as always, one is casually watching us.

Archimedes sighs, and scratches something on the piece of clay pot that he has been carrying for notes. "You're going to have a beating again tonight," he says. "We can discuss old history. But slaves have no room for seditious statements, no matter how oblique."

I cower in silence for a while. Unlike Shimeah, Archimedes can administer exquisitely painful beatings, without affecting the victim's ability to work the next day.

Then I think of an escape. "I meant the Greeks," I say, with a sly grin.

He grins slyly back at me. "Now you get five more strokes, for insulting the foreman." He duly marks *that* down. "And as your teacher, I fault your lack of vision, for assigning a universal law to an overly narrow subject. Nobody rules without hate. You drove your Greek rulers out of Palestine, a few decades back, and within a generation you were crying to Rome to save you from your own priest-kings."

"The Maccabees were great men!" I reply hotly.

"The Maccabees killed more Jews than the Greeks and Romans combined," he says. "One of them executed all of his own brothers when he became king. Then he had his mother starved to death. And you just raised your voice at me." He steadies our bread with the good fingers on his left hand, tears off a lump with his right, stuffs the piece into his mouth, and belches politely.

This man's countrymen once sacrificed swine to Zeus in our Temple. They dragged my grandfather out of his home, and made him eat pork at spear point, because he was a Levite. . . . "My humblest apologies, sir," I tell the foreman. I'm learning rapidly.

VII.

How do you deal with love? They called me the Eunuch—the other slaves did. That was one reason why my masters never freed me. It was a common enough practice to free slaves. But it was also a common practice to set, as a condition for freedom, the siring of one or more healthy slave children.

I would not.

I lived with the rumors: I was a homosexual; I'd had an accident as a child; I'd been a harem attendant, and had been altered for my job. As a teen-ager, I'd been shocked by those rumors at first. So had the first slave who'd tried to act on one of them. He'd gone to Archimedes afterward, half-emasculated himself. I'd gotten a thorough lashing. Then Archimedes had arranged to have the other slave sold.

Archimedes probably knew the truth, or guessed it from my few outward signs, after my pallet was moved to his quarters. I was attracted to women. But I would not breed slaves. So certain nights, after Hermione had drawn the cloth shut that separated my pallet from their bedchamber, I would lie quietly until I neared dreaming, and then would lie in wait outside the villa of my master or one of his rich friends, until a daughter or a young wife, or at least a prized concubine, would come out for the night air. I would seize her, stuff a rag in her mouth for silence' sake, and carry her off into the wild hills above Magdala. There, in one of the many caves, or in a secluded canyon with the stars watching, I would have her, and then apply a stolen lash to her until she stopped cringing at the blows, and then have her again, until she died. There were a lot of robbers and revolutionaries in the hills in those days; women were always disappearing.

So I fed my love to hate. I did it all in my mind, in my imaginings, where I could never be caught.

A vision of those days:

"I hate them all," I say, panting.

It is another noon, another lunch. We are reclining under an olive tree, across the valley from where Archimedes had found me with my broken ribs. Archimedes has been supervising the tally of the olive harvest—counting the baskets of fruit from each grove, so he can tell my master which groves have been the most profitable and which ought to be rooted up or traded off. All morning, I have been running from hill to hill, counting the baskets. All morning, I've absorbed the jeers of the Hebrew olive pickers for being on such fool's errands, and for being a Greek's houseboy.

"Why hate them?" queries Archimedes lazily. "What's to hate?"

"They sell their own children into slavery. They cut their babies' penises and scar them for life. They taunt

44

everyone with their stupid holiness. They make a virtue of arguing, instead of thinking."

"Why 'they'? Why not 'we'?"

"I'm not a Jew," I declare.

"Then why doesn't your male member look like a human being's?"

"That was an unfortunate accident," I huff.

Archimedes adds another date to the cud in his mouth, and chews thoughtfully. "I rather admire the Jews," he remarks. "They have a law for everything. We Hellenes have to think things out each time we do something. But the Jews always have some statute to tell them what to do." He crams in still another date. "They probably have a law for choosing which olive grove to keep, the rascals. I wish I could ask them without losing face. . . . Besides," he chuckles harshly, "they're the only people on earth who have the Romans afraid of them."

"Hoy!" I cry, derisively. *"They* fear *us?"* I catch myself, and hastily add, "Uh, if they're afraid of the *Jews,* then why isn't there a legion camping in Yerushalayim?"

"Because they're afraid of the Jews. You stupid people are the only nation on earth who can look at Rome with all her legions, and still think yourselves superior to her. The Romans know that if they put a legion in Yerushalayim, they'll provoke a blood-bath that will be no end of trouble. And furthermore, *they'll wonder if they had a right to do so."* He swallows his dates. "What are the Romans proudest of?"

"Their soldiers," I answer promptly.

"Wrong," he says. "And here I thought I'd taught you how to think. What are they always bragging about to everyone?"

I don't know. I keep silent.

"Their justice," he answers himself, finally, "and their peace. But here are you stupid Jews with your laws, that are more just than anything Rome practices—if you would only practice them yourselves. And to make matters worse, you claim that these laws come straight from your very own god, which is the one thing that the Romans haven't got—they're so desperate for divine sanction that they worship their own emperors. So that leaves the Romans with nothing but their peace." He chuckles. "Of course, you Jews are wretched at peace. But if the Romans can't keep you off each other's throats and off their own, they know that they'll have to kill you. And worse than that, they know that you'll sneer at them as you die."

A faint sneer wrinkles my own face at the thought. "No, we won't," I tell him, not even noticing my shift in allegiance. "We'll sneer at them as *they* die."

"And we Hellenes will sneer at you both, and live." His hairy lips curl into a grin. "By the way, I thought you weren't a Jew."

"Adonai won't let his people suffer much longer," I declare.

"Why not?" Archimedes says, still smiling. "He let you become a slave."

VIII.

"But what is freedom?" Yeshua once asked. Or was it Archimedes? Both. The vision clears itself.

Archimedes gets his say first. This is as it should be; he entered my head first in real time. A vision of how I earned another beating:

A hot warehouse, greasy with seeped olive oil, sour with hanging skins of wine, with generations of harvests gone stale. . . . Each wineskin has at least two smudges in its coat of dust, where my thirteen-year-old finger has pressed its reality into my uncertain tally. All but a few sacks have just received smudge number three. XLV, XLVI, XLVII. . . .

Sweat runs into my eye like a bee sting. Rub, rub. . . . Archimedes has stripped to his Greek loin-cloth; the sweat beads on his oiled flesh as he counts the huge amphorae of oil. My own skinny, self-conscious body is trying to sweat itself out from under my Hebrew robe. Where was I? XLVI—no, XLVII, XLVIII. . . .

Life explodes.

A bird has swooped through the doorway. Confused by the sudden darkness, it thunders by my ear, rams a wineskin and bounces down to the free air below, thrums to the ceiling and down one wall, whips sideways past Archimedes' wild pounce, hits the opposite wall and drops, stunned, between two jars. Then it is clawing its way into the air again, just away as my arm intercepts the point where it nearly was. It twists wildly among the wineskins toward the light of the entrance, dodges around Archimedes' hastily interposed bulk, and shoots back out the doorway. . . .

I lean against an oil jar—not necessarily a wise thing to do. "Whew!" says Archimedes to no one in particular, meaning me.

"What kind of bird was it?" I ask.

"I couldn't see. It wasn't any good for *you* to eat, though." The master likes all of us slaves, even the non-Jews, to eat kosher. Archimedes, as bookkeeper for the household, thus knows the dietary laws better than most Hebrews, although as a free man he often buys pork for himself.

"Then why were we chasing a bird, if we can't eat it?" I ask.

"Because it didn't belong in here dropping birdshit on the stores. Besides, it's the nature of people to chase something, especially if it looks trapped or crippled."

"Well, I'm glad it got away," I declare, ashamed that I'm not really glad at all. "It deserves its freedom."

"Why do you say that?" says Archimedes, with a curious glance.

"Well, uh . . . " I start.

48

"And you Jews think you can argue!" his voice drips.

"Uh, he showed so much *courage* and *vigor.*"

"Aha! Two more Greek words slipped into your Aramaic! Even granted, though, that such noble words fit a bird's emotions—that particular bird was just panicked out of its skull."

"Even so," I maintain stubbornly, "I'm glad it's free." Then, despite my better instincts, I blurt, "I'm glad when anything is free."

That ends the games. Archimedes eyes me gravely. "I shall have to beat you again tonight. But first let me ask you a question. What is 'freedom'? Why do you think that bird is 'free'?"

"It can fly wherever it wants. No one gives it orders—except," I add hastily and piously, "Adonai."

"Yes," says Archimedes, "I'm sure it wanted to fly into the wall like that."

"Well, almost wherever it wants."

"Can it fly in here when the door's closed? Can it fly in a high wind? Can it fly through the water, or through the earth? Or through a wineskin?"

"But, but . . . why would it want to fly through the earth?"

"Oh, ho—then freedom is the ability to not want to do what you can't do anyway?"

"Uh . . . uh . . . no!" I'm not sure what's wrong with that definition, but if it's right, then I can see bad things coming from it. . . .

"Then what is freedom?" presses Archimedes, his eyes as bright as beads of sweat.

"It . . . it's just the ability to do what you want. It's got nothing to do with what you don't want or would never think of wanting to do, like flying through the ground!"

"Very well. Does the bird have freedom? Can it do what it wants?"

"Yes!"

"What does it want?"

I pause. "To fly, to eat . . . it wanted to get out of the storeroom!"

"Then why did it come into the storeroom?"

"Maybe it wanted some wine," I joke desperately.

"But it didn't get any. Is the bird free, then?"

I pause again. Archimedes presses his advantage. "Why did the bird want to leave?"

"Because he wanted to be free!"

"But freedom is doing what you want. How can you want to do what you want? That's intellectual masturbation. It may feel good, but nothing grows from it."

Sullen, I wait him out. If I'm going to be beaten physically anyway, there's no point in taking this verbal bruising as well.

"The bird didn't want freedom," the overseer continues. "It wanted light and space to fly properly. It wanted to escape the danger of us mad people who don't like to see other things free. Did it get what it wanted?"

"Yes!"

"Then I agree with you. It's free, for now. Or at least, it's more free. Perhaps it's hungry; it won't be free of the hunger until it eats. Then it will probably notice that it's tired, and will not be free of tiredness until it leaves the sky and rests. And as it rests, it will begin noticing feathers out of line, and must free itself of the need to preen them, and then it will decide to sing itself free of whatever demon makes birds want to sing. Even before it's free of one want, another will begin arising. It will never be completely free until it's stopped . . . wanting." He gazes at me, and his eyes are wondrously both hard and sad. "But the bird is permanently free of at least one thing. It will never mistake its real wants for a slippery abstraction, any more than it will try to fly through the ground. We invent words like 'freedom' as a convenience, to help us lump together and sort out real things—then we start mistaking the words for realities themselves. That's when they become dangerous; that's when we start saying stupid paradoxes like 'I want to be free!' and getting ourselves killed for them—or at least beaten."

I shudder, thinking of the whip to come.

"How many skins of wine?" he asks.

I curse, and squint in the dim light, hoping I can spot the last skin with only two smudges. . . .

51

IX.

A vision of the time in the desert of the Dead Sea, after the death of Yohan the Baptist:

It is noon when the lizard, who has gone mad, emerges from its crack. It hesitates only a moment at the heat of the limestone slab before it, then skitters across and plops down on the other side. It is the wrong side, the western side; there is no shade here. Heedless, the lizard charges onward. It crosses the white alkali flat, powdering itself with the stinging dust; charges down the red and white banded side of the ravine, and scrambles up the other side, popping over the rim with a mad leap. Then its course takes it uphill, up the slope of the wind-scoured brown mesas. It skitters over a tan outcrop of rock that makes the air above shimmer with heat: the soles of its feet begin to burn at the touch of the stone, but it continues. A snake is under a nearby rock, but the lizard ignores it. The snake ignores the lizard, too, because the snake is sane; it won't emerge under this noon sun, even to eat.

The lizard runs onward, uphill. A spur of the mesa juts out into the valley; the lizard goes up this, even though the lizard's body is rapidly drying up from the heat. The heat only adds to its madness. It reaches the backbone of the spur, where the wind and sand have sculptured the rock into knobs and pinnacles. The lizard starts up the nearest of these, then falls; its burned foot-pads don't grip the stone as they should. It lands on its back, and thrashes to right itself. Then it finds a wind-scoured crack in the south side of the little pinnacle, and gets enough of a grip there to scuttle upward to the flattened top. There it stops, with nothing else to run up. Its sides heave in and out; its lungs are still sane, and are desperately trying to shunt the heat out of its body.

Far below, the Dead Sea shimmers, brick red with the reflections of the hills beyond, and the white alkali flats of the valley blaze like a flat sun. The lizard remains where it is, until the heat makes it jerk and writhe. It flips on its back; its mouth opens and closes. By late afternoon, it is only a small, dried husk.

Hours later, when the sun that killed it is near setting, a shadow falls across the lizard's tiny mummy.

Yeshua sits down on the rock, notices the corpse beside him, and jumps up again. He bends over the dried lizard, looks carefully without touching it, and then kneels to examine the ground around the rock. He shifts positions twice, waddling on bent knees to look around the other side of the pinnacle.

"Stand back," he says. "There's been a demon here."

Shimon the Zealot perversely springs forward, peering over Yeshua's shoulder. "Where is it, Master?" he asks.

"Don't disturb the marks," the rabbi rebukes him, "or we may never know." He peers a moment longer, then points to tiny tracks in a pocket of fine drift-sand near the base of the pinnacle. "The lizard came here, from across the rocks."

"Was the demon in the lizard," I ask, "or was it in the stone?"

"In the lizard. If the demon were in the stone, it would have taken the lizard for a better host."

"But couldn't it be a curse-demon?" points out Shimon. "Couldn't it be confined here, just wanting things dead?"

Something inside me tightens. Why had Yeshua been drawn to sit on this particular rock?

"Why would anyone waste such a curse on an ordinary stone in the middle of the desert?" scoffs Yeshua. "Anyway, if there were such a demon in the stone, I'd know it. Demons know not to tempt me, now."

I wonder at the story that must lie behind that word, *now*. But I ask, "Why did the demon bring the lizard here?"

"I don't think the demon did, entirely," says Yeshua. "I think the lizard brought itself here to get rid of the demon."

I stare at the pathetic little corpse. "By cooking itself?"

"It must have been a very bad demon," remarks Yeshua.

"But you can't escape a demon by killing yourself!" the Zealot bursts out. "Rabbi Hillel told us that suicides are tormented by demons in Sheol."

Yeshua doesn't reply immediately. He just stands there, pulling the sweat from his beard and staring thoughtfully. I am thinking hard, as well.

"Rabbi Hillel was talking about *human* suicides," I say. "But lizards. . . . Tell me, Master. If a lizard's body can hold a demon, can it hold a soul, also?"

Yeshua laughs. "Ask a lizard."

I am tired of having questions answered by enigmas. I turn to the little corpse and bow mockingly. "Rabbi lizard, did you have a soul?" I wait a respectful interval, then turn to Yeshua. "He says nothing, Master. Can you explain his answer to me?"

"Do corpses usually say anything?" he asks, smiling. "Do stones? Shimon, what does Rabbi Hillel say about stones? Can they hold demons?"

"Of course," says the Zealot. "Houses, too. My uncle's house once had a demon in it. It took the priests three months to get rid of it. They finally had to bring in two Levites from the Temple and a prophet from the hills; the local people kept botching the rites."

"Do houses have souls, then?" Yeshua smiles at our silence. "Oh, well. Whether or not lizards have souls probably isn't of much concern to us, anyway. Our job is with our people." But he scoops out a pocket in a little patch of tan gravel, picks up the lizard with two fingers, and buries it.

"But if the lizard had no soul, then how did it choose to die on the rock?" Shimon blurts, suddenly.

"Maybe Adonai chose for it," I answer, rather pleased with myself. It seems a good, safe solution.

"Then the lizard was a sign. Hmm." Yeshua frowns

55

in mock puzzlement. "A sign for whom? Not me, I think. Perhaps for you, Teoma, or you, Shimon?"

"For Israel!" explodes Shimon. "It tells what we have to do! We have come to the high places to win Israel's freedom! We have to free Israel, even if we die!"

"Even if we kill Israel?" Yeshua asks, quietly. And something that was in Shimon's eyes, dies. I avert my eyes, embarrassed; Shimon is a belching camel when he talks on such matters. The rabbi turns to me. "What about you, Teoma? Can you prophesy from the lizard?"

I kneel by the little grave, at a loss. "I'm no prophet. That's why I travel with *you*."

Yeshua sighs. "What is freedom?" he asks.

I've considered that question too many times since Archimedes first put it to me. The stone which the lizard climbed still radiates heat; in the motionless twilight, I can feel the dry warmth against my face.

"Freedom," I say, "is the ability to choose among various sufferings and deaths."

Yeshua smiles. "Poor Teoma," he says, and stands up. "The others are probably starting to worry. Let's go down."

X.

A vision of my first night with my master Yeshua:

There is a bright dusk this evening; the sun has hardly set when the moon climbs out, glowing with what seems like unnatural brightness. It gives a silvery cast to the pinkish twilight that covers the stony hillside. The young healer picks his way deliberately along the wild goat paths that thread the rocks and thorn-bushes; he seems to know where he's going. But it's obvious that we will spend the night in these highlands, under no roof at all but the stars.

This is the very wilderness I've fantasized about in my dreams of escape and vengeance. But my dreams hadn't included this poor young humbug of a prophet. Since leaving my former master's house, he has walked in front of me all afternoon and evening, not saying much, pausing only occasionally to admire some tenacious desert plant or some hilltop view, while I ponder whether killing him would be of any use to my dreams at all. Now, with night upon us, he continues walking until he reaches the crest of the ridge, and then begins casting about for firewood.

"Don't!" I hiss, when I realize that he is going to arrange his wood right here on the ridgetop. "You'll tell every thief and Zealot in the country that we're here!"

"What do we have for them to steal?" he asks.

"Food," I answer. "Robes."

"*You* have robes worth stealing," says Yeshua. The hem of his new tunic has been shredded already, by the crowd at my former master's gate.

"I'm a slave," I tell him. "I don't have anything." I gather the wood up, and haul it down the slope to a small dry ravine, where the fire won't be seen. "Do you have a fire kit?" I ask him. He shrugs, and shakes his head once. I shake my own head in despair, and walk down the ravine until it runs across a flat outcrop of limestone. I dump the wood on the stone shelf, then pick out a relatively straight stick and a chunk of wood to use for a fire drill.

"A knife?" I ask. He shakes his head again.

I sigh. *He has a working-man's body,* I think, *but I could probably overpower him.* Protruding like tumors from the outcrop are hard, bluish nodules of flint: the same flint that makes so much Galilaian limestone unquarriable. Some of the nodules seem to just begin to grow up out of the stone; others seem to rest on the stone's surface, but in reality their bases are still fast to the rock: a practical joke by Adonai on the toes of unwary travelers. In the little drop-off below the outcrop, I find some nodules that are truly free of the stone around them. I pick up two, and set the smaller one on the rock shelf, and smash the larger one down on top of it; it splits open, yielding a couple of sharp-edged flakes. With these, I begin shredding some bark for tinder. Yeshua settles beside me, and watches. "You may be useful after all," he remarks, after a time. "I know about wood for carpentry, but not for fires."

"I know carpentry, and stonecutting," I say, without looking up. "We use fire for splitting rock sometimes."

"I've seen that done," he nods, and begins rummaging in the little cloth bag I've been carrying. It holds bread and cheese and some dried figs, all filched from my former master's kitchen for us by another of his servants. "I worked on the New Temple for a while," Yeshua adds, and then falls silent, watching me work.

"You know he made a fool of you back there, don't you?" I remark, by way of conversation.

"Who?"

"My master. My old master. Don't you realize why he gave you the clothes?"

"Yes." Yeshua smiles dryly in the half-light. "He wanted to show off his piety."

"He wanted your old tunic," I reply. "He'll cut it into finger-sized strips, and sell each strip to the sick for ten shekels apiece." I sharpen the end of the fire-drill with one of the pieces of flint. "I almost decided to foil him, you know. I nearly suggested that since I was supposed to be you, *I* should wear your old tunic out the front gate."

The healer smiles more broadly. "So why didn't you?"

"My own tunic is better."

"No matter," says Yeshua, stretching his legs. "He can sell pieces of cloth if he chooses."

"That's right. You're a wandering healer. You don't mind bilking the poor."

"They'll heal the ones they were meant to heal," he says. "And the others will spread the word that your old master is a cheat, and he'll lose a lot of business."

"And just who were they meant to heal?" I retort, carving a tinder-cup in the chunk of wood.

"The kind I stopped for in the crowd," he replies, seriously. "The ones I healed."

"The beggars you shocked out of their acts?" I ask incredulously. It is finally dawning on me that this fellow might not be acting—that he might actually believe he is healing people. "You healed them, all right," I snort. "You healed them of their beggary. They'll have to go to the next town, at least, before they can take up their trade again."

He smiles faintly. "You're full of hate," he says. "It must be agonizing."

"Tell me, Master," I ask, "was Nuba meant to be saved?"

"Who?"

"The slave. The one on my work gang. The one you sent that strip of cloth to."

"Oh. No, probably not. But he'll be all right. He'll be healed for Alexandros' sake."

"But his whole foot was smashed!" I explode. "What was that little scrap of dirty cloth supposed to do? Stretch into a giant bandage?"

Yeshua shakes his head amazedly. "You don't see at all, do you? No, the cloth won't stretch into a bandage. It won't need to. In fact, it wasn't really needed at all. But your man was in pain, and the token made Alexandros believe more quickly."

"So Alexandros the slave boy is a healer, now?" I query sarcastically.

Yeshua smiles again: a small, pursed smile that barely offsets the darkness of his eyes in the twilight. "No, probably not a healer."

"You're dangerous," I tell him. "People need their skulls trepanned, or their wounds bound up, or their fevers cooled, and you send them bits of cloth. People could die from you."

Yeshua's smile disappears. "Perhaps they will," he says.

He lapses into silence, apparently considering this new idea. I ponder the terrifying possibilities of what he might be—perhaps no quack, not even a fool, but a madman. Even violence may be no answer against the possessed; they may have the strength of a legion, and even if you kill them, the demons may enter you instead. But the mad, whether their demons be foul or holy, may use violence against others.

I try out the fire drill, because that is what I would normally do next. To my surprise, the tinder lights almost instantly. I hastily dump the coals out on the stone, and add more shredded bark, then bits of twigs. I think, *What does he plan to do with me?* The little coals gobble the twigs merrily. Soon I have a small but eager blaze going. *And if he isn't mad? To whom would a charlatan sell a slave?* I break a larger branch to pieces, and place the smaller pieces across the fire, and lay the largest piece beside me. Yeshua sets a piece of flat-bread on the stone near the fire to warm, just as any man would. Then he gets out the cheese, and breaks off a small chunk. "Here," he says, and holds it out to me.

61

I freeze.

"Slaves don't eat with their masters." I say, finally.

He shrugs. "There's no point in waiting."

"The Romans say a slave is free if his master invites him to dinner," I remark.

"Are you a Roman?" he asks.

"No," I say, slowly. "But we're south of Mount Tabor. This is Pilate's land, not Herod's."

"If you want freedom, go," he says. "Or stay. But I don't have a house or land. I don't need a stonecutter."

I silently shove another stick into the fire, considering. Yeshua's hand still proffers the cheese.

"Go where?" I ask, finally.

He shrugs again. "Home, perhaps." The hand remains outstretched.

"If my father is alive, I don't want to see him," I say.

"And your mother? You said you had a brother, too."

"My mother helped to sell me."

"And your brother?" The faint wind shifts, blowing smoke in my face. I cough and close my eyes.

"I paid for my brother," I answer. "He belongs to Adonai. He's a rabbi's student somewhere, or a Temple attendant, or a Nazirite. I wouldn't know where to look."

I lapse into silence. Freedom, at last. But I have no home, love no one. When I try to conjure up the image of a home or family, the best I can do is Archimedes.

"Then you don't want to be free?" queries Yeshua.

"Yes!" I say, then "No!" I pause, confused.

Yeshua looks disgusted. "My arm's getting tired," he complains. "Let me ask a different question. Are you hungry?"

XI.

Anand, whom I once saved from a snake, visited me today. He brought me fresh fruit—green, lumpy things with pale sweet flesh and many black seeds—as well as more of the flat tree leaves, beaten flexible, that they use in place of papyrus here. He also told me that the king still vows to let me rot here, unless Migdonia relents and returns to her husband, the king's brother. Migdonia is the daughter of a Greek merchant—there is a tiny community of Greeks, even here in Mylapore. She has declared that she belongs to Yahweh, and won't sleep with any man.

"It's not just!" Anand told me. "It's not your fault she's married to a goat."

"Careful!" I admonished him. "The goat is the king's brother. You're in the king's prison. You want to get out again."

"But you could get out if you wanted to. You could get us both out. You could command the guard, or have Yahweh break down the wall."

"The first idea would get the guard into deep trouble," I noted, dryly. "And the second wouldn't do much good, as I believe this level of the palace is underground."

"I don't understand," he complained. "If your god lets you do such wonderful things, why don't you *do* them?"

"Suppose," I countered, "that a miracle suddenly happens. Suppose that a giant crack suddenly opens up in the earth, and part of the King's house collapses above this cell, and an old man somehow climbs out of the rubble unscathed, and goes his way.

"What does the local ruler do? He probably goes hunting, with spears. He starts at the houses of all the people who know the old man. Besides," I added, leaning against my favorite stone, "This place isn't really that bad. It's cool, and I have time to think."

But my young friend left still unsatisfied. I wish I gave answers as good as Yeshua's, or even Archimedes'. But then, I remember how many times I heard those answers, and refused to accept them myself. . . .

When he was safely gone, I moved my back away from the stone, and once more felt it give, slightly, as my weight came away. The stone was small enough and loose enough that even an old man could work it from its place. Once it was out, another one to its left could be loosened; then the one above. . . . My builder's eye has traced the pattern up the wall several times. I have difficulty with miracles, but I could create one here, if I chose: like Shimshon, a great ancestor of my people, I could bring a mighty building down on my head.

Then, however, even if I survived, things would probably happen just as I had told Anand they would.

Anand believes in true miracles. He has to. He is one. I should write that memory down, sometime. But not yet.

Last night, I remembered this:

"This is the way of Yahweh," says Yeshua. I feel the old Pharisee behind me scowl at the use of Adonai's real name in public.

"There was a shepherd," Yeshua continues, "whose father-in-law gave him three fat sheep. . . . "

Suddenly a beam of light strikes Yeshua's face. He looks up, questioningly.

"What's happening?" whispers Yohan, beside me. "Is he being transfigured?"

Even I wonder wildly for a moment. Then my eyes follow the beam of light toward the ceiling.

The hole there opens wider, as a brown hand tears more of the roof away.

"Romans!" someone yells.

"Our roof! Stop it!" yells Shimon the Rock, as he frantically pulls Yeshua back from the growing pool of light and dust. The packed crowd surges to its feet, rumbling. I feel Yohan's hand grab my wrist, the way Shimon the Zealot has taught us: *In trouble, make a fence, hand to wrist; circle Yeshua.*

If this is trouble, it's hopeless, I think. The house is packed solid all the way to the door; the massed heat and odor of people clogs the air itself. There is no hope of even forming the Zealot's circle, much less of escape.

Yeshua shrugs himself out of Shimon the Rock's sweat-slippery grasp. "Quiet," he tells the crowd. "There's no danger here, except the heat! Be still!"

The pool of light is growing rapidly. Then, suddenly, it is gone. An object blocks the new hole. It begins to descend, blackened by a corolla of light that grows around it again as it comes lower. It is long and rectangular and bulgy. It is a litter. It holds a man.

People squeeze backward to keep it from landing on their heads. The noise is deafening.

"Quiet," Yeshua repeats, and everyone hears him. His speaking voice has improved greatly in the past few months.

The crowd surges in again, to help steady the litter. The young man who lies on it twists weakly; I catch sight of a fragment of his motion between the intervening bodies. Yeshua calls for people to make more room.

"Rabbi," a voice quavers from the litter. "Rabbi, I can't walk."

Yeshua kneels beside the man.

"Don't!"

Yeshua looks up.

"Don't!" comes the voice again, from just behind me. It's the Pharisee who had disapproved of Adonai's name. "Don't!" he repeats. "It's the Shabbat!"

"Who's crying?" says Yeshua.

"It's the Shabbat! You mustn't work!"

"Who's working?" replies Yeshua, mildly. "I'm merely sweating."

"It's the Shabbat!" the Pharisee turns to Yohan. "He can't heal today!"

Yohan only shrugs. The Pharisee starts forward. I find Yohan's wrist again, and grip it fiercely; the old man is brought up short by our arms. The damp coarse wool of his prayer shawl scrapes across my wrist; the sweat drips from his nose, and his eyes are wild. "He mustn't disturb Adonai's peace!" he pleads with us. "He can't turn a demon loose on the Shabbat!"

"Have you read the Scriptures?" Yeshua asks him.

The old man's mouth drops open. His hands go to the tassels of his prayer shawl. "I read the Torah in this town's synagogue before you were born!" he replies, his voice low with outrage.

"Then tell me the verse that says this man has a demon," says Yeshua. "Maybe he only suffers from his own sins." He turns back to the paralytic, and tells him, "Whatever you've done, you're forgiven."

"Blasphemy!" explodes the Pharisee.

"Is it?" Yeshua keeps his temper, but his eyes are like two bright coals among tinder. "Is it easier to tell a cripple he's forgiven, or to tell him to walk?" He looks down, and says something to the paralytic; I can't hear what, in the noise of the crowd.

"But Adonai didn't work today!" cries the old man.

The crowd rumbles—for or against which side, it is hard to say. Everyone is on his feet, craning to see. No one can. Yeshua still kneels beside the pallet, but even I can only glimpse bits of what is happening. I do see, between legs, Yeshua's hand touch the invalid's palm.

"Get up!" comes Yeshua's voice. "Take your pallet, and go home!"

The end of the pallet suddenly sticks up above the crowd. Then everything is out of control.

"It's the Shabbat!" the Pharisee bellows beside me. "It's a trick!" But his voice is ignored in the chaos. Yeshua appears above the crowd, borne on someone's shoulders.

"It's a trick! It's the Shabbat! Only the demon left!" the elder shouts frantically, clawing his way around Yohan. "The man's still there! He must be! Make room! Don't trample him!"

Yeshua is being carried toward the door. I release my grip on Yohan, and worm my way desperately down through the pool of light, trying to catch up with him. The sweat glistens like jewels on the foreheads around me.

"It's an illusion! It's sorcery!" the elder still cries behind me, in great sobbing bellows. "It can't be! He's still here!" Then I am out of the light, into the stinking mass of shoulders and backs that surge toward the door.

I try, later, to remember if I had stepped on anything that felt like flesh.

XII.

We northern Jews were a bastard race, and a minority in our own land. Our homeland's very name, *Galilaia,* was a Greek amalgamation of some Hebrew words which I forget at the moment—words which meant, roughly, *land of foreigners.* Only a small portion of the people in Galilaia were Jewish, when I was a child; the rest were Greeks and Persians and Idumaeans and Chaldeans and half-breeds, the conquerers and refugees from the centuries of wars since the fall of the kingdom of Israel. And most of us Jews had no pedigree to prove it: we were a mixed lot, the sons and daughters of the escapees who'd returned when the Ten Lost Tribes were carried into exile, and of the settlers who'd returned with Nehemiah from Babylon, and of the guerrillas who'd hid in the hills in the meantime, and of the converts whom the Maccabees had circumcised with the points of their spears in our grandfathers' time, when Israel was briefly a nation again. We spoke Hebrew, if at all, only in the synagogues; in our homes we spoke Aramaic, the tongue of the Persians and Babylonians who had once ruled us, and at the marketplace we often spoke Greek, after the men who had conquered Persia. We were looked down upon by nearly everyone, including the Jews in Yerushalayim, and we despised everyone back, with the tired, congenial hatred of a people whose whole history was a long sentence of war.

But our land was beautiful. I was reminded of that as I wandered, newly freed, through the tawny highlands with Yeshua the healer, who often stopped to revel quietly at a patch of purple-blue flowers, or to marvel at swallows circling by a red bluff. He would study ants as if they were the words of rabbis; as the days passed, he seemed more like a wise child than a madman.

At the end of three days, we stood on the cliffs northwest of the white city of Tiberias, and looked out across the little green-and-gold valley of Ha-Yarden, and the jewel-blue of Lake Kinneret, which the Greeks called the Sea of Galilaia and the Romans named the Sea of Tiberias. On the far shore, misty with distance, rose the craggy red highlands of the Gulan: I remember trying to pick out the canyon there which held the spur of Gamla, where I was born. But I couldn't decide which one it was.

A vision of the end of that journey:

Kafer Nahum is a large city, as the towns of Palestine go: a jumble of stained white walls and plastered houses and crammed narrow streets, sprawled along the northern shore of the lake. It isn't pretty, like the new town of Tiberias, I think as we sit on the wide low hill to the west of it, waiting for the dusk to deepen. Still, I feel some urgent emotion, a tightness against my lungs, at

70

the sight of those houses: nostalgia, perhaps, but also fear and anger.

"Don't worry," the man had told my mother. (I remember the words, but not the man's name, or even his face. Perhaps I had never dared to look up at it.) *"Don't worry. I know a good Jewish landowner who needs farm help. The boy will go where he can grow up in his own faith. . . . "*

"We should escape notice, now," says Yeshua. "Let's go down."

I was just four months from my bar mitzvah, I think. Slaves never come of age.

When I was a child, this place had marked the beginning of the outside world: the market town which our family had visited most often; the caravan town, its shops full of cheap wares dumped off tired Syrian camels and lame Phoenician donkeys, its inns teaming with swearing caravaneers and rude beasts, there to rest one last night under a roof, before pushing on to Damascus or Tyre or Yerushalayim. As a child, I'd delighted in the big dusty marketplace, and had been awed by the huge limestone synagogue, with its lushly carved capitals and wondrously bright interior.

Now, though, as I go through the western gate with Yeshua, I am hardly impressed at all. As a slave, I've worked on the buildings of Tiberias and Caesaraea, and have helped to build Roman aqueducts. I've also learned how much easier limestone is to work, when it is free of flint, than is the hard black basalt of the Gulan where I was born. The main thing that impresses me now, as we walk through the dusky streets near the synagogue, is the odor. After my time on my previous master's rural estate, I had almost forgotten how a large town shoves its smells against you: urine, dung, slops, fresh bread, overripe fruit, human body odor, spices, smoke, the dung and hides of beasts, and above all, everywhere in this town, the relentless pungency of live and drying fish.

My brother had his coming of age, I think, *if there was any silver left at all from my sale.* I don't remember much about the place where I spent that first night in captivity, except that there was a little straw. . . .

"No!" I shout.

Then the breath explodes out of me, and I suddenly find my self in the dirty straw on the floor. Cloth jerks up around my head and is gone.

"No . . . " I sob between gasps, trying to get my breath back. It was our law: even when a man pledged his cloak for pawn, the moneylender had to give it back each night, to sleep in. . . . "No. . . . "

"Now, take off that tunic," says the slave-agent, "and put this one on."

"No!" Jews were never naked! "No. . . . "

The man squats. His huge hand grips the back of my neck firmly, so I feel its strength. "You should forget that word, child. Change. Now." He gives a slight shove as he lets go. I fall on one elbow, and writhe away from him.

Miserably, I roll around so that my back is to the slave-dealer, and pull off the tunic my mother sewed, and pull on the one he has dropped. It feels coarse and thin— threadbare in some places, crusty in others.

"You'll learn, child. It's different now, but you'll learn." Suddenly the slave-dealer's voice seems gentler, almost fatherly. "Just forget the word 'no.' And get some sleep now. You've got a long walk tomorrow, and the day starts early."

When the man shuts the door, he takes most of the light with him. In the sudden darkness, the urine-stench of the room is like a solid thing. I sit in the middle of it, and hear the heavy crossbar slide into place behind the door, and shake with rage.

"He's right, child," says a voice in the darkness. "It's hard at first, but you'll learn."

Startled, I scuttle backwards through the straw, away from the voice, until my back jams hard against a cool brick wall.

"It's all right. I'm not a demon."

As my eyes adjust to the dim light that seeps under the door, I can just barely make out the figure of the man, crouched against the opposite wall. "He just sold twelve men out of this room this morning," said the figure. "You're lucky; otherwise you'd have backed right into somebody, who might have been worse than I am."

"Who are you?"

"Enoch, call me Enoch. Where are you from, child?"

"Gamla. He can't do this."

"Yes, he can. I've never been to Gamla. Where is it?"

"But he took my cloak!"

"He'll take whatever he wants. It's not yours. Is Gamla west of here?"

"Northwest. In the Gulan."

"Ah. I've never been there. I've been north to Damascus, though. Beautiful city. . . . "

"Where did the other men go?"

73

"Who knows? To pick olives, probably. Most slaves around here pick olives, if they don't know a craft. Let me tell you about Damascus."

"Why didn't they pick you?"

"Me? I'm hard to sell. No toes on my left foot. I didn't learn very well, when I was young. But I work hard."

The air in the cell is already getting chilly; even in low-lying Kafer Nahum, the air of Galilee can be cold at night. "He took my cloak, Enoch," I tell him. "What am I going to do?"

"There's straw."

I grab a handful of the damp stuff. "I can't keep warm with this."

"And there's body heat."

"What?"

"You're unlucky; there were twelve men in here last night. We stayed pretty warm. But tonight there's just us. Why don't you come over here, and we'll share heat?"

"No!" I grab another handful of straw.

"It gets cold at night here."

I scrape more straw together, frantically dragging up fingernails full of the stuff. Then, with the straw, my nails dig into something else, something soft and damp. I smell excrement.

In my panic, I can remember only a few of the thousand things that make a Jew polluted, but shit is surely one of them. I think, *There must be some ceremony to remove this uncleanness. My father will know. . . .*

"Let me tell you about Damascus, child," says Enoch. "There's a temple there with a thousand slaves. Some of them are girls, some boys. . . . "

I wipe my hand frantically on my filthy tunic, and shiver, pressing harder against the wall, against the brick like a parent's flesh gone cold. . . .

We cross the square before the somehow shrunken synagogue. I stare up at its modest Greek-style columns, at the carved, painted friezes of the fruits of the harvest and the lost Ark of the Covenant, and I recall: . . . *and in the morning, as my new master's slave-buyer led me away, there were voices chanting in the synagogue.* Then we thread our way through one of the narrow streets toward the waterfront.

A short distance down the street is our destination, apparently: a rather large, old mud-brick compound, much like the one where I was kept that night. We cross the little courtyard, and Yeshua pauses to touch a small Jewish prayer box over the house entrance, and then walks in. I hesitate, wonder whether I should touch the box also, poke at it half-heartedly, and follow him.

"Rabbi!" A middle-aged woman runs from the dinner she has been setting out, and embraces him. She is followed by an older man, undoubtedly her husband; by a small, plump younger woman, and by half a dozen young men.

"Is this one of your brothers?" the matron asks Yeshua, when she notices me standing on the threshold.

"No, Estere," he tells her, "just another stray sheep." I scowl at the description. "Can you put him up somewhere? He's a builder; he can probably help you fix the boats. His name's Yehuda."

"There's room on the roof," says Estere. "Another Yehuda? I hope he has a nickname."

75

"Teoma," Yeshua says, solving that problem neatly, "this is Estere. I healed her once. And this is Yona, her husband, and those are her sons Shimon and Andreas. . . . "

And so, a few hundred paces from where I became a slave, we recline for my first meal under a roof after becoming a free man. Prayers are said that I don't completely understand, and hands reach for the lids of dishes. There are bowls of sweet red wine, flat loaves of barley bread, lentil soup with onions, fresh figs and fried sweetcakes with wild honey, and of course, fish. I stuff myself at first, tasting fig and onion in the same happy swallow. Then suddenly I find that my hand has entered the fish-stew bowl at the same moment as another hand. It belongs to one of the brothers—Andreas, I think. He withdraws with a muffled apology, and waits for me to soak my piece of bread in the broth, and then fishes out the soggy bit of bread that I had knocked out of his hand. I gulp my bread down, suddenly self-conscious, and hesitate before grabbing another. Then I look around at the other faces. No one is staring at me. But suddenly I notice how carefully the others are making each mouthful last, and realize how many hands are scooping up small portions of this seeming feast. I break off another, smaller piece of bread, my face burning. *These people are real Jews, a real family,* I think, *and you only know how to eat like a Greek bachelor slave.*

My hand is reaching with its bit of bread toward the common bowl, when the vision returns—no, not the vision, the touch and the smell, the slickness and the clinging straws, and the feeling of clamminess I had reached into, a little like thick stew drying on fingers. I see my hand about to reach again into the common bowl, and I rush out, trying to control my gorge.

I am unclean, stained with excrement that will never come off. That night, I go up to the roof with my expensive cloak, and spread it alongside the plainer ones of Yeshua and Andreas, and Mattathias the little tax collector, and another man named Yehuda. I lie down, and stare up at the stars until they outline the blackness of the sky, and I feel utterly, irretrievably lost.

XIII.

A vision of another evening, on the roof of Yona the fisherman's house in Kafer Nahum:

"How do you see visions?" I ask Yohan.

"How do you *see*?" he replies, shrugging in the light of the half-moon.

But I press him for a less cryptic answer. "You studied with the Essenes," I observe. "Did they teach you a specific method?"

Yohan considers me silently. The half-light suits him; he seems as natural and insubstantial as a fish in a murky pool. "I fast for three or more days," he replies, finally. "Then the emptiness in my body fills up with angels."

Shimon the Zealot guffaws. "How does an angel taste?" he asks.

"Not the way you or I taste," replies Yohan, seriously. "In fact, they don't see, or hear, or smell the same way, either."

"Do you understand what they do sense?" I ask him, deadpan.

"No," he replies after a moment.

"Then why do you see visions?" I snap at the weak spot.

"Why do you *see*?" he snaps back.

"Because I can't keep my eyes closed all the time," I reply, unphased.

"How can you keep them open?" Nathan'el sleepily joins in the argument.

"Have you ever seen an angel?" Yohan asks me.

"Several times," I reply, "but they were always married."

"Angels don't marry," declares Nathan'el. "Remember what Yeshua said. . . . "

"I was joking," I tell him. "I wouldn't marry an angel if he asked." I lean back on my mat, and wait for Yohan to get over his shock.

"What *would* you marry?" Nathan'el suddenly asks me, his eyes boring through the dim light.

I know, then, that Yohan is safe for a while. They've found another victim. That's all right. I'm used to it.

"Not a Greek," I answer. "They have faces like bricks, and they smell like pigs."

"I'd have thought you'd like that," said Nathan'el. "I'd have sworn I smelled a Greek at the market this afternoon, but it was just our little unwashed Twin."

"You were just downwind of your words," I reply casually. That mark was too easy; Nathan'el suffers from a minor demon, that periodically enters his throat and tonsils, giving his breath an odor like that of carrion. He glowers at me helplessly, unwilling to admit his affliction.

"How about marrying a Roman?" proposes the Zealot to me. "They just smell like an old olive press."

"Really?" I enquire, innocently. "How did you get close enough to find that out? Are you sure that's not just how their sandals smell?"

Shimon the Rock claps Shimon the Zealot on the back, to keep him from coming for me. Mattathias, who likes me for some reason, interjects playfully, "Perhaps a Samaritan, Yehuda?"

Charity is more humiliating than insults. I smile wickedly. "Perhaps."

"You filthy goat's tail," says Shimon the Zealot, matter-of-factly. "Why do you call yourself a Jew?"

"Because my mother and father were Jews, unfortunately," I tell him. "And my brother is a priest in the Temple—I hope. I paid for him."

"He should be revolted at the sight of you."

"He probably would be," I say thoughtfully. This hadn't occurred to me before. But I add, "I haven't looked him up," with a properly curled lip.

"Moon's up high," intercedes Shimon the Rock. "Time to go fishing." He starts down the ladder. Shimon the Zealot and Nathan'el follow him down, looking disgusted. In his corner, John sits hunched, staring at his angels for a few more moments before going down.

I lie back, grinning in the moonlight. The secret of winning an insult match is not cleverness or profundity, I rehearse to myself. It is saying stupid jibes and smiling at how clever they are, and listening to your opponent's abuse and smiling at how stupid it is.

And most important, it is telling the truth, and smiling at how deadly it is.

I won't be wanted on the fishing boats. But in the morning they may need me to fix something. I pull my cloak around me, and relax, and think briefly of my brother. Before I go to sleep, I decide never to visit the Temple in Yerushalayim.

XIV.

A vision of Yeshua's preaching, on the high hill north of Kafer Nahum:

Here, it is a joy to stand. The cool wind, blowing down from Mount Hermon and the Gulan, rolls around our backs, while before us the orange glow of the evening lamps in the town echoes the wild orange half-moon, which is just rising on the waters of Kinneret.

Shimon the Rock doesn't like it. "We'll catch our deaths up here, this time of night, in the winter," he mutters. "Or worse, *he* will."

"Then why did you come?" I ask. "Shimon the Zealot could have come, or Mattathias."

"I don't trust the Zealot," he grumbles, "and Mattathias wouldn't be any help in a fight."

"You really think there could be a fight?" I laugh. "We aren't worth robbing."

"There are a lot of people who don't like your master," he says.

"My master?" I grin in the dark, irked at him. "He's not yours?"

"You know, there are a lot of people who don't particularly like you, either."

"I know," I assure him. "I have an ugly mouth."

"You're so crammed full of hate, you stink of it."

"I know. You live with fish, you smell like a fish. You live with hate, the same. Good metaphor, fisherman."

"Fish smells better than hate."

"So tomorrow, I'll rub myself with a fish," I promise.

Shimon starts to reply, then turns his back instead. He knows he can't win when I laugh at him.

"Who would harm Yeshua?" I ask.

Shimon's back remains turned. But the question salves his ego. His big dim shoulders straighten. "Pharisees, for one. He's clipped their tassels more than once."

"But they live by the Law. He worries them so much that they'd ambush him at night, at prayer?"

"Not themselves. But they might hire robbers to do it, and not bother themselves about the details. Some of them would have him dragged to the synagogue and stoned in broad daylight, if they dared. The Law is their whole lives. He finds the Law unimportant."

"I'm not sure you're right about that last, Shimon," I tell him. "It's more as though he finds the Law incomplete." I pause, thinking, and then add, "He threatens fishermen, too, doesn't he?"

That brings the big man back around. "What do you mean by that?"

"Half a dozen people have babbled to me about how he fed two thousand people with a couple of fish, out in the wilderness. Assuming that's not just the usual rumor—who's going to buy your father's catch, if *that* starts happening regularly?"

Shimon shrugs, and turns away again. "Maybe he'll teach me to do that, and we won't have to catch but one fish a day."

We are interrupted by the sound of footsteps sliding on the rocks of the slope below.

Shimon's hand slips to something hidden inside his robe. "Who's there?" he calls.

"Pilgrims," comes the answer. "Is Yeshua the Healer there?"

"Not here," says the fisherman. "What do you want with him?"

"To hear him." Four figures resolve themselves out of the dark olive grove below us: a small man, a woman, and two young boys. "Are you Shimon bar Yona, the fisherman?" the man asks.

"How do you know me?" Shimon demands, nonplussed.

"You can always tell a fisherman upwind," I remark.

"They sent us up from your father's house," the man explains. "They said that the Rabbi was up on the mountain with you and a slave. There's a big crowd gathering, waiting for him to come down. We—well, we thought we'd come up," he finishes sheepishly.

"The Rabbi's praying right now," says Shimon. "You shouldn't disturb him."

"We wouldn't dare do such a thing," says the small man. "Would you mind . . . could we just wait here?"

Shimon sighs and settles back on his haunches. The small man takes that for consent; he squats also, a little downslope from us. The woman and the boys sit down beside him. One of the boys gives a long, hacking cough; the woman gathers him against her. Even in the rising moonlight, the boy looks gaunt.

As the night wears on, more and more people come up the slope. Shimon grows frantic trying to intercept them before they disturb Yeshua. Soon the crowd begins to police itself: a sort of boundary line comes into existence by mutual consensus, and anyone trying to cross is swiftly drawn back by jealous hands and hissing voices. Shimon stations himself upslope, as a sort of final line of defense; I try to forget my low freedman status and remember my old foreman's stance. Only once is there real trouble: a lurching figure in a dark-striped robe bursts up the slope, bawling people out of the way in a slurred but commanding voice. Shimon isn't in position to stop him, as he staggers free of the crowd.

"Please, friend," I say, moving to head him off. "The master is praying."

"I've got to see him!" he cries. "My Rachel hates me!"

I step in front of him. He tries to bull his way past. I grab his arm. He drags me forward. "Let go!" he says. A fist hits my jaw and a knee sinks into my stomach simultaneously. Then a half dozen men from the crowd are on him, dragging him back. I sit down on a terrace and swallow my vomit to keep my dignity. When I stand up, the drunk and his escorts have disappeared downhill.

Toward dawn, the wealthier townspeople and the Pharisees begin to arrive. They settle uneasily behind the crowd of beggars and pilgrims, telling each other what *they'd* heard was happening up on the hill. If Yeshua is going to call down the end of the world, then they feel it is their civic duty to be present.

As the sky begins to lighten, I notice the woman who had come first stand up. She helps the sick boy get to his feet; then they start down the slope together, picking their way through the terraces and the hundreds of huddled, napping forms. I hesitate; the crowd is growing around the edges, but seems quiet for now. I walk down to where the woman's husband sits with their other son, and I squat beside them.

"Where is your wife going?" I ask.

"The night was too hard on the boy," he says. "I'll stay, though, and listen. It might help. When will the Rabbi begin his sermon?"

"I hadn't known he was going to give one," I tell the man. "Maybe he will, though." *You fool,* I think, *making your sick child sit out all night on a cold hillside. . . .*

"The latecomers all said he was going to speak," he tells me.

"Wait until later, when this crowd begins to leave," I tell him. "Perhaps I can help you to see him then."

I get up, and walk back uphill, beyond the crowd. Shimon meets me there. "You fool," he says, quietly. "We can't play favorites like that. You could start a riot."

The sky continues to lighten over the canyons of the Gulan. The small hunched figure of Yeshua gradually becomes visible, kneeling a few strides below the hill's summit. He remains still until the first ray of sunlight breaks over the Gulan, and shoots across the darkened valley to strike the red massif above Magdala. Then he straightens slowly, stretches, turns toward us, and starts at the size of the crowd. He stands surveying them for a while, then turns and beckons wearily, and starts up the gentle slope toward the summit.

86

The crowd surges after him, trampling the winter wheat above the olive grove. They sweep Shimon and me along with them. A beggar runs up the slope past us, and almost tackles Yeshua. Startled, Yeshua turns, and then embraces the dirty young man, while the crowd catches up. For a few minutes, then, Yeshua does his usual act, touching the beggars and sick people, healing them or convincing them or whatever he does. There are no spectacular cases in this crowd—no paralytics, no lepers.

Then, after a while, the healer turns again, and walks on to the hill's summit, and stands peering at the crowd from out of the deep wells of his eyes, not replying to the dozens of shouted questions and entreaties, keeping the beggars from his robe with his silence. Finally he gives a little wave of his hand.

"Quiet!" bellows Shimon bar Yona.

Yeshua gives him a sharp glance.

Shimon subsides uneasily. "There's too many of them," he mutters to me. "He'll be all day sorting them out. What should we do?"

But his bellow has already been effective. The crowd settles into a precarious silence. Yeshua and the crowd watch each other.

"Blessed are the poor," Yeshua says. . . .

XV.

Time passes in a trickle, here in my prison: a stream so tiny that it is either unnoticed or maddening. The man in the next cell has died; he was bitten by a centipede of two hand's length, when the creature came inside to escape the floods of the rainy season. I share my own puddled cell with three displaced scorpions. But they are not as aggressive as centipedes, and Yahweh has given me the gift of some control over time. I sit for hours now without moving, and when I do move, I move so slowly that the scorpions easily scuttle out of the way.

The creatures have divided the room into three territories, and have left me a fourth. One habitually posts himself in a crevice near the door; my jailor has noticed it, and has named it my "guardian," and is spreading wild rumors about it. Another scorpion keeps watch in the corner behind my water jar; a third patrols an irregular territory which starts at the base of my sleeping pallet. At night, and at dawn, I lift the blanket carefully, to make sure it is not exploring underneath; I remember waking one morning to feel it scuttling down my leg. But I don't mind it too much; it keeps the bed free of other vermin. And none of the three have bothered the corner where I sit to think and write.

Migdonia, the king's disobedient sister-in-law, was here to see me yesterday. She brought me food and a new bathing cloth and some scented oil. The king had thought, she said, that seeing me in my cell might make her realize what a poor fool I was, and go back to her husband's bed.

"But I know you wouldn't want me to do that," she added smugly.

"Why not?"

"Fornication is an evil and ugly thing," she said.

"Did I teach you that?" I asked.

"No, not directly," she admitted. "But we all know how you live."

"I must be seventy years old!" I protested.

"Did you ever?" she asked innocently, and settled back to hear my divine revelation.

"Ask Yahweh," I replied. Even holy men deserve some privacy.

"But I belong to Yeshua and Yahweh!" she said. "You can't mean that I should share my body with another man?"

"Yeshua has died once already," I pointed out. "He doesn't need your female organs."

"But isn't it better to be celibate?" she persisted.

"I don't know," I told her tiredly. "I never really needed any guidance on that matter."

But that wasn't quite true. I remembered one day, on the shore of Kinneret, by a grove of ancient trees west of Kafer Nahum:

"Teoma, have you met my wife?" Yeshua asks.

"Your wife?" I repeat stupidly.

"My wife," he confirms. "My holy one. My other part of me, who gives me a reason for living."

"Your *wife*?" I repeat, even more stupidly. "You're married?"

"That's the purpose of a woman, you know," he continues. "To keep a man living. And the other way around. What does Shimon bar Yona say about his wife?"

"He adores her," I answer. "He complains all the time we're traveling and she's not with us, he describes her with more flowing words than a Pharisee has at prayer, he drives the rest of us wild. Then when we get home, he yells at her."

"But she's barren."

"They say the mother of Yohan the Baptist was barren, too, until she was an old woman. But about your. . . . "

"Would Shimon stay with us, do you think, if she had children?"

"I don't know. He complains loudly enough as it is."

"He loves his wife, then. Why does he come with us at all? Why doesn't he stay home and comfort her?"

"I don't know," I say, growing frustrated as usual. "Why don't you stay home, yourself?"

"I have a task," he replies. "And why haven't you married?"

"When?" I ask. "How?"

He shrugs. "Many slaves marry."

"Many slaves' wives get sold," I answer. A fish leaps, out on the blue-grey water. (Another vision begins to intrude: two dozen men and torches, leaping wildly, drunk-

90

enly, in the night.) I reach suddenly for a stone, as if I could hit the fish if it leaped again.

"She wouldn't be a slave for long," Yeshua insists. "The Law frees Hebrew slaves after the seventh year. You could have married in the sixth."

"How can you be so wise, and yet so damned innocent?" I snap. "If a Hebrew owns you, and he obeys the law, he frees you in the seventh year—if he doesn't sell you to an Idumaean during the sixth year. My father sold me when I was eleven years old. I'm twenty-eight now."

"Still, your first master wasn't an unkindly man, from what you've said," he persists, unphased. "If you knew you would be sold anyway, you might have attached yourself to a wife, and then he might have kept you, knowing that you would have stayed to take care of her when you were freed. A man of your knowledge soon becomes more valuable as a free foreman, giving strong orders, than as a slave. And then you could have saved money to buy your wife out of slavery."

It seems like a wonderful scenario—but it's so far from reality that I don't even want to discuss why it wouldn't work. (The dancers leap again, legs wide, arms wide, half-turning in midair in ragged unison, torches clacking perilously together in mid-flight. Archimedes laughs and claps loudly.) "You argue like a Greek," I tell Yeshua.

"I argue like a Jew," he replies, smiling. "So why, really, didn't you marry?"

The torches snap and roar like flags in a high wind. One of the dancers throws his torch high in the air: it flips end over end, once, twice, thrice, leaving a cartwheel

91

of blindness in my already-aching eyeballs. Somehow, when it comes down, the dancer catches it again, but he falls over backwards in the process.

"Brave man!" bellows Archimedes, clapping. The dancer staggers to his feet and falls back into the line, while another leaps forward to try the same stunt. "I'd rather see this dance than the one in Yerushalayim!" the foreman tells me.

"You can't see the one in Yerushalayim," I remark. I *have* witnessed *Simchas Bess Hashoevah,* the Torch Dance of Water-Drawing Ceremony, in the Temple's Court of Women, where Greeks are not allowed. I saw it from my mother's arms, while my father danced. But that was so long ago that all I remember is fire.

"I don't need to see the one in Yerushalayim," says the overseer. "That's a ceremony. This is a celebration."

"This is probably sacrilege," I reply, grinning tightly. I am sixteen, and bulging with acne and new muscles; I might be able to beat up Archimedes, now. But if I did, he would either have to kill me or sell me. So he lets me argue more, while I am careful not to push him too far.

"How can slaves commit sacrilege?" the old man counters. "Your master's in Yerushalayim right now, for the whole harvest feast. You couldn't go. So you do what you can—Dung-eater! Your daddy was a jackal!" He stops to cat-call at a dancer, who had managed to coax four complete loops of fire from his thrown torch, but then panicked and dived out of the way of the plummeting flame. "If you do something wrong, it's your master's responsibility, not yours. Besides, if Dionysus can forgive

92

that dirt-gulping excuse of a play that our Greek friends put on this afternoon, then surely Adonai won't mind a few dropped torches."

"Dionysus let a batch of women tear him to pieces."

"Ho! You've mixed up the stories! It was the Titans who tore Dionysus apart! But then he put himself back together, and rose again. . . . Well done!" Another dancer, torch-end in teeth, has bent over backwards from his knees until his head rests on the ground. Then, more astoundingly, he gets back up.

"Excellent!" cries the overseer. "Hmm. Speaking of women who tear men to pieces, I think I'll go off for a while."

"I'll stay here."

"To each his own sacrilege. Come back to the house before long, though. I have a present for you." He lumbers off.

Since Hermione's death, no one besides me has lived in Archimedes' house with him. But he has eaten at the quarters of various slave women, and brought some of them home for the night. When this happens, I prefer to be around no longer than necessary. I spend most of the night at the fire dance, at our little Jewish slave travesty of one ceremony of the great *Chag ha-Sukkos,* the Festival of Booths. Skins of wine pass freely among the spectators; the festival coincides with the end of the grape harvest, and Archimedes has ordered the old wine out of the storehouses to make room for the new. I have plenty myself, even though I don't like wine that much; it smells like rotten fruit, and it makes my head ache. The Greeks say that Dionysus, their god of wine, grants sweet visions to those who love him, but drives those who oppose him mad. So be it. When I finally leave, I am quietly and savagely drunk.

As I approach our house, I'm surprised to see light flickering through the doorway. I enter: a single oil lamp burns in its niche. I glance toward the curtain that divides off Archimedes' sleeping room. It's drawn shut; beyond, I hear an irregular snoring, like that of a man on the edge of sleep. Or perhaps there are two people snoring. My senses are muddled.

"Oh . . . " says a voice.

Startled, I glance toward my sleeping mat. A girl has just sat up there.

My reaction is swift and decisive: "Wha . . . who . . . ?"

The girl is even more succinct. She says nothing.

"Archimedes?"

"Uhh. Yehuda?" Along with his voice comes the sleepy moan of a woman. *The old he-goat! Two in one. . . .*

"She's yours, Yehuda," says Archimedes, from behind the curtain.

"What?"

"Her name's Penelope. She's the best of the ones we brought back from Tiberias last week."

Penelope looks my age, or younger. She is plump, with long black hair tied back, and a small, slightly doubled chin. She wears a coarse, beltless woolen shift, such as the slave dealer had given me in Kafer Nahum.

"Why?" I ask the voice behind the curtain.

"You're a man now," it replies, unconvincingly.

"Penelope. That's not even a Jewish name!" I erupt.

"Pan's dung," Archimedes grumbles. "And I thought you'd be grateful. You can't circumcise a woman."

94

"My mother's Jewish," the girl suddenly blurts.

"No. No, I can't. I can't do this."

But for some reason, I shamble a couple of steps toward her.

Archimedes' head appears over the curtain. "Yehuda, I know your people's history," he says. "Name me one of your kings who didn't have concubines."

"I'm not a king."

"No, you're not. You're a slave. So it makes even less difference."

She has large eyes, made larger by fear and lamplight. But they aren't innocent. They remind me suddenly of a wild dog I'd seen, once, when we'd cornered it in the den it had dug under a terrace.

"She's clean," says Archimedes, as his head disappears again. "I inspected her myself. But you do as you like."

A thought marches with terrible clarity across my foggy brain: *This girl may be a virgin, but she has already been raped.*

With sudden compassion, I reach down and touch her forehead. I hadn't realized until then that I was that close to her. She has oiled herself, or been oiled; her skin is warm and slippery to the touch. It feels smooth, but there is a large pimple welling up in her left eyebrow. I fight back the sudden urge to pop it.

Then she looks up at me, at the acned drunken young slave. Shaking, her large eyes full of loathing, she reaches up with her plump hand, and clutches my own, and guides it from her round face down to the damp cloth over her breast.

In horror, I pull away, and retreat across the room, and blow out the lamp that lights the sight of her eyes.

Then, in horror, I stumble back across the room toward her.

But in the dark, she becomes a set of smells: olive oil, and stale sweat in wool, and the odor of breath and armpits, and strong cheap perfume that reminds me, to my added horror, of Hermione, and finally an odor like that from soiled undergarments, but much stronger. I claw myself to my feet and rush out toward the first faint hint of dawn in the doorway and stumble outside, then fall in the rough grass beside the house and vomit.

Inside, I hear her sobbing loudly, and then hear low voices. Then she comes out, wearing her woolen shift, and carrying a hand-basket that must hold her other belongings. I realize now that her face and body are much like a young Hermione's.

"Damn you," she says, and runs away, towards the slave quarters.

I lie in the grass beside my vomit, and think, *This is something only angels can do without blasphemy.*

Archimedes comes out. He adjusts his beltless tunic over his belly, leans against the doorpost, sighs, and stares sadly down at me. "She could have cooked for us," he says.

"I argue like a Jew," Yeshua replies, smiling. "So why, really, didn't you marry?"

"Because I'm too stupid to think like a Jew."

"You're not stupid."

"Then because I'm stubborn like a Jew! I won't bring a child into slavery!"

"You've done more selfish things."

The arrow strikes home. "Yes," I mutter.

96

"You've wanted to marry?"

"Yes."

"You've wanted more than once?"

"I've raped every moderately attractive woman I've ever met," I reply, "in my head."

"Wouldn't it have been better to choose one, and love her?"

"Yes."

"Why haven't you?"

"Because she would want children. And we could never afford to buy the children out, as well as my wife. So we would stay slaves, and the children would grow up as slaves, and as Jews, and then they would die. And she would die, or I would die. . . ."

"You're afraid of that?"

"Of course I am!" My voice cracks.

"But you'll die anyway. And she'll die, too, only unloved."

"Someone will love her."

"Then you'll die unloved."

"No!" I start. "At least. . . . "

"Why didn't you marry, Teoma?"

"Because I wanted to be the *Meshiha*."

"You, too." Yeshua sighs. He picks up a pebble, a small lump of shale, and tosses it into the lake. It leaves a grease of dissolved mud on his fingers. He rubs them absently together. "Well?"

"What?"

"Are you the *Meshiha*?"

"No." I answer. "I doubt it." I pick up another lump of shale, and watch my fingers crumble it. "Tell me about your wife."

He smiles his small sad smile. "I've never met her."

Perhaps holy men don't deserve privacy.

"I'm sorry, Revered One," said Migdonia. "Should I go back to my husband, and free you?"

"Maybe not," I told her. "But I want to know the real reason why you shouldn't."

She collapsed against the wall again, apparently no longer worried about being smudged. The scorpions, praise Yahweh, were nowhere in sight.

"His teeth are crooked," she said.

"What?" I answered, alertly.

"He has a narrow little mouth, and no chin. His front teeth stick out and cross each other, and the eyeteeth curl backward like a dog's fangs. They're all thin and sharp, and they smell like rotten meat."

"And you have no chin either," I noted, "and your bust is rather too large and sags a little too much, and your nose is the size of a Nabataean's. If he can love you, why can't you love him?"

"You don't understand yet," she said. "He has two older wives and a dozen concubines. Most of them have white scars on their shoulders. So do some of the village girls on his lands, and several of the whores in the city. The scars all match the pattern of his teeth." She stood with her silk-draped back sagging against the damp stone wall, and watched me as I pondered.

"Have you been bitten?" I asked her, finally.

"Not yet," she replied.

"Then there's a little hope, maybe. If he can get his brother to throw me into jail for influencing you, then he

98

could probably have forced his own wife into bed with him, if he really wished. You must still have some power over him."

"I think I'll lose that power," she said, "after I've been chewed."

I considered all this for a moment. "Meet with him," I told her. "Choose a safe place. Take friends or members of your family for protection, if you think you need them. Tell him about Yeshua. Tell him all the things I've told you. Perhaps you can teach him real love, so that he knows he doesn't need to bite prostitutes. But don't go to bed with him, ever."

"When you go to court, always make friends with your accuser," Yeshua once told us. As Migdonia left, I wished I'd had a chance to meet with her husband. He sounded like he needed friends, desperately—he, and all his victims.

XVI.

A vision from the time in Kafer Nahum:

They come searching for him at the fish market at midday. The three men, in the rough, undyed loincloths and tangled hair of hermits, stop a fishmonger by the stone tanks in the bazaar east of the synagogue. "We're looking for Yeshua the Prophet," they tell him. "Where is he staying?"

"The Nazarene?" the monger asks. "The healer?" He eyes them cautiously, afraid of the holy vows they have taken, but contemptuous of their dirty rags.

"The Bet-Lehemite," says the spokesman for the three. "But yes, he heals."

I am standing across the fish tank from them. I turn away without speaking, and make my way back through the fish-stinking alleys, to the house of Yona, Shimon's father. "Where's the rabbi?" I ask Shimon's wife.

"With the men at the boats," she said. "They're stepping the new mast. Is something wrong?"

"No," I tell her, and hurry down to the beach. The new mast lies on the shore beside Shimon's boat. Over it squats Yeshua, with a mallet and chisel, chipping the base so that it will fit more precisely. He has disguised himself by tying his hair back, stripping to his linen undergarment and girding his loins like a common workman. Dressed that way, he reminds me of the three wild men. Shimon the Rock stands by the bow, supervising.

"Did you get those nails?" he asks me.

"What's *he* doing here?" I ask.

"Setting the mast," he answers, with a shrug. "I know. I don't like it either. He insisted. There'll be a crowd here, soon."

"I could do the job," I protest.

"You're still sick," he says. "And since you're too stubborn to let him heal you and too stupid to lie down, we send you to the market for nails."

"I'm just a little queasy."

"You still don't look good," he answers. "Did you remember the nails?"

"No. I mean, I didn't forget them. But something else happened. There may be trouble at the market."

Shimon rolls his eyes skyward a moment, and waits for my explanation.

"Three wild men," I tell him, "like hermits, or maybe Yohanites. They're asking for 'Yeshua the Bet-Lehemite.'"

Shimon scowls. "Yeshua was born in Bet Lehem."

"I thought he was from Nazerat."

"No. He just grew up there. Well, it's against my good judgement, but I suppose we'd better tell him."

Yeshua pauses, mallet in hand, long enough to hear my news. "As far as I know, *they* aren't mad at me," he remarks, when I finish. "I should go wait for them at the house." He picks his tunic off the prow of the boat, puts it on, and starts back into the village. Shimon, swearing under his breath, follows.

I stand, watching them leave, then pick up the chisel and mallet from where Yeshua had dropped them. The fish smell in the air makes my stomach lurch. The two workmen, who'd been hired to help with the mast, shrug and sit down in the boat's shade.

Old Yona, Shimon's father, returns from the market just then. He's been at his fish-tank all morning, waiting for the last of the catch to sell. "Where's Shimon?" he asks.

"At the house," I tell him, "with Yeshua."

I expect him to explode. He doesn't. He just leans sadly against the boat.

"He promised," the old man says. "We've been two months with only one boat. He said he'd set the mast today."

"We will," I say angrily, and turn to one of the workmen. "Eleazar, go to the Street of Smiths. Get half a *mina* of nails, three fingers' length." I grip the chisel in my slightly shaky left hand, and the mallet in my right, and bend over the mast.

It is late afternoon when the mast is finally set, blocked, and tied. I walk slowly back to the house afterward, burning with fever and slow anger, and genuinely sick.

Shimon meets me at the gate. He doesn't look too well, himself.

"Don't," he says, at the glare in my eyes.

"Why not?" I ask. But his face has turned my impending tirade into a two-word whine.

"Yohan is dead," he says. "No, not our Yohan. The Baptist. Yeshua's cousin."

"How?" I ask.

"Herod Antipas," says the big fisherman. "Those men at the market were Yohan's men. They were fasting outside Herod's palace when the news came."

"How would he dare?"

"They said Herodias' daughter seduced him into it. The filthy Greek-lover. Or perhaps it was Herodias herself. They weren't very clear about that."

"Where's Yeshua?"

"Come inside, first." His big arm propels me into the courtyard. "Good. Yeshua's on the roof, praying. But he won't be for long. If Herod Antipas is taking heads, we should get the Rabbi away from here."

"But I thought the centurion here was friendly to us."

"He is. Yeshua healed his daughter. But his men only protect the caravan route and the customs station. They aren't supposed to interfere in local affairs."

"He could go to your brother Andreas' house, over at Bet Saida."

"That's Herod Philippos' territory."

"Exactly."

"No." The fisherman shakes his head emphatically. "Herod Philippos may owe his brother a favor. We'll go to Sidon or to Judaea. Maybe to the Essenes. Just for a while. Just in case."

I sit down in the courtyard, and shudder from the fever. Yohan—our Yohan—comes in with Yehuda Ishkerioth.

They've been at the house of Yohan's brother Ya'akob. Shimon repeats his story, and then sends them off to find some others of Yeshua's followers. Then he bellows to his wife to bring me a blanket.

"You ass of an ass," he tells me. "Why did you spend all afternoon out in the sun?"

"Why didn't you?" I retort.

"I had to be with Yeshua."

I huddle under the blanket, feeling the fever creep over the skin of my back. "Your father hates you," I tell Shimon.

"My father understands," Shimon says. "What I owe him is given to God."

"A clever word-slip. Does that fix the mast?"

"If Adonai had wanted the mast fixed today, he wouldn't have killed Yohan," Shimon replies, with typical Shimon logic.

Just then, Yeshua comes down. He is wearing a striped pilgrim's mantle, the one he uses to travel anonymously. "Shimon," he says, "I'm going to the grove east of town. Come for me tonight, with a boat, after you've finished fishing."

"So much for what Adonai wants." I grin savagely at Shimon.

"You'd better heal Teoma before you go," the fisherman tells Yeshua. "He's starting to babble."

Yeshua glances in my direction. "He doesn't want to be healed," he tells Shimon, sadly.

"I want. . . . " I start, then stop. "You're right, as usual."

Yeshua draws the shawl up over his face, and goes out. Shimon stares after him, and then stares

104

down at me, and finally turns away in disgust and starts bellowing orders.

I go up on the roof, and lie down on the reeds where the late afternoon sun might drive some of the chill from my bones. I shiver, and think, and presently sweat begins trickling down my skin under my robe, and bile crawls in the back of my raw throat, but still I don't move. The sun is nearly down, when Mattathias comes to the roof and stands for a moment, watching, fingering his black beard.

"I hear you're sick," he says. "Why?"

"That's a strange question to ask a sick man," I reply. "Sickness happens."

"Why are you *still* sick?" he persists.

"Because now I know I'm sick," I answer. "If I let him cure me, then I may still be sick, but not know it."

"What? Never mind. You're harder to follow than he is." Mattathias scratches his beard. "Shimon says the rest of us are leaving. But I'll stay with you, if you like."

"That's all right," I tell him, shivering. "I'll keep Shimon's wife company."

"Is there anything I can do before we go, then?"

I shake my head, as my teeth chatter.

"Okay, I'll leave you with your stupid demon. Just don't let it eat you up, or let Herod burn you, while we're gone."

"I won't. I may follow, when I'm better. Mattathias?"

He pauses at the top of the ladder.

"Could you write down what he says," I ask him, "so I can read it?"

"That's a good idea," he says. "'Bad luck that I burned all my papyrus, when I came here. Have care for yourself." He goes down the ladder.

105

Another shudder racks my body. I lie back to study my demon.

"Teoma!" calls Shimon the Rock, from the courtyard. "Thanks for stepping the mast!"

XVII.

I was more than a week in recovering from my illness. It took me another week after that to discover Yeshua's whereabouts. It wasn't that he'd dropped out of sight—on the contrary, it became obvious almost immediately that Shimon had failed to persuade Yeshua to go into hiding. Instead, the healer had left Kafer Nahum for the countryside, and the countryside was alive with rumors in his wake: lepers healed in Samaria, a demon driven into a dog in Magdala, a dumb man singing psalms near Korazim. . . . I began to hear the same rumors over again, only grown and moved to different towns. Everywhere, it was miracles, miracles! I wondered if he'd divided himself like a loaf of bread, and a hundred Yeshuas were roaming about Galilaia simultaneously.

Then, at last, there was the shore of Kinneret again, and the remnant of a huge crowd, stuffed and dazed. They sat on the trampled ground, muttering, or wandered from huddle to huddle, re-garbling the same stories:

"I saw when he started. I was right at the front, not ten cubits from him. He just had three fishes, and one loaf of bread. I saw it!"

"Shemuel said he had two loaves."

"Was Shemuel there?"

"How did it look? Did the bread stretch, or what?"

"It just, well, happened. He took it in his lap, and broke off a piece, and then another piece, and just kept breaking."

"He must have had some under his robe."

"What did he teach you about?" I ask them.

"There were seven loaves," maintains an old man with a bald spot.

"He couldn't keep enough bread for five thousand people under his robe!"

"There weren't five thousand people here! Five hundred, maybe."

"Very good. Let's see you stick enough bread for five *hundred* people under *your* robe!"

"What did he talk about before he fed you?" I try again.

"He healed me," interrupts a plump, middle-aged woman, sticking her hand in my face. "See? See, I chopped it with a fish-knife, I thought I'd lost it. Not even a scar!"

"No, not a scar," I agree, though I think I see a thin white line. "What did he tell you when he did it?"

But she is already waving her hand in the bald man's face. "And did you see him leave? He told them to get the boat ready, they were going to Bet Sayida, and then he talked some more when they were pulling the boat out from shore, and then he just walked off across the water out to the boat, like it was dry land. That boat was seventy cubits out, if it was a finger!"

"They went to Bet Sayida? You're sure?"

"Well, I think so. Maybe it was Bet Pagge."

"*Raka,*" The bald man spits. "Bet Pagge is by Yerushalayim, not on the lake. I think one of them said they were going to Magdala."

"When Yeshua stayed behind to speak with you, before he walked across the water—what did he say?"

No one remembers.

XVIII.

Galilaia is green. Fruit grows there: grapes, figs, apricots, pomegranates. The little plain of Kinneret, which the Greeks call Gennesareth, is lush with grainfields. Even the hills around Nazerat are covered with vineyards and olive groves and terraced fields of barley.

This is not so with the province to the south, which the Romans rule and call Judaea.

Before we entered Yerushalayim for the first time, Yeshua led us on a secret pilgrimage to the desert south of the river Ha-Yarden. There the stones lay flat and brown like baked Passover bread, and not even the bitter herbs grew. To the west, the highlands were like red ghosts wavering in the heat, and to the south the ash flats of the desert were blinding white, all the way to the Salt Sea, which the Romans and Greeks call Lake Asphaltitus, where the salt turns the waters of Ha-Yarden into not real water, but some bitter, nasty stuff that flows like clear oil, but will not burn.

There were times in those days when it was so hot that sweat was not enough, and skin cracked and blood dried on our fingers and chins. Yeshua led us down to the whitened edge of the dead lake, where Sodom and Gomorrha lay drowned. We each tasted a little of the bitter water, and watched it drifting over the salt-encrusted pebbles of the shallows—it was so thick that we could see the currents, like those of melted wax in a candle. I remember that we could see the air also, writhing above the hot stones of the shore.

"The demons of the air," Yohan muttered once, pointing at the nothings which quivered between us and the tawny mountains. He had been almost in a walking trance, ever since the journey had begun.

We stopped at the little oasis of En Geddi, where the fruits of a Sodom-apple tree were bursting their fluffy white seeds into the heat-tortured air, and we filled thirteen skins with water. "Herod took the water south of here," Shimon the Zealot observed to me. "The mountain runoff is all caught in aqueducts, and sent to Mezada." Still, we headed south, into the warren of gullies beneath the great yellow massif of Mezada itself. There Yeshua had us scoop caves in the stinging alkali soil, and we spent a secret time, fasting for six days.

A vision of the evening of the third day of our fast:

My cave, like the others, is dug into the side of a red and white gully. I picked the site for it carefully, with my builder's eye: the entrance is on the south side, in a deep hollow carved by the long-vanished runoff of a branching gully from the north. The wind off the mountains has further scooped out this place, creating a little amphitheater that shelters me from most of the day's sun. Now it is evening, and my bank is already in deep shadow. I sit at the mouth of my cave, and watch the golden light on the opposite side, creeping up the alternating bands of red-brown and white, of clay from the mountains and wind-blown alkali sand from the valley. One by one, each layer, turned copper or gold by the sun, slides into sudden darkness. I sit, remembering another evening so many years ago, watching the sunlight in the ravine below Gamla. . . .

Yeshua's face intrudes suddenly on the view. "Water," he says, and walks on.

I stretch my cramped legs in front of me, then arise and walk down to the base of the gully to join the others. Ya'akob, Yohan's brother, is already unearthing a half-empty skin of water. He draws it from its pit, shakes it as free from dust as possible, and carefully unties the knot in one leg of the skin. Then he gingerly fills a large gourd that Yohan holds for him, and re-ties the leg. We seat ourselves in a circle in the lengthening shade. Ya'akob tips his head back so that we can all see his throat, and lifts the gourd to his lips, and takes four swallows of water, then passes the gourd to Shimon the Rock on his right. Each of us takes four swallows, and then passes the water on; anyone who drinks more will be stealing from his fellows, in full view of them. Three times, the gourd passes around the circle.

"What have you learned?" asks Yeshua, when the gourd has made its last circuit. "What questions do you have?"

"You could hide a whole army in these gullies," says Shimon the Zealot. "But how could you get them enough water? Could you take the poison out of the Salt Sea for them?"

Yeshua smiles. The white dust caked on his face reminds me of a death's head. "No," he says. "And what about you, Teoma?"

"I've learned that this powder itches," I reply. "When you sweat, it begins to burn you even more than the heat. I've learned that if you sit in one position long enough, a little pain in one knee can fill your whole body and make you choke on your own scream. I've learned that a breath can start at the bottom of my stomach and go up, or at the top and go down, and still fill my lungs, either way. I've learned that pain is boring, and that boredom is terribly painful."

"You haven't learned to see visions?" he asks me.

"No."

"That's too bad," he clucks. "I see that both your temptations are continuing. What about you, Yohanan?" He addresses Yohan by his full Hebrew name.

Yohan *does* look like a death's head. His naturally thin face now seems downright gaunt, under its coat of alkali; his eyes look sunken and feverish.

"This is Sheol, isn't it?" he says.

Yeshua looks startled. He scrambles up the slope of the gully, and peers sharply about. Then he returns to the circle, and settles himself warily. "Why do you say this is hell?" he asks Yohan.

The young seer hesitates, then shrugs helplessly. "It just seems so," he answers.

"This place is not Sheol," says Yeshua. "It's hot, and it lies below most land, but the dead don't dwell here. And this certainly isn't *Hades*." He pronounces the Greek word with a Greek accent, to make sure we understand that he means the Greek underworld. "But Shaitan sometimes comes here. Did you see him?"

"No," says Yohan. His voice cracks on the syllable.

"I met Shaitan here, once," says Yeshua. "He took me to the top of the mountains behind Mezada, and showed me the Red Sea and the Mediterranean, and Yerushalayim and Galilaia and Petra and Damascus and Babylon. . . . " He singsongs the names of a dozen more places. "He said Yahweh gave them to him, and that he would give them to me, if I would only give him back the honor due for such a gift. I told him I only served Yahweh. That was the second thing he tempted me with, and the easiest." He turns suddenly to Shimon the Zealot. "What would you have told him, Shimon?"

Shimon stares at Yeshua, then at the ground. "I don't want Babylon," he says at last. "I only want Israel." But his gaze is on the ground, still; he isn't through thinking.

Yeshua lets him think. He turns to Yohan. "Are you hungry?" he asks.

Yohan nods mutely.

"I could make bread for us," Yeshua proposes.

"You brought flour?" I ask suspiciously.

"Who needs flour? See that little flat red rock over there?" he points. "It looks a little like flat-bread already, doesn't it?"

Yohan stares at the stone, which lies about ten paces away. Suddenly he springs up and runs toward it, and snatches it up. He is about to cram it in his mouth when Yeshua calls, "Yohanan, why are we here?"

Yohan stares at the stone in his quivering hands. "To fast," he says, finally, and casts the stone away.

114

"That was the first thing he tempted me with," says Yeshua.

"That was cruel," I tell him.

"It never was bread to you, was it?" Yeshua says. "You're a lucky man, Teoma. Miracles don't tempt you."

"Yes they do!" I protest, then subside in confusion. I want to say that they tempt me every moment, that I want them desperately, but that statement is just as wrong as Yeshua's—though just as true, somehow. There are no words to fit my relationship, or non-relationship, with miracles.

Yeshua knows that, too. He leaves me to hunt the answer to his inexact statement, and goes on. "But the biggest temptation was the last one. He took me to the top of the Antonia, that big fortress adjoining the Temple, and he set me down on the parapet overlooking the Court of the Gentiles. Then he said he'd let me prove I was the Chosen of Yahweh. He said if I was the *Meshiha,* I could jump, and angels would catch me before my feet struck a stone, just as the scripture said." He spreads his arms suddenly, palms out, fingers tense, like a frightened wrestler. "People were beginning to gather down below. A young man started yelling for me to jump. The soldiers were going to arrive up there at any moment."

"And you think I'm not tempted by miracles," I say, quietly.

"Would you have jumped?" said Yeshua.

"If Shaitan himself had suddenly taken an interest in me, and if I were suddenly transported a week's walk, and landed on the highest point in Yerushalayim . . . yes, I might have been tempted," I admit. I think of the north side of Gamla, where the cliff falls nearly a furlong down

115

to a rocky gully. As children, we had thrown stones from our uncle's rooftop into that chasm, and watched them fall so far that we could barely see them land. I'd always wondered that when I pitched a stone upward, I could make it hang for a moment in space before falling—as if part of my will, given to the stone, had for a moment gained a power which I could never have inside my own body. . . .

"Why didn't you jump?" Thaddai asks Yeshua.

Yeshua leans back against the bank of the gully. "A good question," he notes.

"The scripture said angels would guard his heels," Shimon the Rock snorts. "But what about his head?"

"Don't be like a Scribe, Shimon," Yeshua rebukes him. "You think Yahweh would let the *Meshiha* split his head on a point of rhetoric?"

Yohan stretches out, with his head on the master's feet. "Perhaps he did jump," he says, with a strained giggle. "Perhaps we're following Yeshua's ghost, or maybe Shaitan himself. Maybe Shaitan has led us all out here to die of the heat."

"Why didn't you jump?" Shimon the Zealot asks, slowly. "You could have given us everything without a fight. Even the Romans wouldn't have dared to touch you, after such a sign."

"Perhaps he was afraid," I say.

Yeshua laughs. He is no longer nervous of his laugh, as he once was; now it is high and clear, like the sound of the *kinnor* harp that shepherds play. "How profound, Teoma," he says. "Of course I was afraid. I'm standing atop a Roman fortress, with Yahweh's demon beside me, and I'm not supposed to be afraid? Do you know what the

Romans do to people who sneak inside their fortresses?" He coughs on the dry air, and then stares out across the darkening salt pans below the gully. "It would have been very easy to jump," he says.

"When was this?" Yohan suddenly asks.

"Another good question," says Yeshua. "It was before I knew you, before my cousin's wedding in Canna. I'd never done a miracle."

This penetrates our thick skulls slowly. "You really were afraid," Yohan says, at last.

I think of the power standing on that pinnacle, and of the danger. Such a balance: the decision teetering back and forth like a nightmare. . . .

"Teoma," Yeshua says, as if reading my mind. "Teoma, what was I afraid of? Falling on my head? Or hanging by my wrists?"

I think of a thousand answers. "Huh?" I say.

"If I had jumped, would it have been a sign of faith, or of despair?"

I sit silent, reeling with possibilities.

"Merciful Adonai," breathes Shimon the Rock. "How did you escape?"

"I quoted a scripture to him. I told him we weren't allowed to tempt Yahweh. But you leap around my question like mad gazelles. If I had jumped, would it have been from faith, or from despair?" he repeats.

Yohan, for all his swollen tongue, beats me to the answer. "What's the difference?" he asks.

Feverish as I am with heat and hunger, I understand why a question should answer such a question. And then I forget it all for many years: I leave the conversation, and go back in my heat-delirium to the rooftop in Gamla, and my brother, and our pile of stones hauled up from the street. Once we had competed, arguing hotly about which stone had sailed the farthest out before dropping. But now, that game has faded: wordlessly, almost in a trance, we stoop for stone after stone, and feel their rough surfaces for the best grip, and hurl them up to hang on the blue air, as if we expected one of them, someday, to stay there. But always, they only pause a moment, almost until the beginning of hope, and then fall and fall like little bodies, until they are so far down they might be either bodies or stones, except they shatter differently from bodies when they land. . . .

XIX.

Another night, in Magdala, after the death of Yohan the Baptist:

The new moon has not risen yet when I wander into town, and see the light in the house of Miryam the prostitute, and feel a sudden hope. I go around to the back, and step cautiously up to the rough doorway that has been cut into the back wall.

An old clay urn is fastened to the door with an iron band. I feel cautiously inside it: there are no coins there tonight. I pick up a shard of pottery from the doorstep, and toss it in the jar. It makes a satisfying clank.

"Who?" comes Miryam's voice from inside.

"Yehuda the Twin," I answer.

The door opens a little. Miryam peers out at my face, then lets me in.

She is a plump widow in her mid-thirties. Her husband's family are Hellenists, Greek-loving Jews; when he died, they turned her away from their house in Yerushalayim, despite their obligations to her under Hebrew law.

119

So she had wandered up through Judaea and Samaria, feigning madness to collect alms, and finally had returned to the house of her dead husband, and cut the door in the back wall. Then she had met Yeshua.

"*Shalom*," I tell her. "Is he here?"

"*Shalom*," she replies. "Yes, he's here. He's asleep in the other room, with Shimon bar Yona and Yohan and some people I don't know. Are you all right? You don't look well."

"I've been sick," I reply. I could use some wine."

She pulls a round-bottomed urn from its hole in the corner, and fills a bowl with wine. It is a real glass bowl.

"I thought you were staying with Ya'akob bar Yosef now," I tell her.

"I was," she says. "Thaddai came to their house last night, looking for a place where the Rabbi could rest. We thought this place would be better. Men can come and go quietly."

"But the neighbors!" I protest, in a low voice. "You don't want them to think. . . . "

She shrugs that off. "I'll always be a whore, to this town. I've made excuses to one man tonight already."

"I'm sorry," I tell her. Inwardly, I curse at the little knot of shame I feel; I had been thinking of Yeshua's reputation, not hers.

"Here's your wine," she says. "I'm sorry, too. I can't love them here. They won't let me." The smoothness of the glass feels strange in my rough workman's hands; the coolness of the wine seeps easily through the thin walls, as if the drink itself were leaking out. Through the milky translucence of the vessel, I can see my own fingers; the wine stains them deep red.

Miryam settles the jar more evenly in its pit, and sits down against the opposite wall. "What is Herod Antipas doing? Did you see soldiers?"

"Hardly any," I answer, sipping. "The rumor is that he's pulled all of them into his garrisons until the people quiet down. A couple of his estates got burned."

"Yohan's followers?"

"Maybe they did it. Maybe it was the Zealots, pretending to be Yohanites; maybe just people with a general grievance. The Baptist was a good excuse." I take a good gulp of wine. "But they're all just kicking a little, like a body without a head."

She frowns and looks away. "You use ugly likenesses sometimes," she says, after a moment.

"I have an ugly world," I answer. But as soon as the words are out, I feel ashamed again. Is my world uglier than this woman's?

She is silent again for a moment or two, staring at air. Then she says, "We can't stay here very long. If I frustrate too many customers, they'll come back with rabbis and stones." She pauses. "Oh, Adonai, I don't want to think this way again."

I've always thought that way, I tell myself silently. *Hard thoughts, expecting people to be bad. . . .*

"Why are they afraid of us?" she says. "We just want to love them."

"They don't want love," I tell her, my voice hardened with habit. "They don't need to love carpenters, or whores, or slaves." With each word, though, something inside me cries like a slave breaking down under the whip.

"You aren't really a follower of Yeshua, are you?" Miryam says quietly.

"I've just walked his trail all over Galilaia!" I erupt. Then it's my turn to pause. "You're right. I'm not a follower. Not like you," I admit. "I'm his slave."

"He freed you," she says.

"He didn't know how," I tell her. And inside, the voice screams and sobs.

"Thank you for the wine," I tell her. "I think I'll go to sleep now." She nods.

I go into the next room. There are five figures sprawled there already. I recognize Shimon the Rock by his snore, and by the little figure of his wife beside him. I know Yohan by the striped cloak folded neatly under the dark blur of his head; Yohan almost never sleeps in his cloak. And I know Yeshua because he sleeps apart from the others.

I find a place apart, too, in the southeast corner of the room. I pull off my cloak, and spread it on the floor, and curl a little of the top corner to cushion my head, and lie down and pull the rest of the cloak over me.

"Teoma?" says Yeshua, softly.

"Yes?" I answer.

"Why did you follow us?"

"Why shouldn't I?" I whisper back, after a moment.

"You don't believe what I'm doing," he says. "You don't believe, even when it happens in front of your eyes."

"That doesn't mean I don't want to believe," I answer.

I wait for his reply, but none comes. In its place, the voice in my mind keeps chanting to itself, repeating the little psalm that Yeshua gave us, blessing the poor and the humble and the mourners and sufferers on the hillside above Kafer Nahum. I can't believe in this man's miracles. But I pursue his words.

After a while, I hear soft snoring from his corner. I tuck the cloak more securely under my chin, and turn on my side, and try to sleep, myself.

XX.

A vision of the time after Yohan the Baptist's death:

The walls of the town, which guards the northern approach to the valley of Gadara, stand knife-edged with afternoon light and shadow: just small enough and high enough to seem not quite real. The spur of rock on which the town perches is not as high as that of Gamla—at least, not as high as the ridge of Gamla that rises in my childhood memory. Still, it dominates the little plain that stretches between it and Lake Kinneret. The inhabitants of the town are pagan; we know that, from the creatures that snuffle across the grass nearby.

"They'll eat anything," says Shimon the Rock, disgustedly. He kicks a clod of earth back into the crater at his feet. "Anything. Roots, manure, their own young. There was a Greek farmer who had them, over by Bet Sayida. One day, one of his neighbors had a calf die of scours. The neighbor decided to burn the carcass by the lakeshore, so it wouldn't attract wolves. He built a big fire over it, and let it burn down some, and then left—stupid of him; the fire might have spread. But when he came back the next day, the coals were smothered with hog manure, and the calf was eaten."

The gouge at Shimon's feet is shallow, perhaps a span in depth, but three or four spans wide, and long enough for a man to lie down in. The gentle slope around us is leprous with such gouges, from the necropolis at the base of the ridge all the way down to the date-palm grove at the water's edge. Just to the southwest of us, in the direction of the river Ha-Yarden, are the beasts who made those craters. There are scores of them: big and squat and brown, flat-nosed and flop-eared, rooting and basking in the afternoon sun. The still summer air is thick with their dusty-sweet odor, and with the stench of their fresh manure.

Scattered around the swine are a half-dozen naked herdboys and their dogs. Much to our discomfiture, Yeshua has gone over to talk with the nearest herder. We stand, shifting nervously from foot to foot. A huge brown female hog, her belly of full milk-teats dragging on the sparse grass, wanders to within a couple of paces of us, pauses, and grunts: a sound like a quarry-block dragged in an empty canyon, only deeper. Her lazy, malevolent little eyes peer suspiciously at us from under the shade of her ears. Andreas shouts and waves his arms at her. She emits an explosive, barking grunt, whirls, and gallops awkwardly but rapidly back to the herd. They greet her with a cacophony of barks and grunts, and mill uncertainly. Three or four young hogs bolt, and the herdboys and dogs, Yeshua with them, rush to head them off.

Then suddenly the crisis is over, and the herd is as it was before. Yeshua starts back toward us.

"I still don't like this," Nathan'el declares. "The Ga-
darenes may not be beholden to Herod. But they're still
Greeks. . . . "

"*Mostly* Greek," Shimon the Zealot corrects him.
"There are also Syrians, and some Jews in the main city.
Maybe in the towns, too."

"Well?" Shimon the Rock says, as Yeshua reaches us.
"Are the gates open? Is there a synagogue?"

"Yes and yes," the rabbi replies. "There's a synagogue,
a small one, in the city. The gates are open until dark."
He pauses, studying the scarp of the village before us.
"The boy said be careful passing this village, though.
He said there's a madman living in the necropolis, who
sometimes attacks people passing by. He said they can't
even keep chains on him." He pulls at his beard thoughtfully, scanning the base of the scarp for the openings of
the tombs.

"You aren't," says Ya'akob.

"I think so," says Yeshua. "Ya'akob, come with me, if
you would. Also Shimon the Rock and Yohan. The rest of
you please wait here."

The four of them walk up the slope toward the tombs.
Standing on the plain, we others watch the events open
themselves like a strange dance, a drama-ritual such as
the Greeks do. As Yeshua and his companions walk up
the rise, the scarp seems to grow in comparison to them,
until the men are to it as dung beetles are to a man. Finally, clambering over the ancient mounds of debris from
old rock-falls, over the piles of trash thrown from above,
the four men near the base of the bluff. Around them, the
openings of the tomb-caves pock the earth like the dens of
unknown animals.

126

Then suddenly the four men jump back into a wary semicircle. A creature has leaped atop one of the rock-piles, and crouches facing them. It shouts something— the words are blurred by the distance, but the tone is not pleasant.

Yeshua motions to the other three to stay where they are, and takes a step toward the thing on the mound. It hops backward, spewing a torrent of hateful, unintelligible language. Yeshua stops, says something, and then resumes his slow approach. The creature cowers, whining, jabbering, threatening. Yeshua reaches the base of its mound, and reaches up, and grasps its hand.

A scream erupts: a howling, shrieking, indescribable noise, a thousand horrible emotions brawling over a single voice. The scream strikes the bluff and seems to grow and divide, until a horde of screams echo out across the valley.

The swine go wild at the sound. Squealing and bark-grunting like women in bad childbirths, like soldiers under burning oil, they wheel and stampede away from the bluff, towards the date-palm grove and the lake. The herdboys scatter out of the way, while the yapping dogs, uncommanded and frenzied with pursuit, harry the herd's flanks. I see one black-and-white dog fasten its teeth in the hind leg of a big male hog. With terrifying speed, the hog whirls like a stiff-legged dancer, throwing the dog into its tusks. The dog goes down, ripped open. Thrashing and yiping, it tries to bite at the terrible pain in its own belly, while the hog charges on with the herd.

Within a few moments, the entire herd has charged down through the palm grove and into the water. With their noses slung lower than their arched backs, they are not designed to swim.

The screaming stops. In the silence, I see most of the herdboys fleeing up the path that mounts toward the village. One or two of the boys linger by the water, staring numbly at still-thrashing corpses of drowned hogs. Another boy has returned, crying, to the dead dog. He picks it up, carefully, belly up, so that the spilled intestines don't dangle, and stumbles up the slope after his fellows. As he passes, he looks at us. Behind the grimace of sorrow, his eyes shoot pure hatred.

"Yeshua!" cries Mattathias.

Yeshua and his three companions are returning. With them is a naked man. He is thin and unshorn and filthy, and he looks dazed and frightened. But he doesn't look mad.

"Teoma!" says Yeshua. "Do you still have that spare cloak?"

I hesitate, put off for a moment by the thought of the man's filthiness touching my one good possession.

"Master," says Shimon the Zealot, beside me, "I don't think we should go to Gadara now. I think maybe we should go back to the boat."

I follow the Zealot's eyes up the path where the herdboys have gone. High up the slope, on a switchback of the village trail, I see the glint of sunlight on iron spears.

XXI.

A vision of the land between Tyre and Sidon, in the province of Syria:

"Is this Zarephath?" I ask.

"I don't think so," replies Ya'akob bar Yonah, uncertainly. "I think Zarephath is bigger. That's all right. We don't want to find a place with *too* many Jews in it. The Rabbi needs rest."

We are walking down the waterfront street of a small fishing village. Ya'akob is eyeing the doorways of the mud-and-wattle houses on our left. I am distracted by the sound and sight of the Great Sea on our right.

I saw the sea from a distance many times while working on the aqueduct to Caesaraea, but this is the first time I've actually stood on its shores. For as far as the eye can look, there is nothing but water. I'm terrified by the hugeness of the thing, by its noise and noisomeness. There is no storm, but even in this partly sheltered bay, the waves roar in at the height of a medium-sized dog. And the animal smell of the seawater permeates the air. I wonder, for a moment, why Yahweh would make a thing so huge, and make men so small; which did he really care more about?

But even the ocean-smell cannot overwhelm all the other stenches of the village. Feces lie scattered across the beach, awaiting the cleansing of a high wave; the fishing boats are out (fishing in daylight?) but the smell of fish is everywhere. The fish smell adds to the wrongness of the place, because I smell it and expect Kafer Nahum— but here the smell blends with the sea, and with the stench of pigs in their sties behind the houses. We are definitely not in Galilaia; I wonder if we will find any Jews at all here.

But just then, Ya'akob spots a doorway with a tell-tale prayer box beside it. He touches the box ritually, and slips inside. A brief time later, he emerges again.

"We've found a place for the night," he says. "Teoma, would you go tell the Rabbi?"

If you trail after people long enough, they start giving you orders. I don't feel like arguing, though; I can put off meeting more Jewish strangers for a little longer.

Yeshua and a few others are waiting down the coast a bit, on a stretch of white sand beach. We would have camped for the night there, if Ya'akob hadn't found Jews in the village. When I get back to the beach, Yeshua has spread his cloak on the sand, and is lying spread-eagled upon it. Yohan and Yehuda bar Ya'akob have shed their tunics and girded their loins, and gone into the sea to bathe.

Yeshua notes my approach, but barely moves. I sit down beside him, so we can speak over the roar of the waves.

"Sand is one of Yahweh's great creations," remarks the healer. "One bit of it in the wrong place is torture, but a whole beach of it is better than a king's cushions. When the Kingdom comes, we'll all sleep on sand."

I carefully avoid the "Kingdom" talk. "I'd rather sleep here tonight, myself," I agree. "But Ya'akob has found Jews."

"They're everywhere, aren't they?" remarks the rabbi. He is growing a little bitter. Lately, a horrible pattern has been emerging: whenever he arrives somewhere, he's adored at first for the beggars who drop their crutches at his feet. But then he starts talking about the Kingdom, and people start getting afraid—especially the landowners, and the powers of the synagogues. They begin showing up with words like sling-stones, then with the stones themselves. Lately the Pharisees and landowners have been spreading rumors ahead of us, so that the stone throwers arrive along with the beggars, and Yeshua has been forced to hone his wits as sharp as iron arrowheads. It's a comfort to spend a few days away from the synagogues.

"It's a poor village," I encourage him. "I doubt if there's a roof and floor anywhere in it that will be as comfortable as this sand."

Yeshua sighs. "*Shalom*, Teoma. Sand won't feed us." He levers himself upright. He has a little belly-fat from all the dinners he's been given in the past few months, but he still looks slightly gaunt.

We call the two bathers back from the sea, and start up the beach toward the fishing village. The sea roars at us all the way into town. The sand grabs at our ankles.

131

When we reach the village, a knot of people has already gathered around the house that Ya'akob entered. They chatter in Greek and Aramaic, just as our crowds in Galilaia do—only here, there is more Greek than Aramaic, and the Greek is different. There's something in their 'r's and 'o's that reminds me of Hermione's speech. I'm not sure which of these people, if any, are Jews. Ya'akob emerges from the crowd. He has his hand around the elbow of a bald fisherman, who looks a bit confused.

"Master, this is Malachi bar Saul," says Ya'akob. "He's the eldest here, though there aren't enough men for a synagogue."

"*Shalom,* Rabbi," said the bald man, nervously. "Would you stay at my house this evening?"

"Gladly," said my master. "Do you have room on your roof for my students?"

"How many?" the elder asks, suspiciously.

"Just those you see here," said Yeshua. "I've sent the rest off for a while. And one of these says he prefers to sleep on the beach."

"Ho, he does? The man obviously doesn't know about sand fleas," says our host, suddenly chuckling. "Perhaps he'll take supper with us, anyway."

Dinner this night consists of only two fish. But no miracles are needed. The fish are enormous, a cubit each in length. They have been roasted over an open fire of wood from the twisted, thorny trees that grow just above the beach on this coast; the smoky flavor is delicious. But I have no name for either the fish, or the trees. The marble-sized eye of the fish peers up from its increasingly bare bones. I think, *I'm eating the unknown.*

But the arguments are familiar.

"I don't really see that much difference between what you say and what the Pharisees tell us," maintains Malachi. Wine has washed away much of his timidity. "Some of them also say it's not purity of the food, but the purity of a man's soul. . . . "

"Those vipers?" Yeshua interrupts. "Look at what they *do,* not what they say. They put the tassels on a prayer shawl above a human's life. They'd let people die in agony, rather than heal them on the Shabbat."

"Maybe some would," says our host doubtfully. "But it's so easy to lose the Law, especially in a town like this. My own daughter wants to marry a . . . what's this? Tamar, what's this woman doing in here?"

One of the townswomen has come into the room with Malachi's wife. I only glimpse her—a square jaw, slightly plump arms—before she prostrates herself in front of Yeshua's reclining body.

"Holy man, I'm told you cast out demons," she says, in the local Greek. "My daughter. . . . "

"I'm sorry," said Yeshua. "I'm having trouble with this woman's accent."

"Tamar, this is a private dinner!" explodes our host at his wife. "It's bad enough you gossip with this woman in the marketplace, but this . . . !"

"Teoma?" Yeshua queries.

"She says her daughter has a demon," I tell him. I've heard this dialect before. It's not quite Hermione's, but it was common among the slaves; the Romans have reconquered towns in this region several times.

"It's a mute demon, but it throws her all over the room," says the woman. Talking into the mats on the floor doesn't improve her accent. "My girl breaks her own bones. I can't light lamps in the house, for fear. . . . "

"Is this woman a Greek?" asks Yeshua.

"Her family's Greek, yes," explains Malachi, embarassed. "Tamar, would you get this woman out of here?"

Malachi's wife kneels beside the prostrate woman. "Let's go home, Penelope," she says.

I wince at the name.

"I have enough to do with Hebrews," says Yeshua, angrily. "I can't start casting out Greek demons, too. You have to feed the children, before you throw bread out for the dogs."

The men around the table grunt their approval. Most of the older men at the table remember the reign of the Greek Antiochus, who once ruled Syria and Palestine, and disemboweled men for not eating pork. The Maccabees had finally thrown Antiochus out of our homeland—but the Jews here had never escaped, and had suffered all the more for it.

"What did the healer say?" asks the woman.

"He says he has to feed the children of Israel first, not the dogs of Greece," I tell her.

Someone drops a piece of fish on the woman's head. "Oops, I'm sorry," he says, grinning.

"Tell the healer," says the woman slowly, raking the fish from her hair, "tell him even the dogs under the table lick up the children's crumbs."

"I think I understood that," says Yeshua, suddenly thoughtful. "Go home, woman. No mute demon can withstand a reply that eloquent. Your daughter will be fine."

The woman backs away on her knees. "Thank you," she said, and left.

There is an uncomfortable silence until she has gone. Then several of the men mumble excuses and stand to leave. "You comforted a *Greek?*" says Malachi.

Yohan is reclining next to me. He looks about, confused, at the men who are standing up. I lean over and whisper to him, "I think the Children are about to spit up again." Then I arise also, and walk back to the beach outside the village, and spread my cloak on the sand. The moon has risen. The sea is a thousand moving shades of black and white and grey. There is something strangely peaceful in the roar of the waves; I sit watching them, entranced as by a campfire.

Finally I hear the sound of footsteps and low voices, and look down the beach to see the figures of men approaching, black against the moon-grey sand. It's the rest of our party. They quietly lay their cloaks down on the sand around me.

Then I finally doze off. A little later, a bad dream pushes me awake, then retreats laughing into the blackness. I lever myself up on my elbows. The moon is about to set. Yeshua is still sitting, staring at the waves.

XXII.

I was never an easy person to get along with. I was self-righteous, excitable, and insecure; curious to the point of nosiness; obsessive about my own problems and bored with the problems of others. I still am. But I got along better with slaves than I did with Yeshua's other followers. We were *all* self-righteous, insecure and excitable.

And worse, none of us knew who we were. We Jews were not like the folk here in Mylapore, whose castes tell them exactly what to do. Our last kings, the Maccabees, were both warriors and high priests; Yeshua's followers saw themselves as everything from soldiers to mystical prophets. Their own ideas of themselves often turned them into swaggering, half-blinded exaggerations, like Greek actors in giant masks and foot-tall shoes. Shimon the Zealot was a reasonable man, normally—but whenever he came in sight of Yeshua, his mouth filled with military words. I sincerely believe that he thought Yeshua walked around in a sword and armor. Yohan, dancing in his ecstatic trances, saw Yeshua in a prophet's goatskins. And I don't know what Shimon the Rock saw Yeshua as—maybe Adonai himself—but a glance from Yeshua turned the stolid fisherman into some sort of fawning comic servant, so attentive on the man that he fell off boats following him around. Whatever the men themselves might be, their masks were insufferable.

And it didn't help that they saw me as a former slave, and harassed me for being able to write Greek.

But eventually, I did form a sort of alliance with one of them: Mattathias, a short, black-haired young man with baggy, sad eyes and a mellifluous voice. Mattathias was a former tax official, which made him even more despicable than a former slave; I didn't really like the man much at first, myself. But he was sociable enough, in a shyly desperate sort of way: hesitant to start a conversation, but often loath to break it off. And he had a very good head for numbers. So we built a little wall around us, of mathematics; I taught him what my Greek taskmaster had shown me of Pythagoras and Euclid, and he learned eagerly, which flattered me.

So when Yeshua sent us out to work miracles on our own, it was only natural that Mattathias should ask me to go along with him.

A vision of that journey:

"I wish he'd let us take spare robes along, at least," says Mattathias. "It will get cold, if we have to spend the night up here."

"What spare robes?" I ask sardonically. "But I can understand that command, anyway. That's so we can't just hide out in the hills until it's time to go back."

"Why should we want to hide out?" says Mattathias. I don't look over my shoulder to see, but I'm sure he wears an expression like a puzzled dog's.

"Look," I tell him, "what did he say for us to do? Spread the word, heal the sick, cure the lame, cast out demons? I can deliver the message, whatever that's good for. But I don't know anything about curing. And I haven't got the least idea of what to say to a demon."

"I think you just tell it to get out," he volunteers. "Anyway, I wish we had spare robes, because I think we're lost. We should have been in Caesaraea Philippi by now."

"Are you sure it's east of the Yarden valley?"

"Northeast of the headwaters. This road should have bent back north a long time ago."

"This 'road' is turning into a sheep path. We should double back to the river valley. If we can't find the main highway again, then at least we can find a village."

"We'd never get back there before dark," he says.

I look at the shadows creeping up the sides of the narrow valley we've been ascending. "You're right," I tell him.

"Maybe we should climb the hillside, and see if we can spot a village."

"That's not a hillside. That's a canyon wall. And if you want to try climbing up through all those seventy-seven varieties of thornbushes, go right ahead," I tell him. "This is sheep country; if a plant can't stab things, it gets eaten."

"I wish I'd grown up in the countryside," Mattathias says sadly, after a moment. "I feel so ignorant. What kind of flowers are those?"

138

I waste a moment of precious sunlight to turn around and stare where he's pointing. A cluster of bright purple blossoms hang above a clump of grey-green leaves—all liberally bristling with the inevitable thumbnail-length needles. Such flowers used to grow around Gamla. . . .

"I forget what they're called," I tell Mattathias, gruffly.

A quarter-mile later, the sun has disappeared from the valley. We reach a fork in the trail. One path, the broader of the two, leads on up the valley to the northeast. The second climbs up a narrow side-canyon to the north.

"Which way?" says Mattathias, coming up beside me.

I survey the two paths, and then notice a few puffs of smoke hanging, still rosy with sunlight, in the sky above the canyon rim. "This way," I tell Mattathias, and plunge up the side-path.

It is twilight when we finally climb, shaky with fatigue and thoroughly be-prickled, out of the canyon, and discover a little cluster of black stone houses on the plateau above. Mattathias hauls on my arm as I start toward them.

"Do you think they're Jewish?" he asks.

"Probably not," I tell him. "Around here, they're probably Syrians."

"But he said we should just go to our own people."

"I'm hungry," I tell him, and walk toward the huts.

There is a large, full sheep pen next to the six houses, which cluster roughly around a small well. As we approach, four black-and-white sheep dogs rush up, barking. They stop three or four strides short of us, though; after a moment, I start forward again, warily, and

Mattathias follows. We enter the village square, which isn't square at all. To my private relief, I notice a little Jewish prayer-box by the door of the first house we pass.

A young girl is drawing water from the well. She peers anxiously through the twilight at us. Then suddenly she abandons her water jar and rushes toward the nearest house.

"It's the *Meshiha!*" she yells.

In the doorways, the silhouettes of cautious heads peer out at us. The girl from the well reaches her own door, and drags out a balding man in a ragged smock. "See?" she says, pointing at us.

The man stares at us. "I don't think so," he tells her. But he advances toward us uncertainly. "*Shalom,*" he says. "You aren't Yeshua of Nazerat, are you?"

"No, I just look like him," I reply crossly.

"*Shalom.* We're followers of his," adds Mattathias, quickly. "How did you know about him?"

"We were visiting my cousin in Korazim, when the rabbi preached there." The man shakes his head. "I never saw such an uproar in my life. What are you folks doing here, anyway, without so much as a bedroll?"

"We're lost," I tell him.

"Yeshua sent us," says Mattathias.

"Well," the man says. "Hmm. Would you like something to eat?"

The meal is simple, but filling: wild greens fried in olive oil, with goat cheese and barley bread, all washed down with stiff Syrian wine from a skin that our host has opened just for the occasion. Our host's name is Yosef. His wife's name is Elisheba. She is fortyish, and was once pretty, with somber eyes and a fine straight chin to balance her long, slender nose. But the hard life has wrinkled her early and destroyed her posture. She bubbles about the healings that they'd witnessed in Korazim, but says she didn't quite approve of the way Yeshua had refused to see his family, after they'd come all the way from Nazerat to visit with him.

"But you don't understand," Mattathias tells her. "They'd heard the stories about him, and decided he'd gone mad. They were going to drag him back to Nazerat with them."

Elisheba clucks at that, as she fills his wine bowl again. "Well, still, I just don't know," she says. "He could have talked to them, at least. He did such a good job of persuading everyone else."

"How long have you people lived up here?" I change the subject politely.

"Twenty years at least, hasn't it been?" says Yosef, with a glance at his wife.

"More like twenty-five," she says, nodding.

"We came up from Bet Horon, after Yehuda's rebellion."

"Yehuda the Galilaian?" I perk up my ears. Yehuda the Galilaian was not really a Galilaian. He was a native of Gamla—the town's only famous native son. After the rebellion, the Romans had come to our town and demanded all of Yehuda's family as hostages. We'd told them that the whole family had fled to the wilderness. In reality, of course, all of us were related to Yehuda in some way or another.

"Yes. We got out when the the fighting started. Things were just too unsettled, and nobody was sure what the Romans were going to do once they got control

141

again. I might have joined the fight myself, if I'd been alone, but I didn't want to risk my Elisheba." He gives her brown wrist a squeeze as she passes.

As dinner ends, the men from the other houses begin to appear; with the courtesy of the poor, they have held their curiosity until after the meal, to avoid taxing Yosef's modest larder. But Elisheba and her daughter are kept busy filling wine bowls.

"You say Yeshua the Galilaian sent you here?" says a burly middle-aged shepherd named Dawid.

"Yes," says Mattathias. "He sent us to give you the good word."

"We could use a rabbi," says Yosef. "As soon as Eleazar's son Boaz comes of age next month, we'll have enough men for a congregation. I know we don't have much here, but my daughter. . . . "

"Uh," I interrupt, "I don't think we really qualify for that. We're just followers, not scholars. My Hebrew is terrible."

"Yes, we just came with a message," adds Mattathias.

"What's that?" says Yosef.

I've drunk enough wine to feel reckless. "The Kingdom of Heaven is at hand," I declare.

The whole room falls silent, for the space of several long breaths.

"What does that mean?" says Dawid.

"Uh, he also told us to heal the sick," volunteers Mattathias.

Yosef's daughter has been the model of polite silence throughout the meal. Now, unfortunately, she decides to open her mouth. "They could help Aunt Ruth," she suggests to her mother.

142

"If you could do that, we'd all be grateful," says Yosef.

"What's wrong with her?" I ask, noncommittally.

"She has a demon," says Yosef. "At least, I guess it's a demon. If it is, it's a bad one."

"Where is she?" asks Mattathias.

"Yes, we can look at her, at least," I add. *Adonai help us,* I think.

"She's over in Eleazar's house right now," says Yosef. "We move her every month, to share the burden."

Eleazar leads us all across the darkened square to his house, while Yosef's wife and daughter run to the other huts to cast words of what's happening. By the time we reach Eleazar's door, most of the village is on hand.

I peer inside. Eleazar's house is much like Yosef's: a big square box of rough basalt blocks, with a wooden partition inside, dividing off a living area and a sleeping room. Inside the living room, a couple of olive-oil lamps are lit, but the unplastered black walls absorb the light as if they were cursed. The evening dishes have already been cleared away; in the center of the room, near one of the lamps, a boy and a girl are playing Hounds and Jackals on a crude homemade set, supervised by a woman who is obviously their mother, and obviously sane. She sees us, and stands up anxiously as we enter. "*Shalom,*" she says. But my eyes have already moved beyond her.

In a far corner, by the family grindstone, another woman sits like a discarded cooking utensil. I pick up a lamp from a niche in the black wall, and step hesitantly closer to get a better look. The woman might be in her mid-thirties; it is hard to tell. She is very gaunt, and sits absolutely rigid, with her arms clasped tightly against her chest. A crust of dried saliva runs down the side of

143

her chin from her half-open mouth, and reflects in the lamplight. She smells sour.

"Touch her, if you're sure you're blessed," says Dawid.

I touch her anyway, gingerly pressing my index finger against her forearm. She doesn't even shift her eyes. The muscle of her arm feels like stone.

"Merciful Adonai," breathes Mattathias. "How long has she been like this?"

"Two years, hasn't it?" Yosef looks around for his wife to agree with him. "She and her husband, my brother Boaz, went down to Yerushalayim with us for the Passover. They got caught in a mob outside the Temple—something about Pilate misusing the Temple funds to build something. Boaz got his head broken open by a Roman cudgel, and their little girl Sarah got trampled. We found Ruth in the square afterwards, rigid as a heathen idol, with the child's body clutched to her. She's been this way ever since."

I try to recall what little I know of demons. I know there are two basic kinds: those of the body, which cause disease or leprosy or some kind of crippling, and then usually leave; and those of the spirit, which inhabit the body alongside the victim's soul. Which kind is this? I remember the paralytic who came down through the roof: the old Pharisee had claimed that there was a demon inside the man, but Yeshua had seemed to refute him. Or was it the other way around? The wine has made my memories a little slippery.

"How do you feed her?" Mattathias asks.

"She'll swallow, if we put milk or porridge in her mouth," explains Eleazar.

144

"Can you help her?" says Yosef to me. He seems to think I'm the leader of us two.

You won't have any more courage tomorrow, I think.

"Stand back, please, everyone!" I tell them, in my best gang-foreman's voice. "Unclean spirit, whatever or whomever you are, I'm commanding you! In the name of Yahweh and of Yeshua the Nazarene, stop afflicting this woman!"

Ruth continues to stare ahead.

"Get out of her!" I add.

No response.

I hear some mumbling in my audience.

"Yehuda?" says Mattathias, timidly. "Yehuda, I think I know what to do."

I give him a little bow, and step aside.

Mattathias goes over to Ruth, and bends down, and kisses her grimy cheek. Then he sits down beside her.

"Careful," says Dawid. "Sometimes she shifts—and when she does, it's like the kick of a horse. I lost a tooth that way."

Mattathias gently gathers the woman onto his lap. "Yahweh, help us," he whispers, and hugs her against his shoulder, rocking softly. For a long time, they sit that way.

"Boaz?" asks Ruth.

"No," says Mattathias. "Just someone else who loves you."

Ruth relaxes, and settles against him like a tired child. Then suddenly she shrieks and leaps to her feet, knocking Mattathias against the wall. "Sarah!" she screams, and rushes toward the door, throwing big Dawid out of the way in the process. She stops at the doorway,

145

stares out, and then collapses against the doorpost, sobbing.

Mattathias staggers to his feet, coughing to get his breath back. Then he goes to the doorway, and gathers Ruth against him again.

"She's gone," Ruth tells him, as she cries.

"Yes," says Mattathias. "But not for long."

"So where's the Kingdom?" says Shimon the Rock.

We've gathered on the hillside above Kafer Nahum, to tell Yeshua what we've done on our journeys. Ashamed of my own impotence, I've let Mattathias tell about our adventure in the village of the shepherds. Ruth has come back with us. But many of the others haven't fared so well. Shimon the Rock bears a huge purple welt across his left eye and cheek, proof that his head actually isn't as hard as a real stone. Ya'akob and his son Yehuda were arrested and nearly stoned in Arbela. Shimon the Zealot is ecstatic; after rabble-rousing near Nain, he got himself chased by real Roman soldiers.

Yeshua listens grimly; he himself has been thrown out of his own home town. He sheds garbage better than most men do, but the insults of his old synagogue elders still burn in his eyes.

"I knew this would happen," he says, finally. "They don't want the Kingdom, Shimon." Then he walks up the hill, and turns his back on us, and delivers a methodical tirade against the towns which we've visited and the towns in which he has preached. I won't repeat that speech, as I feel uncomfortable writing great curses.

When he comes back down, he tells us, "It's time to go south. Pack food and clothing this time; we don't want to

146

burden the Samaritans for hospitality. Meet me on the beach this evening."

I wait until the rest disperse, and then tag along after Yeshua. "*Rabboni?*" I ask him. That title means both "teacher" and "Master"; I'd started using it out of irony, but it's now become habit.

"What, Teoma?" his voice sounds a little hoarse.

"The woman from the shepherds' village—Ruth. A question about her."

"Yes, what about her?"

"Did she really clutch her own daughter's soul inside her for two years? Or did she just think she had?"

Yeshua turns, and smiles, and claps me gently on the shoulder. "Poor Teoma," he says. "What's the difference?"

XXIII.

A short vision, of a conversation in Yericho:

"What happened to his father?" I ask, scraping the coals of the fire closer together. We are camping in the courtyard of a Pharisee named Amos, who has invited Yeshua in for supper and debate.

"He died building the Temple," says Philippos. "A big block fell on him."

"No, it was a timber," says Shimon the Rock. "One of the Rabbi's brothers told me."

"You're both wrong," says Shimon the Zealot. "He died at home. I'm his cousin-in-law. I should know."

"Then why should your cousin, his brother, lie?" demands Shimon the Rock.

"Maybe he didn't," says Yohan. "I heard Ya'akob, Yeshua's brother, say once that their father was conscripted to work in the Temple. The way I heard the story, they had to send old Yosef home, because he tried to lift a timber so big that it ruptured his gut."

148

"That *would* be slow death, for a carpenter," admits Shimon the Zealot. "My sister-in-law told me that he never worked much, that he made Yeshua and the other boys do most of the lifting. I thought he was just lazy."

"That would kill a man, if he were proud," I agree. "That would make a son bitter, too."

"Not if the son understood," says Yohan.

"It could make a son bitter with himself, because everyone else would have an excuse," interjects Yehuda Ishkerioth, to my surprise. Yehuda doesn't speak often.

"Not if he understood himself," says Yohan. He's finally had a revelation, and he's hanging on to it.

Yehuda Ishkerioth is a timid little man, but a stubborn one. "But Yeshua said we had to love others and hate ourselves," he argues. "If we understand everyone, but we're only responsible for our own actions, then we . . . we have to take all the blame for the world on ourselves."

Yohan considers this silently for a moment. "But if we understand ourselves," he exclaims, finally, "then we can keep from doing anything to feel guilty about!"

"I don't think we could ever understand ourselves that well," I tell him. "But are you sure that's what happened to his father?"

They are too far gone in their argument, though, to remember where they started. The topics of blame and guilt are turned inside out and tied into knots, but nobody can find a way to get rid of them. I finally leave the group and wander out into the empty market, and watch the moon rise over the parapet of the city wall—the wall that had fallen at the trumpet blast of our ancestor Yeshua, our own Yeshua's namesake, and that our other

149

ancestors had rebuilt so many times after that. I think about a carpenter who had given all his strength to re-build Yahweh's Temple, and had gotten back a ruptured gut and a slow death from humiliation. *If* that was what had happened. . . . But if it wasn't, then something else must have taken its place, to make a young man become so aware of the world's pain that he'd begun seeking a way to end it forever. *I am lucky,* I decide. *I've always had someone else to blame for my misfortune. But who could Yeshua have blamed, besides Yahweh, or himself?*

XXIV.

Brother Yehuda, the letter begins,

I don't know where you are or how you are, or even if you are still alive. But I've met Isam, son of Haban the trader; Isam says he can find you if you haven't died. So I entrust this letter to him and to Yahweh, who, if they will, shall give it to you.

So many things have happened since you left, that I don't know which to tell you. Our people are dying, but the followers of Yeshua are growing in numbers daily. Shimon bar Yona and Saul of Tarsus are both dead, killed in Rome. Judaea and Peraea are in rebellion; Yerushalayim is under siege. Poor Galilaia is already crushed; the Romans are selling whole cities into slavery, and killing all the old and young who can't be put to work. Only Gamla gave them a fight; the Zealots there defeated the Romans twice, but a new general came and besieged the town, and finally broke down the wall. They killed four thousand people there; five thousand more jumped from the cliffs.

*We were all gone from Yerushalayim before the siege
began. Yahweh ensured this; when we had found our best
people there, and had found friends elsewhere to take us
in, Yahweh used his own people to drive us out. Stephenas,
whom you don't know, and Ya'akob the brother of Yeshua
were killed, but most of us escaped safely.*

*We wait and wait, Teoma, and still the Kingdom
doesn't come. Usually I don't care, because the peace inside me is like fine wine. But sometimes I worry, for I
think I remember Yeshua saying that we would not taste
death before the Kingdom comes, yet so many of us have
died already, and we don't rise from the dead again. Soon
we will all be dead, who once kept the crowds from trampling Yeshua. Can something have gone wrong? Does my
memory fail, or did I misinterpret what he said? Or am I
just too ignorant, too stupid to understand?*

*I worry, too, for all the young people. We tell them
about Yeshua, but we can never tell everything. And then
they fill the holes we leave with their own ignorance and
selfishness, so that terrible monsters sometimes breed
from their belief. So I have begun writing an account of
what Yeshua said and did. But as you once said, words
are too slippery to grasp truth for long. I pray that the
Kingdom will come soon, and save my poor words from
the test. . . .*

I put down the letter, and wonder why I'm not crying.
The Romans selling Galilaia into slavery. Nine thousand
dead in Gamla. There were never nine thousand people
living in Gamla; they must have cornered all the Jews in
the Gulan there, and killed them all. My family, if any
were still alive, must have died among them. I know my

152

mother must be long dead, but still I see her now as a young woman, facing the choice of rape and butchery, or of making a stone of herself, of launching her soul shrieking into the canyon below. . . .

I don't cry. The love is gone from there, along with the hate. The people of Gamla have broken their bodies like stones, and were no more hurt by the fall than a broken stone is hurt. The love and the hatred and the pain and the beauty and the ugliness were all immortal; when the bodies broke, those other things just went elsewhere.

I might weep for the Romans. How much of that hatred and pain has gone into them? When they have sopped up all the hatred of the Jews, whom will they spill it out on again? The Parthians? The Germans? Each other?

But after all these years, I am nearly out of hate. Yeshua soaked up most of it and sent it . . . somewhere . . . died and took it with him, somehow. I am an old husk, that has accepted only the love given me for these past thirty or forty strange years. Soon they'll release me from this prison, and I'll die. I want to die releasing only love. . . .

XXV.

A vision of a vision, in my last days in Yerushalayim:

"What's wrong, Teoma?" says the ghost.

I am asleep, I think. I send my gaze slowly around the room, thinking that I should be awake to do this. Then my eyes return to the vision of Yeshua—or perhaps it is my real brother, or even myself. The light is too dim to be sure.

"You saw them today," I tell whomever it is. "Laughing and shouting and spouting out the most unspeakable truths. . . . "

"So were you," the ghost observes, reasonably.

"I was pretending! Faking! *Hoy*, don't you understand?" I snap. "Everyone else is singing like a madman. That makes the one who doesn't sing the one who's mad, doesn't it? You want me to sit there and tell them, 'I don't feel anything?' " I stare at the vision and think, quite rationally, that I'm overwrought and worn out and slightly drunk and very probably asleep, and if I don't stop thinking about it he is going to disappear and oh, Yahweh, what a loss that will be.

"How many others do you think were just pretending?" the ghost asks.

"I don't know. Maybe all of them. Maybe all but one."

"Then one man really was . . . ?"

"One man really *thought* he was," I correct him.

"But what's the difference between what's real and what you think is real?" says the vision, sounding a little like Archimedes. He smiles slyly.

I duck the question. "Maybe more than one of them really thought so. Shimon the Pebble was putting on an awfully convincing display."

But the vision is not to be deterred. "Why do you use the word 'display'?" he asks. "Isn't an event real, if it happens inside a man? What's the difference between 'putting on a display' and displaying what's inside you?"

"Why do you always talk to me in questions?" I demand, exasperated. "You tell everyone else prophecies or stories or, at very worst, parables, but you always tell me questions!"

The vision chuckles. "You're wrong. I ask questions all the time. You just don't hear them unless I ask *you*. And I give *you* questions, because you can believe in them." He leans back against the plaster, smug and amused, and crosses his white ghostly legs. *I should wake the others,* I tell myself. Then I think, *No, I shouldn't. . . .*

"You don't understand," I plead, loudly. Shimon the Rock continues snoring. "I want to believe in answers, too. I want answers I can believe in. I want to have a holy demon inside me, the way Shimon claimed he did. . . . "

155

"I also ask you questions because you never answer them," the vision chides. "I repeat: is an event real, if it happens inside a man?"

"I don't know!"

" 'Real' is a word," the ghost continues, as relentlessly as Archimedes. "You choose the meaning of words. What meaning do you choose for 'real'?"

"I don't know!"

"You mean you refuse to choose." The vision sighs. "Don't cry, Teoma. Try this. Is what's outside you own mind real?"

I stop sobbing, and consider. "Yes! Reality is what's outside my head!"

"Never what's inside your head?"

"Right!" I answer, defiantly.

"So Shimon dancing on the table and shouting of holy spirits, and Yohannan yelling 'God is word! God is word!'—was all that real?" the ghost asks, grinning.

"Yes!" I tell him triumphantly.

"But what was inside them, what filled them, wasn't real?"

"Yes!" I repeat recklessly.

"Yet you want it inside you, anyway?"

"Yes," I answer, doggedly.

"Am I real? Where am I—inside your head, or out?"

I stare at the vision, and consider.

"Yes. . . . " I answer, slowly.

XXVI.

A vision of Yeshua's first preaching in the Temple:

It is dawn. The vendors enter the Court of the Gentiles in a mob; they have been waiting on the Temple steps since long before the first light, hawking their wares and services to the early pilgrims who have also been waiting. In a frenzy of arguments and muffled orders, the vendors scramble to their usual spots. The regular merchants have their places pre-established, but a couple of dove-sellers, here only for the holy days, erupt into a loud quarrel that ends in blows. A Temple guard strides over, parts the two, and angrily rousts out the older of them—a farmer from Bet Sayida, who did not know enough to bribe the guard captain. From the rampart of the Antonia, above the Temple, two of Pontius Pilate's mercenaries watch until the farmer has been ejected.

Shimon the Zealot and I watch also, from the colonnade.

The sun bursts over the eastern portico, and suddenly the vendors are in full cry: dove sellers, with their white robes and manured cages, on the east side; Levites crying from the south portico, selling stone blocks and gold leaf for pilgrims to donate to the ongoing construction; water, oil, and food sellers on the west, between the Lower Gate and the King's Gate. On the north side, against the portico of the Court of Women, the money vendors cry, squatting behind their low tables: the pilgrims who enter the inner courts must first trade all their Greek and Roman money for the Tyrian silver of the Temple treasury. The Temple officials, of course, are said to claim one coin in ten on the transactions, and the money-changers take several more for themselves.

In the center of the court, a stooped figure in an elaborate prayer shawl stops and raises his arms. A crowd immediately starts to gather around him.

"Who is that?" I ask the Zealot, pointing unobtrusively.

"One of the big Rabbis," he answers.

"I *know* that. By Abraham's beard! Which one?"

"Don't swear. Hillel, maybe. I can't see."

Whomever it is, he has a fine, booming voice, even richer than Yeshua's. But even he only tries to teach for a short time; the vendors are just too loud. He finally flaps his arms in disgust, and leads his followers into the inner courts to pray.

"Twelve guards, right?" says Shimon the Zealot.

"What?" I ask. I have been watching for priests more than for guards. Then it occurs to me that the Temple Guards are also Levites; my brother might be among them, as well. . . .

158

"Two over by the center gate. Four by the west portico," says Shimon, a hand's breadth from my ear. "See them, there in a knot, in the shade? A couple more over there talking to that dove vendor. Two following the Rabbi's crowd. And four of them over by the money vendors. They'll be the ones who make trouble. We'll need to draw them off."

"Trouble? For whom? About what?" It's beginning to dawn on me that this is more than a casual visit.

"For Yahweh," is Shimon's only answer. He has gotten more and more cryptic in the past few months. I'm about to try him again, when a lamb merchant arrives with his whole family and three or four slaves, carrying month-old lambs slung from poles by their bound hooves. The group begins unloading their cargo in the shade at our feet. The lambs, still bleating for their ewes, make little hiccupping noises as they land on the paving stones. "Shalom, friends, do you need a fine lamb for the altar today?" the merchant asks us.

"Not today, friend," Shimon tells him.

"Then move," says the merchant.

"Good idea," says Shimon, eyeing the vendor's lambs thoughtfully. He nods to me, and we strike out across the court toward the money-changers. The Zealot obviously has a plan. We pause and kneel as a small troop of Levites pass, dancing with drums and incense in one of their ritual circlings of the Temple grounds. I try to avert my eyes, but still scan their faces with quick, furtive glances. None of them resembles me.

We arise when they've passed, and approach the portico of the Court of Women. Shimon turns and checks the length of the shadows on the columns behind us, then walks up to one of the guards. "Honored sir, excuse me," the Zealot tells him. "Do you see that lamb dealer—the Peraean, over there by the colonnade? No, to the left. Yes, that one."

"The one in the green and red robe?" The guard, a thin young man, follows Shimon's pointed finger. "What about him?"

"Two of his lambs have runny noses," says Shimon. "And I saw a black spot on the left rear hoof of one of them."

"Blemishes? Huh," says the young guard, trying to sound authoritative. "Thank you." He starts off by himself, then reconsiders and comes back for his companion, who is flirting with a money-vendor's daughter. After a brief conversation, both guards head across the court, toward the hapless lamb-seller.

Then we head for the far end of the money-changers' tables, past the other two guards, who stand chatting with a Tyrian goldsmith.

"What's going on?" I ask into Shimon's ear.

"Just follow my lead," replies Shimon. "We just need a small distraction, a diversion. Once things get started, it won't matter." He walks on past the last money-changer's table, and approaches the vendors by the west portico. Suddenly he trips, falling into a stack of big earthenware urns full of lamp-oil. Time seems to slow, as I watch him grab desperately for a hand-hold, wrap an arm around an urn, and bring it down with him, upsetting three other jars in the process. The crockery crashes to bits, the vendor lets out a very profane oath, and perfumed oil spreads in a brown, reeking stain across the pavement.

160

"Shimon, you oaf!" I cry, rushing to pick him up. He flounders around, smelling like a Phoenician whore, and seizes my arm heavily. I slip on the oil and land on my seat. Shimon laughs, and pats my cheek with his oily scented hand. I curse and try to slap the hand away, but my own hand stops in the damp wool that swathes the oil vendor's looming belly.

"You sons of asses!" he tells us, his tenor voice gravelly with rage. "Two hundred shekels' worth of oil!"

Shimon, still seated on the pavement, puts his greasy hand to his nose and sniffs. "Ten denarii's worth of sandalwood, maybe, and a shekel's worth of frankincense. You must have overpaid somebody for the olive oil, friend."

"I want satisfaction! Guards!" shrieks the vendor.

The other two guards from the money-changers' tables appear among the gathering crowd. "Get up!" growls one of them, seizing me roughly by the arm.

But I'm not about to be sold into slavery again, just to pay for Shimon's clumsiness. I give my arm a solid jerk. The Levite guard slips, does a half-spin in mid-air, and lands hard on his back. I scramble away between the legs of two cheering spectators. The crowd hoots with laughter.

Their laughter, however, is soon drowned out by the noise of some larger event, back in the direction of the money-changers. I hear angry shouts, and the sound of wood splintering. I start to get up, then spy the legs of a guard, frantically shoving his way through the crowd on my right, headed for the new disturbance. I squat down and look around. Behind me, through several sets of legs, I catch a glimpse of the guard I had pulled over. He sits up dazedly. He has deep eyes and thick eyebrows like mine.

"Eliya!" I yell my brother's name, and then wonder if I should have. But the whole crowd has now begun to surge toward the money-changers' tables. I scramble up to avoid being trampled.

"Thieves!"

"Snakes!"

"Cheats! Profaners! Throw them out!"

I work my way laterally across the crowd, trying to get to the fringe of it. A knot of temple guards emerges from the Court of Women, then forms a wedge and begins forcing its way through the crowd by clubbing them with spear butts. Freed by this distraction, two other figures are also scrambling for the mob's edge. I recognize one of them: the girl who was flirting with the guard at the money changer's table. An older man, probably her father, has his arm around her shoulders; in the confused glimpses I get, it is impossible to tell whether she is supporting him, or he is trying to shelter her from the blows of the crowd.

As I slip into the shadow of the outer portico, I see a contingent of Pilate's mercenaries emerging from the tunnel that connects the Temple with the Antonia. They form a skirmish line, but don't start into the mob yet. The man and his daughter start toward them from the edge of the crowd. Someone grabs the money changer by the elbows and wrenches him back. The girl refuses to let go, and is yanked back also.

"Profaners! Kill them!" shrieks a voice that sounds like the oil vendor's, but probably isn't. Then I see a large dark fragment, a piece of a table, rise up like a broad sword above the crowd, just behind the couple's heads.

"Don't! You profane yourselves! You'll kill yourselves!"

The new voice is Yeshua's. I rush back into the open court.

But Yeshua's voice has carried, as usual. The crowd hesitates. Two more money-changers emerge, their purses gone and clothes ripped open; they scurry to the safety of the entrances. The Temple Guards pause, startled by the sudden silence, and for the first time realize how few they are. Pilate's men hold their line warily.

I plunge into the crowd, looking frantically around for some sign of Yeshua, of the Zealot, of the other disciples. If the Rabbi is alone in this crowd. . . . "Yeshua!" I call.

"Yeshua!" someone else takes up the cry.

"Yeshua! Yeshua!" The word becomes a chant, swelling.

Then I see him. He is standing on a money changer's table, his arms upraised for silence. In his right hand is a coiled lash. Then, with perfect timing, he drops the whip. The movement catches more eyes: the cheer swells even louder, then subsides at the silent command of the upraised hand that the whip has left behind.

"Remember the Roman emblems?" Yeshua asks the crowd. "Remember how Pilate wanted to bring his pagan banners with their human faces into the Temple Court itself? Remember how your own kinsmen went to Pilate in Caesaraea to protest, and he threatened to have them all killed? Remember their reply? They knelt before him, thousands of them, and bared their necks to the

163

swordsmen. They said it was better to die than to see the Temple and the Holy City profaned. And Pilate relented!" Yeshua's hands turn slowly, dramatically; they become a hand cupped to heaven and a hand raised in benediction. "If you want to die, kill," he says. "If you want to lose your life, try to save it."

An arm in a torn sleeve suddenly reaches out of the crowd, open-handed, toward Yeshua. My master reaches out and grasps the hand gently, and steps down from the little table. Then he seats himself on it. The front row of the crowd follows his lead, and squats on the dirty white stone pavement. The rest of the crowd join them. The guards, suddenly left standing by themselves, look embarrassedly at each other, then turn in a wary clump and edge toward one of the farther entrances to the Court of Women.

The muscles in Yeshua's shoulders relax; I can see their slight slump from my place in the crowd. The people relax also. Yeshua picks up a fallen coin from the pavement, eyes it bemusedly, then tosses it away. People shift, but no one scrambles after it. Yeshua begins to teach.

Stunned, I hunch at the crowd's edge.

Oh, master, I think. *They'll never let you live now. They've found out that you can control these people better than they can.*

XXVII.

From the time on the banks of Ha-Yarden, north of Yericho:

"He's dying," Yishay the slave tells us.

"What type of sickness?" Mattathias asks him.

"Perhaps the food sickness," Lazaros' slave replies. "Perhaps he was poisoned. He has fever and he shakes. He may be dead by now."

"The Master is exhausted," says Ya'akob. "Another journey now might kill *him*. And certainly a trip that close to Yerushalayim would. The High Priest wants him stoned."

"At least tell him," pleads Yishay. "Let him decide."

Shimon the Rock has listened silently up until this point. Now he swears softly under his breath. But he tells Yishay, "I'll inform the Master."

We are staying along the banks of the river, on Herod Philippos' side of it, near where Yeshua had once listened to Yohan the Baptist preach. We've been to the Feast of Booths in Yerushalayim. There were riots there. The

Sadducees have accused us of starting them. (In truth, I'm not sure all of us are guiltless. Shimon the Zealot, for instance, and Yehuda Ishkerioth were both away from our group much of the time.) So we've fled the city, and have erected our booths here, on the west bank of Ha-Yarden, which the Twelve Tribes crossed so long ago to claim our homeland. Many other pilgrims have followed us here—a fact which has probably made the merchants of Yerushalayim our enemies too, I think wryly.

Yeshua's booth is downstream a little, under a large oak tree. As Shimon the Rock gets up to go there, Ya'akob reaches for his sleeve, as if to stop him. But all Ya'akob says is, "Don't say that he's dying. Say he's sick. That's all we know, for certain."

"We can't stay here much longer, anyway," says Nathan'el, when Shimon has gone. "Herod Antipas will think Yeshua is trying to take Yohan the Baptist's place."

"Yes, and if all these people keep camping here, the Romans will think we're gathering an army," adds Shimon the Zealot. "We shouldn't give that appearance, even if that were what we were really doing."

"Yes, and if we go back to Bet Aniya, the Romans and the High Priest will think we're advancing against Yerushalayim. Let Herod think what he wants; the worst he'll do is behead us. The Romans will nail us up," observes Ya'akob, with chilling detachment.

Everyone hates us, I think. The Sanhedrin and the Sadducees hate us, because we've cut their profits and challenged their rule of the Temple. The Pharisees and scribes hate us, because we flout the laws that they live to keep. Herod Antipas hates us, because he looks at Yeshua and sees Yohan the Baptist; the Romans hate us and the

166

Greeks hate us and the Samaritans hate us, simply because we might become leaders of the Jews. How can hate breed out of love so easily?

I leave the group and go back to my own booth, which is on a little patch of ground uphill from the choice sites on the riverbank. Like all my constructions, the booth is something I quietly revel in. Its willow poles support each other in a free-standing dome; it needs only two ropes to anchor it against the wind from the highlands. Its thatch of date-palm leaves is interwoven so that not the slightest sparkle of sunlight shows through, and yet lifts off quickly as six light panels, any one of which can be raised or lowered to take advantage of minor air currents. So can the walls, which are made of deep brown wool cloth that was sent to us by the family of Ruth the shepherdess.

I pull the stakes, untie the rope, pull off the panels, and unwrap the cloth. Then I flip the network of bare poles on its back like a turtle, and dissect it, pole by pole. As I work, I consider the possibilities that radiate from this place. They all seem to lead to the same end. I don't like that end. I never have. Now, though, I hate it more than ever, because it seems so close.

I wrap my few tools and my spare clothing in the brown cloth, and tie the whole thing into a neat traveling-pack, and wonder. I have freedom: I can choose among these various sufferings and deaths, at least for this moment or so. Will I take this pack down to join the others, and go with this mad rabbi back to the waiting soldiers? Or will I shoulder this pack and disappear into the brush of Peraea?

After a long moment, I hide the pack under a couple of discarded roof-panels, and walk back to the river bank.

167

I find the others arguing violently among themselves. Shimon the Rock has returned from Yeshua's booth; he sits a short distance from the rest, and broods.

"When is Yeshua leaving?" I ask him.

"He isn't," Shimon says, without looking up.

XXVIII.

"Of course you're asleep, Teoma," says the ghost. "Why should I wake you up if I just want to talk?"

"But you're gone!"

"We've been over that before," the ghost points out. "Poor fellow, this all still comes hard for you, doesn't it? But it comes easier when you're asleep." The figure settles itself more comfortably against the wall, in a patch of moonlight, so that I am not sure whether its pale color is from the light or from its ghostliness. "Listen," it continues. "I have a job for you. Settle your affairs here, and come to the stall of Enoch the Tinsmith tomorrow, at noon."

"A job? Where?" Then I chide myself. After what has happened, does it matter when or where?

"You're going to the land of the Hindi, to become an example."

"India?" my poor, undisciplined dream-self wails, despite me. "That's months from here, by *sea*." My stomach does a sickly lurch at the thought of it.

"You've always wanted knowledge, Teoma," says the ghost, his smile unchanged by my outburst. "They've pursued knowledge longer there than anywhere in the Roman Pax. A little more knowledge might make believing easier for you."

"But. . . . But. . . . " I blubber, and wake up.

By noon the next day, my pens, tools, and spare tunic are tied up in my cloak and slung over my shoulder, and I am wandering through the market. Most of the stalls are already shutting down for the afternoon's hot hours, but here and there a housewife or servant still haggles with some sweating dealer over a limp chicken. I come to the Street of Smiths, which is even hotter than the rest of the city. Occasionally a hammer still clangs beside a burning forge, but for the most part, the fire-pots have already been filled with coals for the evening rekindling, and a hundred newly quenched blazes have left an acrid, steamy haze over the narrow lane.

In the haze, I see two men talking. One is a heavy, middle-aged, crook-nosed man in a rich but dirty robe. And the other. . . .

"Master!"

The crook-nosed man stares in my direction, then turns to the other figure, who looks like Yeshua. "If he hadn't acknowledged you like that," the first man says, "I'd have sworn he was your brother, not your servant. Sold."

XXIX.

The peoples of Takasilla were barbarous, I thought. They owned incredible temples and very ancient poems, it was true—but they also cursed their own best friends every day, out of habit; they left no corners of the fields for the poor to glean, and if parents outlived their children, or a wife and children lived after the husband, then the survivors were often thrown out by their relatives to beg and to grub for insects, until they died in the monstrous rains that came each year, threatening to break Yahweh's promise to Noah. Some people married their children off before puberty, to insure against this fate. And pestilences were called down upon them such as even the Egyptians never dreamed of: leprosies that rotted through limbs and mouths in patterns like stinking spider webs, and demons that filled their victims with heat and cold and delirium, then disappeared mysteriously, only to attack again just as the poor victim would begin to hope. I learned about all this, after Haban the merchant brought me as a slave to Takasilla, when that city was in eastern Parthia.

The floods must still come to that region. But it is no longer eastern Parthia. I don't know what people reside there, now—probably the same, with yet another new caste of overlords.

I stayed in that region for several years, while Gudnaphar the Parthian ruled. The Parthians, in those times, regarded their Hindi subjects as nervously as the Romans viewed Israel, though for different reasons. The Romans were always afraid that we would rebel and make them kill us; the Parthians were afraid that the Hindi would simply open the jaws of culture and swallow them whole. That, in part, was why Haban the merchant brought me there, after he had bought me in Judaea. As he told the Parthian landowner who came to buy me, "There's only one breed of man in all the world who's stubborn enough to out-argue a Hindi, and that's a Jew. He'll make you a fine accountant."

The Parthian was impressed by that statement—but not very. I recall that he showed more interest when Haban added, "And an excellent carpenter, too. He fixed my ship's rudder, on the way over."

"Hmm," said the landowner—or something like that. I remember that he arched his eyebrows: a favorite mannerism, I discovered later. "A fellow of many talents," he remarked. "What else can you do?"

"I can mend the masts of fishing boats," I told him. "I know stoneworking and architecture. I've built houses, villas, and aqueducts. I can read and write Greek and Aramaic."

I remember, then, the quick but icy glance that Haban the merchant shot in my direction. He had named too low a price. "You didn't tell me you built houses," he muttered in Hebrew.

"You didn't ask," I told him, in Aramaic. I liked Haban the merchant, but being sold made me irritable.

"Yes, a bargain indeed," remarked the merchant, in Aramaic, which the Parthian understood. "If it weren't for his insolence, and for that other little problem. . . . "

The landowner, of course, hadn't believed a word of what I'd said. But he was intrigued when Haban began trying to discourage him. He decided to take a risk, and was very pleased later to discover that I really was an architect, and that I really didn't have the disease of frequent knowledge that Haban had hinted at.

Haban was wrong on another point. I soon learned that we Jews were no match for the Northern Hindi. Even the worst bandits of the Judaean hills still had the Law in their heads, and could only lie or steal with the aid of noble causes and ingenious arguments to soothe their consciences. But some of the Hindi were *expected* to lie and steal—especially when dealing with foreigners. For one such as me, they would quote one price at the beginning of a job and another at its end; they would change the weights on their scales, and then laugh if I caught them. Even though I was a slave, I remained the slave of a ruler; for the first time, I felt the contempt that the downtrodden always reserve for their masters.

Still, I was a good, honest accountant. I quickly learned the Persian book-keeping system that was used there, and cross-checked it with my Greek system. I discovered that only some classes of this society were allowed to cheat, and I got the help of those who had to be

173

honest when I dealt with those who could be dishonest. Soon I had made many enemies without intending to, because my master's foremen and captains no longer dared to steal from their inventories.

Perhaps it was one of those captains who, at the orgy on the night before my master married his fifth wife, suggested something fiendish to him.

A vision of that time:

It is already late in the night when I am called down to the party. The master is lying with his head in the lap of a rather nervous servant girl. He eyes me lazily. "Didymus," he asks me, "Have you finished with the dowry yet?"

"Yes, Protector," I answer. "I've checked it all. Everything that was agreed on has arrived."

"Except the bride, of course," grins my host. "One really should wait until they've started bleeding, at least. Oh, well; her father's rich. Where's the list?" Something intelligent and hard still gleams beneath the liquor-glaze of his eyes.

Fortunately, I had been dozing in my robe before he summoned me. The dowry-list is still tucked in my sash. I fumble for it in a moment of groggy panic, then produce it.

"Read it," he says.

"Two gilded rosewood elephant-howdahs. Four bronze ankuses, with silver inlays; fifteen bronze candelabras; twenty ingots of silver, ten of gold. Twelve bolts of assorted silks, thirty of dyed cotton. Fifteen turquoises of thumbnail-size or larger—those aren't here; they're to be set in the wedding dress. Three fields of forty strides each."

"Bring it all in here," says the master. "Except, of course, for the land." He chuckles more loudly than he should at the joke. So does almost everyone else.

He seems to have forgotten about the turquoises. I don't stop to remind him. As I head for the storerooms, I thank Yahweh that the last of the dowry had only arrived this afternoon; otherwise, it would already have been dispersed to different coffers and jewelers.

I commandeer the help of three guards and a court eunuch, and we all go down to the storeroom and return with our weight in dowry, and pile it at our master's feet. He smiles sleepily at it.

"Tiddly Mouse," he says, and grins at me. "You've been doing a good job. I know, because everyone's been trying to whisper dirty things in my ear about you. But I'm going to give them all a demonstration of my good faith and sound business judgement." He gives everyone else a round scowl, then returns his smile to me. "I'll give you all this . . . "—he flaps his hand over the treasure— " . . . with one condition. You must divest it immediately. With the proceeds, you will go to the foothills and build me a new summer house. It should be of red sandstone and marble, with space to hold myself and my household in the hot season, and ten servants year-round. If you can do this, and not go beyond the funds just given you, then I'll let you keep what's left—and I'll give you that much again to invest for me, with a tenth of the profits going to yourself. If your luck holds, we should both make a good living."

Then he waves me and the wedding spoils out of the room again, without saying what will happen if my luck *doesn't* hold.

175

I go back to my chamber to worry. My boastful list of skills has caught up with me. I have built agricultural structures, such as terraces and storehouses. I have worked on houses, building wings and making repairs. I even worked on the Temple in Yerushalayim, for one day. But my housing work was mostly done under Archimedes' supervision, and done in the Hebrew or Roman country style—not in the manner of the houses of Takasilla, which have elaborately carved wooden doorframes and high vaulted ceilings. And I have never built anything so elaborate as a summer palace. And now I remember, also, how poor I was at managing gangs of slaves.

I lie awake on my pallet for a long time, with Roman villas growing high-arched ceilings in my head, until they collapse of their own weight or twist into grotesque impossibilities: doorways leading into walls, atrium fountains flowing into granaries, all leading, always, finally, to a large stone out of place, and the image of Nuba's mashed foot. Finally, I fall into uneasy slumber, knowing that in the end, as usual, I don't really have a choice. . . .

Judaea, in the desert between two small towns:
Yeshua, waylaid by a group of pilgrims, is answering questions with stories. A heavy grey storm is boiling ponderously up to the west, over the highlands. No one seems worried about that, though; rain almost never passes beyond the ridges to this valley.

A new troop of travelers marches up to join us. They are more orderly than most such pilgrims, and better kept. They are led by a young man in a rich robe of scarlet and ivory-colored stripes—fine Phoenician cloth, limp

176

with heat and caked with pale desert dust. Under the tunic, he wears loose trousers of the same cloth, after the style of Persian travelers; his beard is full, but too carefully shaped to be a Pharisee's. A Sadducee, I decide; or more likely, a merchant's son from the Diaspora: cultured and Greek-like, but devout, and obviously wealthy.

Yeshua is speaking about the Kingdom. "See it!" he tells the crowd. "It's almost in sight of here. Heaven can be seen even across the gulf of Hades, sometimes, and the gulf between Heaven and Hell is ten times that between Heaven and Earth. In some places, such as Zion, they almost touch. Look hard! See it!"

Whoever the young man is, he has obviously recognized Yeshua. He listens for a while with folded arms, then interrupts. "Good Rabbi. . . . "

Yeshua interrupts right back. "Why do you call me good? Only Yahweh is good."

"Rabbi," the young landowner persists, "I would rather do more than *see* eternity. What should I do to enter it?"

"Don't steal," answers Yeshua. "Don't know your neighbor's wife, don't lie, acknowledge your debt to your parents. You know all of that?"

"Since childhood," the young man smiles, unimpressed. "I've kept the Laws, carefully."

"Good," says Yeshua, smiling back. "Now one more thing. Go home right away, and auction off all your lands and belongings. Then give the money to the poor. When you're all done, come join us."

The young man simply stares for a long moment. Then the right corner of his mouth begins to twitch. Suddenly he spins on his heel and strides away. His

177

courtiers break into chatter and follow, clinging to him word-and-hand.

Yeshua lets them go. He is still smiling, but his eyes are sad beneath their heavy brows. "He won't be back," he tells us. "There are too many leeches with a share in that young man's blood." Then he raises his voice to the crowd: "I'll tell you a truth. It's harder for a rich man to find heaven than for a camel to go through the eye of a needle. Things always hold you in this world; you keep needing to manage them and protect them and get more of them, instead of thinking about Yahweh."

"But Rabbi," says Lazaros, who has come to us with a donkey-load of food, "we all have things of some sort or other. Who can get to Heaven, then?"

"Anything's possible," Yeshua answers, "with help."

I am sitting on the edge of the crowd, with Matta-thias the tax-collector and Ruth the shepherdess. At our feet are three small bundles, each made from a spare tunic, with the bottom tied to make a pouch and the arms tied together to make a carrying strap. Each holds extra clothes, a little food or money, a cooking pot. Mattathias, I think, has been disowned twice: by his family when he became a tax-collector, and by his wife and her family when he gave up tax-gathering to follow Yeshua. Ruth, when Mattathias cured her, was already indigent, her husband's flocks long since divided among the relatives who had kept her; when she'd left with us, she'd taken almost nothing with her. And as for myself. . . . *"You don't have things,"* my former master had said. *"I have things."*

How lucky we are, I think sardonically. *What do any of us have to lose?*

In Takasilla, the day after the last wedding festivities, I take the dowry goods to the market. For the howdahs, I must find an agent; I don't dare sell them to any of the local rich people, for it might start a rumor that my master is in financial straits. So I take them, hidden in a cartload of old wineskins, to a caravaneer who has carried my master's goods before: he quickly locates another merchant who is willing to pay gold for them and ship them down the coast to the Tamil states. The merchant also takes the bronze elephant goads, and finds a discreet brass-dealer to handle the candelabras for us. This takes all the morning and noon hours, until the afternoon resttime. When the shops reopen, I take two guards with some of the gold and silver, and go to the grain-dealers' bazaar, and to the stalls of the palm-oil vendors, and to the cloth merchants' street. I bargain carefully and fairly; I don't lie, and I hold my temper, even when the most outrageous lies are told to me. I get fair prices, if not good ones, and I cause no pain or ill will in the process.

It is late afternoon when the guards return with eight donkeys to load my purchases. I've brought buckwheat and white rice, dried mango paste, and cheese; palm oil, a clear but inexpensive grade, for cooking; and cheap bolts of the gaudy cloth that the women wrap around their thighs, and the coarse white cotton that the men wear. When the donkeys are all loaded, we lead them through alleys to narrower alleys, to the beggars' quarter.

The poor people live in whitewashed mud houses in narrow, winding alleys; their homes are not much different from those of the smaller merchants. But the very poor live in shacks of mud and sticks and palm leaves,

179

behind and beyond and between the houses of the poor. These shacks form walls and roofs for other shacks, until they all become one amorphous mass; the narrow streets change into clogged footpaths, then into careful thread-ways. The crops have been poor this year, and the monsoons have struck with more terrible floods than usual; the crowding and stench are even heavier than they are normally. "You're going to get us all killed, coming in here," mutters one of the guards.

We have not gone very far into the warren, when a young woman begins following me, catching at my sleeve. She is as gaunt as the child that rides on her hip, and her face is deliberately smeared with dirt. Her voice is thick with dialect: "Please, my protector, we are very hungry, my child is very hungry, a coin please for milk for my child. . . . "

I've had the flour packed in small bags and stowed in larger side-bags on the lead donkey's packframe. I pull out a bag, and hold it out to the woman. Uncomprehending, she ignores it. "Please, my protector, a coin. . . . "

But an old woman, squatting beside a tiny hovel made from sticks and a broken grain jar, sees the flour and realizes what is happening. She darts forward, snatches the packet, and then runs away without thanks.

Then there is a crowd. "Please, protector. . . . "

I order one of the guards to pass out the cloth, and tell the two servants to keep the donkeys moving, no matter what. But we are soon stalled in a morass of reaching hands. A packet of flour is torn open between two grabbing women, whitening a dozen faces. I pass out the flour as fast as I can, and fill whatever container is offered with the oil, yet I am not enough. The guard who's not

passing out cloth curses and uses the butt of his spear.
Impatient hands reach around me to the donkey's pack. A
fight breaks out. The guard trips, and someone makes off
with his spear. The pressure of the milling crowd shoves
one of the little donkeys off its feet. It brays in terror;
spilled oil rolls over bare feet and packed earth. A hundred people pile on the thrashing animal, trying to scoop
up a little oil from the broken jars. A hand jerks my robe,
trying to tear off a piece. I become separated from the
donkey, and feel another hand groping under my robe for
my purse. There are a dozen fights now, and bucking,
surging donkeys, and brown backs white with flour. I
shout, and can't hear my voice in the babble. A donkey
screams like a big, hoarse woman in pain. I lose my balance
in the press. A knee looms in my face; something crashes
into my chest. Flashes of green, then blackness. . . .

I awake on a pallet and feel cold water dripping down
my neck and beard. A pain sears across my side with
each breath, and something feels wrong with my left leg.
A plump figure looms blurrily above my face.

"Hermione?" I whisper.

Then I remember that Hermione is dead from a tu-
mor in her womb, and that Archimedes hugged me as a
father would when my first master sold me, and that I
am now in eastern Parthia. I suddenly realize that the
wrongness about my left leg is the weight of a shackle. I
look up again, and the plump figure resolves itself into
my current master.

His expression is unreadable. "I will ask once," he
says, "because I am a fair man, and a puzzled one. Why?"

"I told you of Yeshua. . . . " I begin.

"Your old master, who beat you so badly you thought he was a god." He waves aside my protest. "Continue."

I realize, groggily, that Yeshua's name has no authority with this man; I must speak words, and let them stand on their own truth. "Things decay," I tell him. "Moths eat the finest cloth. Metals corrode or wear out; vines tear stones apart. You want a fortune that lasts, a palace that lasts. I was trying to build it in heaven."

I lie back, and try to relax the pain in my side, and wonder if I really had hoped to build such a palace, or if I had just made a grand gesture to avoid failing at a job I couldn't do well. But it didn't matter; the act was done. My master stands silently over me, looking down with his eyebrows arched.

"Yes," he finally says, "You've made me a lot of merit. It would have been stronger merit, though, if you had built me a small temple or a stupa." He sighs and straightens his shoulders. "You are either an idiot or a holy madman. Either way, you're of no use to me." He turns to the guard beside him. "Get this man to the physician. When he's healed, throw him out. Let him live with the beggars."

XXX.

"Master?"

Yeshua lifts his gaze from the river, and turns. "Yes, Teoma?

"Master, Lazaros' other servant is here."

"Who?"

"Lazaros' servant Amoz. He has a message from Miryam and Martha."

Yeshua's gaze returns nervously to the green water. He is sitting by his booth, near the river's edge. It is not as good a booth as mine, I think; really little more than an inverted 'V' of brown cloth, strung over a rope from a staked pole to a large, twisted oak.

"Master?" I repeat.

Yeshua looks up. The hollows in his eyes have deepened lately, I think.

"Teoma," he says, then pauses. "Teoma, suppose you had the power to end the world—all the suffering, all the selfishness, all the taxes and battles and thefts and executions, all the guilt. . . . Would you do it? Would you end it?"

"Yes," I reply, incautiously.

"But suppose that it was the whole world you were ending: the water sparkling in the river, the coolness of shade on a hot day, the touch of a friend's hand, the embrace of Shimon and his wife. Suppose you discovered that suffering was a part of all these: that the most intense love couldn't exist without giving up parts of lives for each other; that if you banished your own death, you also destroyed the chance of ever kissing a wife or holding a child. Would you still end the world?"

I stand silently for a long time. "Yes," I reply, finally.

"Yes? Why?"

"Because some of us will never have sons," I answer. "Some of us will never embrace wives. And there will always be some blind man who will never see the water sparkle, and a harlot who dies knowing that her flesh has rotted without ever feeling the touch of a loving hand. And . . . and the rest will die, and lose what they have. I don't know what life would be like without death, but I would risk learning."

Yeshua stares at the ground by his feet, and nods. "Poor Teoma; maybe this time, for once, you're right." He lifts his head again, and stares straight into my face with his large haunted eyes. "Teoma, what if we really could end the world? What if Yahweh wanted to become a man as much as men want to become gods?"

I look away, boggled and nervous. My eyes fall on Yeshua's little tent-booth, and then suddenly, absurdly, I have a revelation. Yeshua's booth is not inferior to mine at all. It is a masterpiece of simplicity. In place of my elaborate thatched panels, it uses the shade of the big oak; its open ends catch the breeze off the water in the day, and the highland winds at night, just as my vents do. And it is also beautiful: its graceful, simple curves undulate gently in the occasional puffs of breeze, and its brown cloth blends naturally into the browns of the tree trunk and the earth and the river gravel.

"Your booth is wonderful," I tell him.

My mental leap draws a faint smile from him. "Some questions don't like to be answered, do they?" he remarks.

"So what if Adonai wants to become a man?" I retort, surprised by the anger in my voice. "You're right: it must feel like Hell to be a god. But it's still a silly 'What if.' Adonai would know better than to trade hell for death."

"Would he?" Yeshua asks, his eyes staring through me to some point far beyond.

"Wouldn't you?" I erupt. "Wouldn't anyone? Look, I'm not very afraid of Sheol, or Hades, or any other hell you can imagine. If there's a hell, then at least there will always be something to struggle against. What I'm afraid of is what the Sadducees preach: what if, after life, there's . . . nothing? What if I'm just going to die—won't be there, won't see or feel or know, won't even be able to fight *not* knowing? What difference will it make then, if I ever *was*?"

"Your friends will know," Yeshua says, staring like a blind man.

"My friends will die, too!"

"Yes, they will." He seems a little surprised at the thought. "Yohan will die, and Ya'akob, and Shimon the Rock. Mattathias will die, and Ruth. And my mother, and your parents, and your brother Eliya. And me. I'm going to die, too." Yeshua shudders. "I can't imagine that, quite.

185

When I try, I always discover a wall of fear. I can go up to that wall sometimes; I can even face it and explore it for a few moments. But I can't go beyond it, and if I try to look over, I can't see anything that a man could comprehend. I guess that shows me I'm human." He suddenly breaks his stare away from mine. His eyes come to rest on the ground beside his crossed legs, and his finger begins idly tracing some pattern on the sandy soil there.

"All men are mortal . . . " I mutter, in Greek.

"What?"

"Nothing. Just some words an old Greek taught me, once," I explain, gently. I am thinking what the real importance of that syllogism is.

For a moment, Yeshua's face reshapes itself into Archimedes'. . . .

"You think too much about your god," he snaps, sitting at the door of our little house. Inside, Hermione groans in her sleep, dying; even here, outside, her sickbed stench seeps into the air.

"What else is worth thinking about?" I retort. "Women?"

He rubs his bristly chin, and refrains from striking me. Instead, he asks, "How much is the sum of any number divided by nothing?"

"What?"

"Assume any finite number. How often will nothing go into it?"

"I don't know."

"That's the traditional answer—the one the followers of Pythagoras would give you. That's because they don't want to know. The answer is this." He pulls a stylus from its nest in his curly black hair, and makes a mark on the ground:

$$\infty$$

"Infinity," he says. "Something divided by nothing equals infinity."

"What's your proof?" I demand.

"Self-evident proposition. How many times can you subtract nothing from something, when something always remains the same after nothing's taken away?"

"Oh." I squint and sweat, and wonder where this is leading—probably nowhere, probably a game to keep us from thinking of the woman inside. . . .

"Theorem. If something-over-nothing equals infinity, and any number will go into infinity an infinite number of times, then infinity is to something as something is to nothing."

I am too boggled to challenge him. I nod sullenly.

"Corollary. If a god is infinite, then how does he perceive us?"

I begin to understand, but I refuse to answer.

"He *doesn't* perceive us," the architect forges on, grimly. "To an infinite god, we are less than fly spots; we are nothing at all. And worse than that, an infinite creature must perceive *himself* as finite. Even immortals must be mortal, in their own eyes." He spits, and wipes out the symbol on the ground with his toe. "At least our Greek gods have each other for company. I pity your Hebrew god, if he exists: locked away alone, with nothing but his own death to consider."

"But he *can* see us!" I object. "Our whole history . . . "

"... is written by men," Archimedes interrupts. "And men have a vested interest in proving that a god is interested in them. Do you think we Greeks don't have histories filled with divine interventions? That every city doesn't have its personal deity watching over it? You Jews have the mad arrogance to claim that your god is the only one needed. But just because you need something, doesn't mean it exists."

Inside, Hermione awakens, shrieking. Archimedes flinches like an oft-beaten animal, and then gets slowly to his feet. His body sags with fatigue. "Let's go see what we can do for her," he says, and steps inside.

Yeshua levers himself stiffly to his feet. He grasps the front pole of his little tent for support, and nearly tears the stakes loose. For a moment, he stares down at the tent pole under his hand, as if he were a child discovering it. "The scribes have rules for making these things," he says.

"Yes," I reply, after a moment. "We both broke them."

Yeshua tests his left foot gingerly, wincing a little at the needles of returning circulation. "We just have to keep breaking rules," he murmurs. "Poverty for wealth. Abstinence for lust. Love for hate, help for enmity, healing for sickness, death for life. Seek your life, you lose it; lose it, you save it. It's so logical. I don't know why no one's tried it." He tugs at a knot, and the entire tent gently collapses. "You know, Teoma, there's one thing Yahweh always grants: vengeance. Sooner or later, everyone suffers and dies, and that makes up for everything. But what happens if someone refuses to demand vengeance? What does God do, then?"

I shrug, at loss. "If you don't demand it," I offer, at last, "someone else will."

"Maybe," says Yeshua. "But someone should try it, someday. Someone should test. What else could Yahweh do?" He smiles tentatively.

"Let's go hear Amoz' message," he adds, and starts back toward the group.

But I hang back for a moment, to worry. Then my eyes fall on the collapsed tent. As I stoop to gather it up, I notice, beside the fallen tent-pole, the marks that Yeshua's finger had traced in the sand.

They form the image of a stick-man, dragging an enormous cross up a steep hill. At the end of the slope is an abrupt cliff, that falls into nothing.

I drop the tent-fabric, and rush after Yeshua.

XXXI.

"He's only ill?" queries Yeshua.

"He's sick to death," says Amoz, Lazaros' slave. "He was unconscious when I left, and he wasn't breathing well. It took me two days to find you. It may be too late already."

"Don't worry," says Yeshua, in his most soothing tones. "We can bring him back from death's edge. It will be a sign of Yahweh's power. Go home, and tell Miryam and Martha not to worry."

Amoz hesitates, shifting his weight from one foot to the other, looking nervous and doubtful. But he is a slave; after a moment, he turns without speaking, and starts for the ford of the river.

"He's my friend . . . " says Yeshua, to no one in particular.

"Lazaros is a rich man," says Yehuda Ishkerioth. "You yourself said it's impossible for a rich man to go to heaven."

"I didn't say impossible. Just very difficult," Yeshua rebukes him. "I wish you'd learn to listen more exactly, Yehuda."

"But a camel can't. . . . " Yehuda protests.

"I'm tired," Yeshua cuts him off. "Please don't start one of your arguments."

Yehuda opens his mouth and closes it a couple of times, then turns away, looking hurt. He has begun taking his wine with the Zealot, and has gotten more and more volatile, of late.

"I'm tired, Yohanan," Yeshua repeats, resting his hand for a moment on that young man's shoulders. "I just wanted to celebrate the holy days, like a good Jew."

"At least stay until tomorrow morning," suggests Ya'akob.

"I need to think," says Yeshua. He walks downstream a little ways, to a copse of willows, and disappears into them to meditate. At a nod from Shimon the Zealot, Nathan'el and Thaddai go to keep watch near the thicket.

Amoz the servant has crossed the ford by now, and has started up the small rise on the far side of the river. As he walks, he turns more and more frequently to stare back at our camp, looking for some sign that we are preparing to follow. Finally, at the top of the rise, he reaches some sort of point of balance: he reluctantly starts down the other side, then stops and returns to stare, then takes a few steps back, as if to come back and plead with us; then stops again. At last he simply squats, waiting.

"Don't you see? He's not trying to conquer the world!" It has been nearly an hour since Yeshua entered the thicket; I have fallen into an argument with Shimon the Zealot again, and am inwardly cursing myself for getting trapped in such a stupid, useless activity.

"Of course that's what he's doing!" says the Zealot. "He's challenging the Pharisees right and left, calling them out, weeding them, bringing the best of them over to us. When he's done, he'll have absolutely the purest, the toughest, the most resolute men in the whole nation. No one will be able to face us!"

"But I thought our enemies were the Romans, not the Pharisees," I rejoin acidly.

"Our enemies are anyone who does not follow the pure will of Yahweh," interjects Yehuda Ishkerioth.

"How are you so sure," I ask him, "that *you* follow the pure will of Adonai?"

"We're here with Yeshua," Shimon replies smugly, then continues: "He's such a master! Remember how he put those Pharisees to confusion with the coin story? Even Herod Antipas didn't dare seize him after that. I'm telling you a truth: even the Romans will have to do what he says, before he's done."

"And just what do you think he'll tell the Romans to do?" I ask him. "He's not interested in the Romans. He's not even interested in the kingdom of Israel."

"Then what do you think he wants?" challenges Shimon.

"He wants an end," I reply.

Shimon snorts, flabbergasted. He is just formulating a better retort when Yohan quietly interrupts: "He's coming out."

Yeshua emerges from the thicket, and goes back to the site of his collapsed booth. He returns soon after, with a small traveler's bundle slung from his shoulder.

"I'm going," he tells us.

192

"But Rabbi," protests Shimon the Rock. "You heard what those pilgrims said last night. Herod's on the road from Bet Aniya to Machaerus. Annas and Caiaphas are publicly calling for your head. Bet Aniya is in sight of Yerushalayim. You want to commit suicide? Go to Bet Aniya!"

"I will," says Yeshua. "But they won't kill me yet." He starts down the path, crosses the ford, and goes up the rise, toward where Amoz has sprung up to meet him.

Shimon the Rock sits down dejectedly. "What if they do kill him?" he says, abstractedly.

"He wants an end," I repeat. "He sees all of us tearing at his robes, making stupid demands, hating him because he breaks all our rules. So he just breaks more rules. He doesn't want Israel. He doesn't want the world. He wants it ended."

"Well, what should we do?" asks Ya'akob, ignoring me.

"We have to get him back," says Shimon the Zealot. "We have to stop him—kidnap him, if it comes to that. It isn't time yet!" He subsides, though, at the glares of the rest of us.

"We shouldn't all go," suggests Nathan'el. "A big crowd, going up to Yerushalayim just as everyone is leaving? That'll bring attention, if he hasn't drawn it already."

"Just send one or two people," suggests Andreas.

"Yohan, why don't you go?" suggests Shimon the Rock. "He tries to protect you. Maybe you can talk him out of it."

He's breaking every law less noble than the Commandments themselves, I think, while they talk. *He sees the consequences; he knows they're going to kill him eventually. And he does exactly what he's decided to do, anyway. He's free.*

"I think the Rock and the Zealot should go," suggests Yehuda Ishkerioth. "They'd be better in a fight."

I stand up.

"Let's go," I tell them.

"What?" says Shimon the Rock.

"Where?" says Shimon the Zealot.

"To Bet Aniya" I tell them. "To die with him." I start down the path to the ford.

XXXII.

"Lazaros!" bawls Yeshua, like a gang foreman. "Come
out of there!"

I wade through the stench to Yeshua's side, and
touch his elbow. "Master," I plead softly, "Let's close it up."

"Lazaros!" he shouts, ignoring me.

Silence.

Then a figure stumbles out of the low entrance,
tripping over the stained shroud-cloth that it clutches
reluctantly about its loins. Lazaros bends and retches,
then stares about himself. There is wonder in his eyes,
and terror.

XXXIII.

A vision of the time in Takasilla, in eastern Parthia:

It is evening, or else early morning, when I awaken. The room is small and plain; smaller even than my old room by the Master's chamber. It is empty, except for the straw mat on which I lie, and the blanket thrown over me, and a squat brass water-pot by my shoulder. Somewhere, not in the room, I hear voices speaking in Hindi, and the lowing of a cow. I turn my head, and decide that I am in one of the kitchen servants' quarters; through the doorway, I can see the courtyard, and the big earthen oven where the round loaves of Parthian-style bread are baked for the Master's table. From the shadow of the oven, I decide that my room must be on the west side of the compound, and that this must be evening.

Vaguely, I remember fever, and the stabbing pain of broken ribs, and a Hindu physician saying that I was weakened because my organs were bruised. The fever seems gone, now. But when I try to sit up, a violent twinge still pulls at my lower chest.

A middle-aged woman enters. "You're awake!" she exclaims, as if I weren't aware of that. "You look much better."

"Thank you, Laxana," I tell her, remembering her name.

"Would you like something to eat?" She doesn't wait for an answer, but bobs her head respectfully and retreats out the doorway. She returns a moment later with a large piece of flat bread, piled with yellow lentil beans.

"Thank you," I tell her again, for lack of anything more clever. I accept the bread and beans, and suddenly realize that I'm hungry. The lentils are gritty, and flavorless except for the bite of hot pepper, but the bread is fragrant and wonderful.

The woman ducks her head again, and clasps her palms together in front of her chest, and retreats, leaving me puzzled by her show of deference. Is this the way to treat an outcast?

Then Aran the Eunuch comes in. "How are you feeling, friend?" he asks.

"Sore," I answer. "But the shaking is gone."

"That's good," he says. "You need to heal quickly now. The Master doesn't know you're still here."

"I'll leave in the morning."

"No need for that," he replies hastily. "If the Master learns of this, we can always give him his own words. He did say to to throw you out, when you were *healed*."

"Does it matter?" I ask. "Sick or well, how long do you think I'll survive, once I leave here?"

Aran smiles. "Your status has changed, friend. You may find, now, that we're better people than you thought.

But I have to go before the Master misses me. Get a good night's sleep."

He slips out again. I finish my bread and beans, and lie back. Suddenly I realize that the cushion beneath my head is silk. Startled, I roll over to examine it—and catch my breath at the sudden pain in my side. But the pain is less than it has been. I recognize the pillow: I'd ordered it a month before, for use in the harem. I grin at that, and settle back, and sleep.

I awake the next morning, as the first light crosses my pillow. Outside, in the courtyard, women and servants are already bustling about; the aroma of baking bread drifts in through the doorway. I push myself upright, only wincing a little. Carefully, I pull myself to my feet, and take a few experimental steps. Walking, I find, is less painful than sitting up. I pace back and forth with increasing vigor, staying carefully away from the doorway.

Laxana enters with the morning meal: flat-bread again, but this time covered with curry. "You look much better this morning!" she exclaims brightly.

"Thank you," I tell her, accepting the bread. "I'll leave after this meal."

Her look changes to consternation. "Please wait," she says, and hurries out.

A few moments later, Aran appears in the doorway. "Good morning," he says. "You're going?"

"Yes."

"You don't have to. You can stay until you're completely healed."

"No. I'll leave. I don't like being a burden. And I don't want to risk getting the Master angry with you."

"All right," he nods, in his side-to-side Hindu way. "But wait here a short time, please."

He ducks out again. I shrug and finish my curry. Its spice burns pleasantly along the sides of my tongue. I enjoy having an appetite again.

Just as I am finishing the last bit of bread, Aran reappears, carrying a large bundle. He unwraps it, and lays out a staff, a large black bowl, and some loose-fitting, pinkish-orange garments. "Put these on," he tells me. "They'll let people know you're a holy man."

"Thank you," I tell him, bemused. *What kind of holy man?* I wonder. But my own tunic is nowhere in the room, and I don't wish to wander the streets in the loincloth I'm wearing. I put on the strange garments with some difficulty, while Aran assists, beaming.

When I'm done, he hands me the black bowl. "Bring this to the back gate each morning," he tells me, "and the servants will fill it with food. You can also take it to the back entrances of the other rich houses, or to the front doors of the poor who have their own houses. They'll be glad to feed you what they can. It will give them merit."

"I don't understand," I tell him. "You don't feed all those people in the shanties. But you'll feed a foreigner's disowned slave?"

Aran pauses, and shifts his feet uneasily. After a moment, he answers, "We can't feed everyone. And some of the poor deserve to be poor; they're more selfish than animals. But the story of you and your donkeys is all around the market stalls. When a man gives up everything to be more holy, he will be fed—even if his ways are a bit foolish."

199

"I don't agree with you," I tell him. "About what the poor deserve, that is. But if you will feed one poor man, that's something. Thank you." I tuck the begging-bowl under my arm, and bend painfully to pick up the staff. Aran hastily reaches down to hand it to me. Our heads collide. He jumps back, aghast. I straighten, startled, and gasp at the pain of sudden straightening, and then see his face, and laugh, and wheeze at the pain of laughing.

"You don't have to go today," he says, when I've finished laughing and wheezing.

I hesitate. It's not easy to leave the shelter of good people.

"It's time," I tell him.

I go with him to the back gate, and hug his plump body—gingerly, because of my ribs. Then Laxana comes running up. I can't hug her because of the customs of this place, but I imitate her clasped-hand salutation. "Thank you," I tell her, one last time. "Thank you," I tell Aran.

Then I turn to the gate. *Yahweh, I don't know what you are,* I think. *You are somewhere beyond the wall of death, and I can't even picture you. But I'll have to trust you, now.*

I step into the hot, dusty street, free at last, and go to find the poor.

XXXIV.

Near the center of Judaea is a narrow ridge, called
the Mount of Olives, that juts up like a dull knife dividing
two worlds. To the east of it, the ridges fall away into the
tawny lower valley of Ha-Yarden: a bleak, rainless, oven-
hot landscape, punctuated only by the occasional dusty
palm trees of an oasis village—and by the gigantic grey-
white mound of the Herodium, Herod the Elder's burial
fortress, that protrudes from the brownish plains as
shockingly and unnaturally as a dead woman's breast.
But to the west of the ridge, the green begins: first the
pale twisted olive trees, marching in tiers down the
ridge's slope; then the orchards and vineyards and
scrubby evergreen forests of the western Judaean mountains. And in the midst of this new greenness, on the
slope opposite the Mount of Olives, rise the ivory-colored
walls of Yerushalayim.

Just over the summit of the ridge, Yeshua pauses,
sweaty and out of breath, and steps off the path to gaze at
the panorama before us. The rest of us do the same, fan-
ning out on the little terrace that the olive growers have

left for pilgrims such as us. "Isn't it amazing?" gushes Yohan, next to me. "I've seen it at least two dozen times, but I still catch my breath at the sight of it. It's as if we were standing on the wall of Eden again, and Shaitan's burned everything behind us."

I say nothing; I've long since learned the futility of swimming against Yohan's floods. But I think, *This is nothing. Look at the walls before us.*

Across the valley, Yerushalayim sprawls on its five hills: the largest city between Egypt and Mesopotamia. Its white native limestone, even unplastered, gleams in sharp relief in the mid-morning sun; the roof of the Inner Temple, flat and ramparted during my boyhood, now rises to a peak, Greek style, and supports a sheath of gold leaf too bright to look upon directly. And everywhere, surrounding the city, snaking among the houses, are walls and ramparts: the walls of Zion and of the lower city; Nehemiah's walls, the Maccabees' walls, the Herods'—and rising over everything, so massive that I once mistook it for the Temple itself, are the four towers of the Antonia, where the Roman troops live. As a former builder, I can admire the ingenuity with which new walls have been joined to the old. I can also see at least a dozen places where they could easily be breached: weak junctures, poorly disguised with thick layers of white plaster, where no amount of ingenuity could possibly attach some cluster of new houses into the fold of the city's defenses. Yerushalayim has seen too many armies; it is a city that has even walled itself off from itself.

Yeshua calls Thaddai and Andreas over, and gives them some instructions; they set off down the slope, angling southwest, toward the little outlying village of

202

Shiloah. Then Yeshua walks off a little distance, and sits down under an olive tree, and bows his head. I think at first that he is praying; then, faintly, I hear the sobs. I turn away from the sight, troubled. Ya'akob notices my reaction. "We Jewish men are allowed to cry, on important occasions," he assures me. "This is one advantage we have over the Romans."

"I know," I tell him, curtly. But since Lazaros' tomb, *every* occasion seems to have become important for Yeshua. We have seen him more and more often like this: crying like a child. . . . But that is not why I've turned away. I've turned because he has reminded me of something I don't want to remember. I look determinedly back at the city walls, but the memory persists: the first time I looked on those walls. I wasn't an architect then, so I don't remember the walls themselves so much; of that trip, I remember the people, and the animals. . . .

"Remember," my father says, "when we get to the city, don't tell anyone we're from Gamla."

"Why not?" my brother asks again.

"Because," my father explains again, a trifle crossly, "They'll think of Yehuda the Gamlite and the Galilaian rebellion. We don't want to get mistaken for Zealots."

We descend the Mount of Olives on a little winding path toward the Sheep Gate, which my father hopes will be less crowded. As we cross the summit of the ridge, I get my first clear view of the city: lovely limestone ramparts, the color of clean teeth, array themselves all across the next hill. The hill itself is nothing, compared to the mighty spur on which Gamla perches—but the stonework here is the most massive human thing I have ever seen.

"That's the Temple Mount," says my father, pointing unnecessarily.

"And there's the Temple!" adds my mother, also pointing. I try to follow her outstretched finger from my lower vantage point, and my eyes settle mistakenly on the Antonia, with its four gigantic corner towers like the horns of a tremendous altar.

"It's *huge*," I breathe.

We follow the path down the hill to where it merges with the Bet Aniya road, and join the horde of people funneling down it through the Sheep Gate: during the festival of Pentecost, *no* gate of Yerushalayim is uncrowded. Never in my short, sheltered life have I seen so many people and animals: herdsmen, oily-smelling with the musk of their sheep; olive-oil vendors with their balky little pack-donkeys and huge oil jars; caravaneers with donkeys and sturdy ponies and evil-faced camels; dove-sellers and fishmongers and rich pilgrims on horseback, and poor country families, each family with its one donkey for possessions and its one lamb for sacrifice. Agog at all these creatures, I stumble into a grimy shoulder. I instinctively grab onto it for support, then realize that there is no arm in the sleeve, and find myself looking straight into the dirt-smeared face of a beggar. For a moment, we stare at each other: he in surprise, I in horror. Then I let go of his sleeve as if it were hot dung.

"Go," he says angrily, and twists and gives my shoulder a boost with his good arm.

"Mama!" I yell—then realize that I have lost sight of my parents.

"Mama! Papa! Eliya!" I scream.

I run down the street in a panic, shoving past the skirts of robes, burrowing through a muddled herd of sheep, narrowly escaping the splayed cloven hooves of a startled camel. Then suddenly I am at the gate again: I have gone the wrong way. A whole row of beggars, whom I somehow hadn't even noticed when we went through before, sit ranged along the thick, shady wall of the gateway. One of them, the nearest, is a leper, with a triangular hole for a nose. I turn, screaming my mother's name, and rush back up the street, through the robed legs and stamping hooves and the terrible noise and stench of a real city.

I finally slow, exhausted and crying. I look bewilderedly about, for the first time aware of my surroundings as a whole. I am on a street paved with stone—a startling sight for a boy who has known only the dirt lanes of Gamla and Kafer Nahum. It is not a very broad street, though, and has been narrowed to a threadway by the crowds of vendors along both sides. Most of them are brass-vendors; they squat beside their tables of plates and water-pots and branching candlesticks, and yell at passers-by in voices made louder by the stone walls and paving. I stare up the street and then down it, utterly confused: which way, even, is the gate?

"Boy. Boy!"

I suddenly realize that the vendor behind is talking to me. I turn around. He is a big man in a red-and-brown robe and a flowing, grey-shot beard.

"Yes, you," he says. "Move away."

"Have you seen my mother?" I ask.

"How would I know?" says the brassmonger. "Go on!"

But I still stand there, dumbfounded, staring. *This man doesn't know my mother,* I think. *But everyone knows my mother!*

Then I realize how different this place is from Gamla, where everyone knows everyone. I don't know this man, and he doesn't know my parents. I am stupid, ashamed, small. I have been torn from the center of the world.

"Go!" repeats the merchant. I retreat, hurt and astounded, wondering what I've done to make him so rude. But this time I don't run screaming. I walk down the street, holding my panic under the knot in my throat, and dodging the moving forest of legs, and looking for landmarks. I turn from the brassmonger's lane into another, and find it choked with leather-workers and reeking of their acid solutions and curing hides. I retreat, and try another lane. After a few dozen steps, it opens into a narrow court filled with butchers. I press forward a little way, dodge a clump of chattering women with plucked doves that dangle from their hands at the level of my eyes, swat at the hordes of flies that buzz before my face, and suddenly find myself confronting a table full of scalded sheep's heads. They regard me with great sleepy eyes; flies crawl unnoticed over their pink, naked foreheads. After a long moment, I turn away, clutching my fear against me as if it were a heavy, fragile clay pot. I do not begin running until after I've found another alley.

This time I'm lucky. The alley emerges into a broad, crowded street. I follow it around a right-angle bend, and discover my landmark: at the junction of the street and another alley, in a patch of late-afternoon sun, sits the one-armed beggar.

From across the street, he doesn't seem as fearsome: groveling and staring, child-height, crotch-height, opening a little lonely space in the river of legs that flows past. But he is still dirty, and ugly, and mean; his space is a patch of revulsion. Pity balances with terror; finally, I screw up my six-year-old courage, and dart across the street, and inch cautiously along the wall toward him. I stop at the edge of the space that he has cleared with his presence—a space approximately equal to the circle of his arm's reach. From that distance, I can separate his personal odor from the general smells of the city: it is heavy, sour, a mixture of sweat and soiled damp cloth and rancid olive oil, and a strange bitter smell like that of some dye or medicine. If the man notices me, he gives no sign of it.

"Did you see my mother?" I ask, at last.

He doesn't even look in my direction.

I retreat two or three steps, uncertain, then inch toward him again. "Did you see my mother?" I repeat. I try to be louder, this time, but my voice just develops a quaver.

He turns, a little startled, and stares at me.

"My mother," I press. "Did you see her? You shoved me, and now I can't find her, or my father, or Eliya." I feel my chest muscles tightening again.

"You're lost?" he says.

"Yes." I'm ready to cry again now, for certain, but I still hold my fear carefully in front of me. My voice is squeaky with tension.

"Where are they staying?" he asks.

"At Aunt Tabyeta's."

"Where's that? What street? Do you know?"

207

I don't know. I stand there, starting to whimper a little.

"Sit down," he says. "Wait for them. They'll find you."

There is a surprising authority in his voice. I scrunch down against the wall, just out of reach, and wait.

For a long time, as the shadows spread ever so gradually across the frenetic street, I sit at arm's length from the beggar, and watch the feet and hooves of the world go past: soldiers and stonemasons and purple-handed dyers and various lesser priests, wild ragged dancing prophets and shaggy Nazirites from the hills, tasseled Pharisees and rich Greek-robed Sadducees with their entourages, and a gang of ragged older children who dodge laughing and hard-eyed through the crowds, and every type of animal that I can name, except perhaps a lion. The oxen shy and bellow at the noise, and the sheep bleat to each other in terror, as they disappear toward the stock-ramp of the temple. I am battered by the noise of the crowd and the odors of sweat and manure and the endless buzzing of the flies.

The beggar mostly ignores me, too. He works the crowd, never speaking, scanning those who approach until he locks eyes with some unfortunate pilgrim, then following the poor fellow with his gaze and outstretched hand, until either a coin plinks down on the pavement or the victim has hurried guiltily past. The beggar shifts occasionally to stay in the sunlight, always carefully arranging himself with one leg out in front of him. There are several big ulcers on the leg; some have almost healed, but some sort of red tincture has been applied to all of them to make them look raw and wounded again.

Flies alight and crawl on the man's legs and his face; like a sheep's head, he ignores them.

Once, I speak. "What if they don't come?" I ask.

The beggar is silent for a moment, watching his latest mark approach and pass. "If they don't," he replies, finally, "then I'll teach you how to be a beggar."

I don't speak again. I huddle back into the wall, watching desperately, while a noisy procession approaches, led by a huge white ox, its broad horns gilded and its back laden with grain and fruit. It balks and sidles nervously, forcing the beggar to scramble aside, but the priest who leads it quickly regains control by twisting on the rope that goes through its nose. The ox freezes in pain, and the priest jerks it forward again. After the ox comes a column of singing Levites, in gorgeous white robes overlaid with *ephods* of brilliant colors. I stand up, scanning the priests' ranks anxiously; my father is a Levite.

I don't see him. Looking at these men hurts me, because they're not my father, and they're more splendid than he is. I huddle back again, and clutch my knees to myself as if they were my family, and hold desperately onto everything left, even my sobs, while the evening shadow fills the street and spreads up the far walls like a stain. Stinking with all the thousands of odors of flesh, the people and beasts still sweep past, ignoring me, bearing the world's center further and further away. . . .

"Yehuda!"

It is almost dark, and my mother is gathering me into her arms, clutching me the way I'd been clutching myself, sobbing along with my sobs. Then she passes me to my father, who is also crying. *"Raka,"* he curses me fondly. "You made me miss the procession." He pulls me into the crushing love-hug that only men give. The beggar says something to us, but none of us take much notice. . . .

Shaking, I sit up in my cell beneath the King's palace. *My parents loved me,* I think. I am shaken down to the center of my chest by that terrible paradox: that my parents could have loved me, and still done what they did. What had that poor woman felt, half a dozen years later, when she'd taken her second son down to Kafer Nahum to be sold into slavery? What had her husband felt, lying crippled in that black stone house in Gamla, and knowing that he was unfit to offer a sacrifice, was unable to support his family? And I have hated those people all my life, have never tried even to see them again.

I am an old man. They must be long dead by now. I'll cry for a long time tonight: for them, and for the terrible thing I've done.

XXXV.

For the first time in months, I have lost my peace.
The walls, whose surfaces had been growing almost as infinite as landscapes in their detail, have shrunk now into
walls again, and closed in. I pace the cell restlessly, glad
that the scorpions have moved out for the dry season. My
rickety legs complain from the exercise. I try to remember what trade my father pursued; village priests never
got enough from the Temple offerings to survive. One
memory insists that Father was a stonemason, but that
would be too much of a coincidence. Another says he was
a broom-maker. (A fragment of a scene: my mother clear-
ing away the supper bowls; my brother Eliya in a corner,
reciting his Torah lesson to our two younger siblings to
impress them; my father, in another corner, binding a fan
of straws to a cane handle. . . .) Seeking clues, memories,
something, I search again and again through the sheets
of writing that Anand has not yet collected from me, and
examine the phrases in horror. "I step into the dusty
street, free at last. . . . " What a smug, empty illusion!

211

I have committed a terrible crime. I have hated my parents into their graves, hated them until they were beyond the wall of fear, beyond any hope of reconciliation or repair or forgiveness. I have added another small, irretrievable weight to the terrible imbalance of the world. And I thought I was free of hate! I've only shifted the burden of it a little, so that I didn't notice it so much. Now I must hate myself. . . .

And yet, I don't know how I could have avoided this crime. I never thought, *I am doing wrong.* I never saw beyond the wrong that was done to me. How could I have fought an evil that never appeared evil?

A fragment of vision comes to me—a half-formed memory:

It is nearly dusk. With the cover of fading light, Yohan and I have ventured to the entrance of the shepherd's cave where we are hiding. Yohan takes a piece of the flatbread that Lazaros' sister Miryam sent with us, and wolfs it down mechanically, without tasting. He looks like a starved beast, an emptiness with an appetite. I wonder if he will ever speak again.

I am affected differently. My despair is no less great. But I don't have any need for food. I have become a collection of thoughts with no body; there is no room in me for anything but despair. I stare at the rocky hillside, then at the lap of my tunic, then at Yohan, swallowing his great gulps of bread, and I see no particular difference between any of them.

"I'm Miryam's son," Yohan says, suddenly.

Out of habit, my mouth opens and I reply. "Miryam? You can't be. She's younger than you are."

"No. Not her—not Lazaros' Miryam. Miryam, Yeshua's mother. He said I was her son. I was supposed to take care of her. But the women are taking care of us." He rocks back and forth on his haunches, staring at memories, the mangled remnants of the bread still clutched in his right hand.

Out of habit, I ask: "What else did he say?"

"He said he was thirsty. He said . . . what did he say? Why weren't you there? Nobody was there but me and the women. . . . "

"What else did he say?" I repeat, surprised at the sudden anger rising in me. I should strangle this poor creature, this suffering demented wreck of a young man.

"What else did he say?" echoes Yohan, rocking. "I can't remember. He said . . . he said. . . . "

But the vision fades abruptly, like an interrupted nightmare. I can't recall it, can't go on with it now. But I know that it is important—that I must finish this memory someday.

XXXVI.

Changes are taking place. This morning, the guard brought me a substantial meal: vegetables and fish in a brown sauce with rice, and a white, pulpy fruit with a yellow skin. This afternoon, he brought me another meal, much the same, but with ripe mangosteens for the fruit. And this evening the night guard came with a monk's robe of fine cotton, still crisp with the freshness of its dye. I asked who had sent this gift. The guard smiled— smiled!—and said that it was from the king.

I think they have decided to kill me.

I will have some time yet. They will want me well-fed and healthy-looking when they release me, so the king won't take any blame for my treatment. Then they'll incite some hot-headed young Brahmins to do the job for them. I don't need the gift of prophecy to say how kings work.

I can tell all this without bitterness, without hate for any of them. It occurs to me now that a younger Teoma would have hated a king who planned his death. Now, though, that only seems silly. The poor king will warp

214

himself so badly through such actions that he will suffer from them, quietly, desperately, in a thousand subtle and obvious ways, for at least the rest of his life. . . . Perhaps I have finally moved beyond hate, despite my sin. I don't know. But at least by now, I may have loved as much as I have hated. I can take some comfort in that, perhaps.

I've had no visions for weeks now—none since the fragment about Yohan and the shepherd's cave. But time has become too precious. I must write, even if I can only draw from ordinary memory. So I will write about later times, which I can remember more clearly, and with less guilt.

For years after being driven from the house of my master in western Parthia, I stayed in the city of Takasilla and lived as a holy man: helping the very poor however I could, and getting my food from the poor in whitewashed houses and from the servants of the rich. I began by returning to the alley where I had started the riot with my master's charity. There I was recognized by the old woman who lived in the broken grain jar. She said she had no flour left, but would give me her home to sleep in for the night. I examined the hovel doubtfully. The broken jar had been a huge one, nearly the height of a man. It was about two-thirds intact, with a large wedge of crockery missing from one side; it had been tipped over with the broken side down, and propped shakily in place with sticks. A shallow pit was scraped out beneath it, making just enough room for a small person to sleep, curled up or sitting.

"Oh, well," I think I remember saying, "I accept your generous offer. But if I'm going to stay here, I might as well make some improvements for you."

215

I began by trading sticks around and resetting them, so that the crockery roof was higher but more steady. Then I left, and went down to the river that flowed by the city. There, despite the pain in my ribs, I gathered stones and willow branches. Returning, I began setting the stones against the bases of the old branches that propped up the jar, and built up a low foundation wall, and then wove the willows between the larger branches to form a latticework. A small crowd gathered to watch: mostly women and very thin children, with a few old men; all of them ragged. They watched at first, I remember, with the listless curiosity of the malnourished; then, gradually, a few drew closer, and began asking each other questions in low voices.

I had built houses of wood and stone and mud bricks, but never before of pottery and basketwork. But I remember remembering as I worked: the vision of the booth I'd built by the River Ha-Yarden fitted itself like a pattern over the panels I was building, and my fingers, clumsily twining the thick willow stems between the branches, suddenly became Hermione's plump Greek fingers, weaving an olive-picker's basket in the evening beside Archimedes' house in Galilaia. With increasing sureness, I began discovering the forms and harmonies within these crude materials, just as a stonecutter finds them in hunks of marble, or as Temple woodcarvers once drew them out of the rich red grain of cedar. I found the beauty in that ludicrous little hovel, and wove it out until it was plain to every beggar: the sticks that braced the sides grew into a graceful woven archway, while another stick, jutting forward like a spear at ready, became the backbone of a peaked awning over the jar's rim. When I ran out of willows, I discovered that the old woman had already fetched more from the river. Soon others in the crowd had begun making trips to the river as well.

In the afternoon, I returned to the river myself, and showed the old women and scrawny children where to find the best stones, and how to choose good willow branches and break them off cleanly by using two stones for pinchers, and how two or four people could use a piece of cloth to lift loads of stones that they couldn't have budged otherwise. I found some soft limestone that could be ground into mortar, and some smooth, river-rounded granite to use for grindstones, and I think I remember that some children helped me to carry them, since my side was hurting badly by that time. Meanwhile, the others quarreled over stones and pilfered them from each other and sometimes threw them at each other. But they also chattered among themselves, and held up prize finds to be admired, and helped each other carry their new possessions up the riverbank.

By late evening, with the children's help, I had built a curved wall of uncut stones up over the willow latticework. I gave up on using mortar, because I had no fire to char the limestone, and had only my begging bowl and a small, cracked cooking pot of the old woman's to use for carrying water. But again, the crude material had become a vision beneath my fingers; I had worked almost in a trance, and the uncut stones had fitted themselves together almost miraculously, interlocking like the words in a long sentence, so that almost no light at all came through the chinks. Later, I would get some straw and make a clay plaster to cover the entire structure.

When I had set the last stone in place, one of the children tugged on my arm until I followed him to his mother's hut. We threaded through the stinking morass of alleys to a ruined building, the one standing wall of which was lined with crude lean-to's. The boy, his mother, and his two sisters—or was there one sister and a grandmother?—at any rate, the boy's family lived in one of these shelters; it was not much bigger than the jar-house, and was really more of a tent or booth than a hut. The frame was a shaky structure of lashed branches; the walls were a combination of broken bricks and rags. The boy told his mother that I was a great architect who was going to build them a new home. I had no tools, but I showed them how to set the posts more firmly and how to lash them with fisherman's knots, and helped them to restack the bricks so that they were less likely to fall on the family as they slept. Then I went back to the river to bathe, and returned to the jar-house, despite the boy's family's protest that I should sleep with them.

That night, I tried to sleep outside the rebuilt jar-hut, which was now just large enough inside for one person to stretch out comfortably. But the old woman who owned the jar looked thoroughly distraught and insisted that I sleep inside, and in the end Hindu once more proved more stubborn than Hebrew. The woman spent the night beside the mouth of the jar, sleeping squatted over her knees in a position I found difficult to believe. Inside, aching with hunger and fatigue, and feeling my sore ribs with each breath, I recalled a story that Archimedes had once told me, about a crazy philosopher who had also once lived in a jar, and had run around with a lantern in the daytime, looking for honest faces. Grinning, I fell asleep.

By the next day, it had become obvious that I had begun something. All over the slum, people were looking at their hovels, and shoring them up, and building little rough stone walls. It was as if those dirty, hungry people had suddenly discovered a small way to feel good about themselves; they threw themselves on the task of improving their homes with the same desperation that they drew on in their daily hunt for scraps of food. The building went on all day—and the day after that, and the day after *that.* Each morning, I would take my begging bowl, and go off to the back gates of rich people's houses to get food. Usually I came back with enough to feed the old woman as well as myself. After eating, I would go out among the builders to help and advise; each evening I would return to the old woman's hut, fingering the bruises made on my arms by people dragging me off from hovel to hovel.

On the fourth evening, I remembered that it was the Shabbat, and recognized the value of a day of rest. I had no prayer shawl or phylacteries, nor did I know the Hebrew prayers very well—but I went into the jar and slept, and then awoke and sat cross-legged like a Hindu holy man and prayed and thought, until the sun set the next day. Outside, meanwhile, the old woman kept a ferocious shrill guard on my privacy, amid innumerable clanks and bustlings and an odd sweet odor.

When I finally emerged at dusk that day, I remember, I found the exterior of the hut transformed. The clay plastering had been finished, and a little shed of

219

branches, willow slips and clay extended out to one side, narrowing the alley still further. Inside the shed lay the old woman, asleep. And directly in front of the jar mouth, someone had placed a square block of dirty white marble. On top of the block were flower petals, and the burnt-out stubs of two joss sticks (undoubtedly stolen), stuck in a little tray of river sand. Next to the stone sat the woman's cooking pot, filled with rice and vegetables.

I roused the old woman—I can't remember her name!—I roused her, and asked, "What's this?" and pointed at the block.

She stared drowsily at it. "Respect," she said.

I approached the thing again, while gratitude and abhorrence struggled inside me. The block looked too much like an altar. What were they worshipping here?

I started to dump the sand. Then I had a thought. The incense sticks had burnt down to about the length of my middle finger. I pulled a thread from my already fraying robe, and bound the two sticks together to make a little wooden cross, and stuck the cross in the sand. I impaled one of the flower petals on the top of the cross, and piled the rest of them in a little delicate heap at its base. Then, shaking a little, I took the bowl of food over to the old woman, and gave her half of it, and broke my fast.

I lived in the jar-hut for perhaps three years. Every day, I went to assist in the straightening of some hovel or other, or to mediate in some dispute that I barely understood, or to cradle some dying shuddering old woman or bony dying child in my own arms, because no one else would. Sometimes, after I performed this last duty, the woman or child would live a little longer, and the word spread that I had some healing power. But I never noticed anything happen, except that the people in my arms felt someone caring for them again. And as often as not, they simply died anyway. Sometimes mothers would drag their children to me and ask me to teach them; I tried this, though I did not consider myself a learned person. No one in the world, though, was quite as ignorant as those children were, so if they learned to count to twelve before they ran off, then I felt that I had done some good. In the end, they always did run off, but there were always more mothers who wanted to try. . . .

Sometimes, too, another type of student would show himself. Takasilla was somewhat of a center of learning, and sometimes curious novices from the local temples would come in the evening to the stone block in front of my jar. There they would sit, with their eyes averted, until I returned from my work or emerged from my jar, and they would say that they were from this or that teacher, and that they had a question. I was never sure whether these questions would be serious or a joke, so I would answer all of them as well as I could, in my poor version of their dialect. Soon this became a local sport, and all types of strange young personages would appear by my doorway: regal hooded Brahmins, and Zoroastrians with ridiculously long beards for their ages, and bald, orange-robed Buddhists who bathed once a month, and bony, louse-infested Jains who never bathed at all, and who sometimes swept the ground before themselves with a broom, for fear of killing some insect with their feet. Sometimes the questions would even be serious, and long discussions would ensue, in Greek or the native tongue, with each of us toiling to make the other understand some difficult question or answer.

Often these questions would be about carpentry or stonework; as one student explained to me, I seemed to be following the path of *karma yoga,* God-within-work. But I told him that I thought my path was more like *bhakti yoga,* God-within-love—that I did what I did because everywhere I looked, I saw the suffering of my old teacher Yeshua, and only escaped that suffering, as he had, by walking through it. And then, I remember, I saw the confusion in the student's face, and tried to explain by telling some story of the days in Galilaia and Judaea. I forget which story—perhaps about the day on a hill outside a village, when Yeshua had sat with his arms full of wriggling children, and told us that we all had to become like children too. Or the time that his mother and brothers had come searching, thinking he had gone mad, and he had escaped going away with them by claiming a whole crowd as his mothers and brothers. Or perhaps it was about that terrible evening when he had washed our feet and told us that we were drinking his blood, that we would fail him and betray him—and that he didn't mind. . . .

But I can't write now with courage or certainty about those older times. I close my eyes, as I often have done, and watch the green light of the after-images move on my eyelids, and wait for them to follow my memory into visions—but they only shift into ordinary dreams. Later I waken, confused and unfulfilled, with only a few vague and treacherous shards in my head: my first master's beekeeper, puffy-faced and red-eyed from smoke and stings and weeping, come to tell Archimedes that the seven diseased hives have been destroyed; my brother Eliya and I, hysterical with guilt and laughter, watching as a flock of tiny sheep stampede madly out of the way of a stone that we've sent bouncing down the slope toward them. . . . But these images themselves always disperse wildly, driven before the returning thought: *you were hating your family into their graves.*

Perhaps my confusion now is only another stage of wisdom. Perhaps I can't see visions now, because when I try to look at them, I also see the uncertainty of memories, and the wild ingenuity of my imagination filling the gaps. And certainly the words above, when I read them over, seem not much different from my earlier records. . . . Perhaps I have been blinded to my visions so that I can see the need for them, the terrible need to make myself like a prophet, important and meaningful beyond any guilt; to create an order greater than myself and my poor memories. Oh, that Yahweh were as clear and sure in my mind, as is the need for Him!

But this new lack of vision and clarity of vision, this blindness and insight, is a paradox as terrible as any of those that Yeshua threw before us; I can see no way out of it, except by sleeping and thinking and letting time pass. The oil in my lamp is nearly gone. I will stop writing now, and try to sleep again.

XXXVII.

A vision of the time in western Parthia:

It is morning, and I am returning to the jar hut for the last time. The alley is no longer a threadway; now there is no sure path at all. I step carefully over a charred timber, and detour around a low wall of uncut stones. With each step, I still feel the warmth of the ashes beneath my bare feet. Once, I smell roasted meat, and notice the brown carcass of a woman half-buried under some fallen bricks. Her face is crisp and swollen; I don't recognize it. The odor, now, is almost pleasant, in a horrible way; but soon it will only be horrible. I start to pile some more bricks on the exposed part of the body, then remember that the people here cremate their dead, rather than bury them. So I start to clear away the bricks, which are still very warm in my hands. But under them I find the body pinned by a heavy blackened timber, that is in turn jammed under more bricks and debris. So finally I leave her, half-cremated and half buried, and walk numbly on.

To my amazement, the hut is still intact. Nothing large has fallen upon it; the willow latticework inside the entrance has charred, and the adjoining shed, where the old woman slept until she died, has burnt up and fallen, but the clay coating of the hut itself has simply been baked harder by the flames. Inside, the walls are still hot to the touch, and the air makes me blink and pant, but I find my few possessions still intact: the cooking pot; a spare garment of coarse, pinkish cloth; a few worn-out tools given to me by the poor in white-washed huts. My begging-bowl is already outside; I brought it back with me this morning, along with a little food.

I crawl out with the cooking pot, and make my way back through the ruins to the river. Then I return to the hut with water, and rinse the ash off the stone block before the entrance. The tray full of sand has been knocked off, and the sand spilled, but the tray itself is somehow no more cracked than it ever was. I fill it again with sand and ashes. Then I go to the ruins of a nearby hovel, where three children had lived by themselves. If there were bones there, they've been buried or burnt; now there are only ashes and pieces of limestone. I gather a handful of each. The limestone is charred red and fragile; I crush it against the altar stone, mix the lime with the sand and ash, and stir in a little water to make a crude cement. From a fold in my robe, I produce a little wooden cross, and set it firmly in the tray. Then I sit down in the ash beside the entrance, and consider what I should do next.

It is noon, and I am still sitting, when Arul shows up. Arul is a young Buddhist monk, of the mountain sect that wears deep red robes; he has come often before, to argue with me.

"You're alive!" he exclaims. "You weren't even touched!"

"I wasn't here."

"The house, the shrine," he gushes on. "Nothing's touched at all!" Arul likes to find miracles. He reminds me of Yohan.

"I was in another part of town," I tell him, "inside the old city walls, at a poor vendor's house. Those families like to have me visit them. They think I'm lucky."

"They think it's good *karma* to shelter a holy man," he corrects me. "But the hut, the shrine—everything around them is burnt. This is a wonder."

"It was set," I tell him. "The fire was. That's what I heard last night, in the city. Would someone really set fire to a slum full of widows and children?"

"It may have been set," he affirms. "Maybe by a carpenter, or a stoneworker."

"Why?" As usual, the emotion makes my voice squeak.

"They have families, too," he says. "They're afraid of the slum brats. The young men work for almost nothing, so the Parthians have been hiring them instead of real builders." He squats in the ash on the other side of the stone block. "I think good never travels very far before it becomes someone's evil."

"I'm to blame for this, then?"

"No, I don't think so," the young man assures me hastily. "It was still good when it left you." He pauses, then adds, "Will you stay here?"

"Will the people come back here?" I ask.

"Not for a while, I think. They'll find other slums, or go to the villages. The rainy season's too close now to start building again."

"Then I'll leave, too."

"It's the wrong season for monks to travel," he warns.

"I'm not a monk," I reply.

He grins at me. But the grin fades rapidly. This is not a place for grinning. He traces his finger idly in the ash.

"I think I'll go with you for a season," he says. "You're a very holy man."

I say nothing. I watch his finger, breaking the self-disciplined awareness of his monkish order, wandering by itself in the ashy dust. It changes into Yeshua's finger, tracing crosses in the dirt beside Ha-Yarden. Then it becomes Yohan's finger, dangling in the cold ash of the shepherd's hearth. . . .

"What did he say?" echoes Yohan, rocking. "I can't remember. He said. . . . "

"*Raka.*" I spit on the ground. "Yohan, you're a fool."

He doesn't look at me. "We're all fools," he says. "All liable to the fire." He rocks back and forth and back, and then adds, "This is what he said. He said he was thirsty."

"You already said he said that," I tell him.

"He said Miryam was my mother—he told me to look at my mother. She was all tired and crying, not pretty at all. Crying isn't pretty. She was wrinkled and old, like my mother would have been. My mother's dead, you know."

"I know." Yohan's mother had died pushing him from her womb.

"She's going to die all over again." He suddenly scoops up a handful of ash and bathes his face in it, as if it were water.

Something inside me is chuckling at this ludicrous scene. Something else is glancing about for a suitable stone to brain this poor suffering idiot. Something else doesn't care. "What else did he say?" I ask again.

"He prayed. He prayed twice. He asked Yahweh to forgive them, because they didn't know what they were doing."

"What?"

"He asked Yahweh to forgive them, because they didn't know what they were doing."

"Forgive whom?"

"Them."

"The Romans?"

"Them! The Roman guards. The Sanhedrin. The pilgrims standing around, waiting for some kind of show. Shimon the Rock. Yehuda Ishkerioth. Us."

I am crying, finally.

"He asked Yahweh why Yahweh had forgotten him," continues Yohan. "He said it was finished." He gouges up another handful of cold ash from the fire, and throws it over himself, and then grabs another. His frenzied face is grey with ashes, and rosy with dying light.

I sit, stunned, and consider, and stare at the stone walls of my cell. It has been so long since a vision came, and now these two together, both so terrible. . . . Already I feel more visions building in my head—some even darker than these two. I will have to begin writing again. But first I must pray. Yahweh, my father—whether I am the son of ashes, or the son of light, or the son of nothing at all—Yahweh my father, forgive me, forgive us all, for we don't know what we do.

XXXVIII.

A vision of the last days in Parthia:

The dominant element of this season is dust. It is everywhere: in every cup of wine or water, in every morsel of food, in each breath of hot air sucked into the lungs. It settles in dull layers on the goods in the market stalls, and forms a gritty mud between clothes and body. It transforms the few green leaves of the few trees, and the bright cotton clothing of the women, and the white-washed huts of the moderately poor, all into various shades of reddish tan. . . .

I awaken from dreams of choking, and find that the dust has already filled the shaft of new light from the white-washed mud window: a glittering gold column descends, like a stack of ingots knocked askew. Outside is shouting and braying and bleating, and all the other noises of a people moving hurriedly. Inside, my hostess and her family are busily gathering up and bundling their few possessions.

"I'm sorry," the woman tells me. "We have to leave now. The armies will be here soon."

"We learned early this morning," the husband explains. "There are refugees everywhere, and soldiers pretending to be refugees. They say the Sakas have broken the walls of Takasilla, and that Gudnaphares was killed."

"But. . . . " My mind is still sluggish with sleep. This whole scene burns with the feverish hopelessness of a nightmare. "But you aren't kings. Why should they bother you?"

"They'll take everything," says Tamad, my host. "They'll take the grain and the animals for their army. They'll take the women."

Ten years, I think. *Is it ten years I've been a holy beggar? All the people who have taken me in, have given me food and lodging for the sake of my poor stumbling words—they'll all be scattered now, like my own people after Babylon came. . . .*

"Go call the other people," I tell Tamad. "Tell all of them to come here."

"They've already gone," he replies. "Most of them, anyway. We're late. We didn't want to wake you."

I groan. "Go find the ones you can, then."

Tamad barks some orders to his two sons, and the three of them leave to scout the village for laggards. Ratana, his wife, brings me a large piece of flat-bread and spiced beans for breakfast, while the grandmother continues to direct Ratana's sister and their collective daughters in the packing. By the time I've finished eating, and they've finished tying bundles, a small knot of people has gathered outside the door.

I go out to meet them. Looking at their faces, I feel something inside me twist. They are the abandoned of the abandoned: the old, the crippled, the foolish. They've gathered around this hut because they could find no hope elsewhere. I stand there staring at the little twists of hope in their own faces, while they stare at me. Then, for lack of anything more constructive, I walk around and hug each of them: Laksmi the one-eyed root-gatherer; old Laxana, who claims that her arthritis improves when she gives me food; Rugan the humpbacked slave-woman, thrown out on the street when her master died. I hug even the ones I'm not supposed to touch; some of them shrink from me at first, but I persist, and then they clutch me so hard that their fingers leave bruises on my ribs.

"How will you destroy them?" old Yasodhara enquires eagerly.

"I can't," I tell her. Their faces begin to change, and I add hastily, "Yahweh wouldn't let me. I wouldn't anyway. That's not Yahweh's way."

"What is his way?" growls a beggar at the back of the crowd.

"To hold each other," I reply, hesitantly. "To help each other. To love. If necessary, to die loving." I think of Yeshua's nail-wounds, and shudder. "But first, to try getting out of the way."

"But how do we get out of the way, when every ox-cart in the country is clogging the road?" demands Laksmi.

"Does anyone here own an ox-cart?" I ask them.

People shuffle. No one answers.

"Then why do we need a road?" I ask them. "We'll travel across country. It's the dry season now; we won't have to worry about crossing streams and trampling crops."

"But how will we take our food, our things?" Tamad asks.

"What food?" I counter. "Half of you beg, anyway. And what do you own that you really need, that you can't make yourselves?"

"There will be plenty of unguarded granaries along the way," suggests a man from the crowd's edge. I don't recognize him; he wears an old traveler's cloak drawn up over his head against the sun, but he looks healthier than most here.

"Let's go," I tell them.

"All right," says Tamad. "Everyone get your things, quickly, and meet back here at my house."

"No," I tell them. "If you go back to your huts, you'll be tempted to take too much. Let's go." I start walking.

"But where are we going?" asks Tamad, while his wife, sister and mother hastily gather up their pots.

I pause for a moment. "To the sea," I tell them. "To the sea, and then west or south. There will be ships."

"And how are we going to get passage on a ship?" asks the man in the hood.

"We'll find passage," I reply doggedly. "Trust Yahweh."

Then the wonder of those words, in my voice, sweeps over me. *If the Yahweh exists, and he cares at all, then he is laughing right now,* I think. Whether laughing ironically, or from joy, I'm not sure.

"Trust Yahweh," I repeat, to hear the words myself. I begin walking again.

232

XXXIX.

A vision of the fall of western Parthia:

The moon tonight is almost full. Not long after twilight, the broad disk rises golden over the mountains, then shrinks as it rises, washing away the golden dust of the earth in a flood of light that is more silver than silver itself. I watch it rise, and wonder what to do with such beauty in the midst of disaster: whether to see assurance in it, or mockery, or simply beauty.

Then, for some reason, I see none of these—only the memory of Arul, smiling his calm moony smile. I haven't seen Arul in years—not since he had walked away one summer afternoon, saying that it was hot, and that he wanted to go back to his mountains to think in the coolness. I wonder, now, if he had safely reached his monastery again—and if the Sakas had gone into the mountains that far, also. . . .

The after-images of the moon leave a string of glowing pearls across my vision; when they have faded, the cleanness of night-sight, the pure lines of moonlight's silver and shadow, transform even the dirty abandoned village where we have camped. There is not much of value left here; this place is too far from the fighting for that. The owners had time to collect their belongings before they left, and other refugees have already picked through the leavings. But we've found a little grain that was spilled around the bins, and Mataya, a young "untouchable" widow, has captured a stray nanny goat which badly needed milking. She offered to kill it for us—her caste would allow her to do that—but I told her to keep it; her children could use the milk. She divided the milk among us all anyway—at least, among those who would accept it from her hands. I was surprised at how far the milk went.

The hooded man who joined us was wrong about finding full granaries, but has still proven himself useful. At his suggestion, we've posted a watch tonight around the perimeter of the buildings, alternating our few men with the older children, who can see as far and run faster. The stranger reads the terrain beautifully, showing us where to put our fires so that they won't show, and where to put our lookouts so that they can see the most without being seen. I've let him make his preparations, although we have nothing to fight with and nowhere to run. Yahweh will protect us from bandits and stray soldiers if He wants to, and lookouts can't hurt. Now the stranger and I sit on one of the rooftops, digesting the meager meal the women have cooked. He scans the milky plains below our little hill. I watch the moon, scudding among clouds that seem finely carved out of translucent marble.

"You're going that way?" the stranger says suddenly, pointing to the southwest.

"Yes," I tell him.

"They'll cut you off."

"Perhaps. But we'll at least avoid the worst mountain passes. We'll follow the valley down to the sea."

"They'll reach the coast, too."

I shrug. "Maybe we won't be there by then. Besides, Gudnaphar had garrisons on the coast; they may still rally."

The stranger shakes his head. "He pulled most of his men off the coast for the battle before Takasilla."

"You're a soldier, aren't you?" I ask, in my most polite voice.

He shrugs. "I'm a *Kshatriya*, from an old family. Gudnaphar found me useful. You're Toma the holy man, aren't you?"

"Yes," I answer. "But not so holy, I think."

He chuckles suddenly. "You must be. I use your name like I would a servant's, and you turn the insult into a demonstration of modesty."

I feel my cheeks flushing, and am glad of the disguise of moonlight. I had simply forgotten, despite all these years, that no one addressed a holy man by his informal name here.

"You know, there are still people in the court who hate you," the stranger remarks. "Or at least, there were. I suspect most of them are dead by now. It's a better time to be a holy man than to be a soldier."

"You're changing careers?" I smile thinly.

He shrugs again. "I wasn't born to that."

"I've heard that too often among you people," I tell him. "You aren't born to anything. I've been a free Hebrew, and a slave, and a foreman—an architect, a shipwright, a bookkeeper, a holy man. . . . " I nearly add, *and a man of hate*. But something warns me not to make such a boast aloud.

"Why didn't you content yourself with being good at one thing?" the warrior asks, dryly.

I wasn't allowed to. . . . Those words start to form on my tongue. Then I look at the soldier's moon-hollowed face, and finally I know what prophecy truly is. I look at the words on my tongue, and look down them and beyond them, and see that they lead back to hate, to death, to the hard look behind this man's eyes. . . .

"Perhaps you're right," I tell him, shaken. "Perhaps you were born to be a soldier. But if you were, we're all damned."

The glint in the stranger's eyes goes out for a moment. Then he laughs. "I like you, Your Reverence. You're no holy man. You're just honest. You scare the dung in my bowels."

"Do you like me enough to come with us," I ask, "even if we're going the wrong way?"

"Oh, well," he says, still chuckling. "The right roads are all clogged, anyway."

XL.

A vision of the week before Yeshua's death:

Even at night, Herod's Temple dominates its surroundings. It is felt as much as seen: the torches along its massive walls, each torch with its patch of lit stone, are utterly dwarfed by the towering black absence of stars above them. Along with the other carpenters, I crowd into the wooden barracks to escape its bulk. But even as we huddle around our lamps, we can feel the presence beyond the barracks wall; no one sits on the east side of the room, with his back to the Holy of Holies.

The Temple itself has just claimed another victim: an old man, a carpenter like us. He was on the wall, fitting a roof-beam in the portico of the Court of Women, and had leaned out too far, like a green apprentice. Or at least, most of us have that impression. But Moshe, who was closest to him, thinks differently.

"He dropped his hammer before he even started to lose his balance, I tell you," he repeats, his voice growing a trifle louder. "What good carpenter would do that? And

I saw his face: the fear was on it, before he buckled over. Adonai took him up there on the wall; he was dead before he fell."

"At least nobody went with him," grumbles another worker, whose name I don't know. "The wall is no place for an old man. They should never have conscripted him."

"He wasn't that old," says Hoshea, who is himself rather grizzled. "Maybe not fifty-five. And the wall's killed more young fools than veterans like Yosef."

"Well, he couldn't have died better," remarks a younger man, "not as a carpenter."

And here's the young fool himself, I think, revolted. I'd seen the aftermath of the accident, before they blessed Yosef's smashed remains and carried them away. "I'm going back to my family for the night," I tell them, casually. "I'll return tomorrow, if they still need men."

I slip out of the barracks, and across the deserted plaza, and then make my way through the darkened alleys toward the Golden Gate. It isn't a good hour to be roaming the streets, but for some reason I feel curiously immune tonight. Perhaps I have really begun to believe that if I am stabbed in some alley somewhere, Yeshua will bring me back to life. Or perhaps I am assured by the reports that Pilate's soldiers have recently captured one of the chief bandit-rebels of the area, along with most of his men. But mostly I think I am just lulled by the numbness that always follows an accident, and by the dreamlike stillness of the city: the hypnotic flicker of the oil-lamps in the few open doors, the dim bands of moonlight that roof the crooked open streets. These half-seen alleyways and old Yosef's shattered skull are both visions, equally unreal.

The city gates are open—another sign that Bar Abba and his band have been taken. One of Pilate's mercenaries lounges quietly in the shadows of the gate; he shifts to study me as I pass, but he says nothing. I emerge from the gate, and take one of the branching paths up through the gardens of Gat Shemaneh, on my way over to the Bet Aniya Road.

In the light of the almost-full moon, the twisted olive trees look even more tortured and alive than they do in daytime. A stray breeze stirs the dark leaves, as it passes like some nocturnal animal through the orchards. I should be nervous, I think as I walk: even if there are no thieves here, this is still a good time for demons to be about. But still I seem more alive in my thoughts than in my aching abstract muscles, and the moonlight is like a gauzy curtain across the world.

Then I see the figure beside the path.

At first I am sure that he is crouched, waiting. I freeze, and study the faint outline of him, and then I realize that he is not crouched, but kneeling. As I watch, his face rises from his cradling hands, and he stares at me.

"Teoma?" comes Yeshua's voice.

"Master?" I start to ask, then cut myself off. This is the time of demons; if I am mistaken about this creature's identity, then the word "master" might have horrific consequences. "Yeshua?" I amend.

"Don't worry, Teoma," says the figure, wryly. "It's me."

Which is precisely what a demon would say, a part of me thinks. *Would a mere man guess your thoughts so precisely?* But Yeshua is no mere man; for a non-slave, he has always had the most extraordinary knack for guessing men's thoughts. I curb my suspicions reluctantly; it

239

would at least have been interesting to meet a demon who deigned to speak with me.

"Where have you been?" Yeshua asks.

"To the Temple," I tell him. "They needed builders to finish the new portico before Passover began. I went to help."

Yeshua sighs. "That was foolish. Now they'll have your name on their rolls. They could conscript you."

"Probably not," I answer. "I told them my name was Eliya ben Yishak."

"Why bother?"

"What?"

The ghostly figure settles itself cross-legged. "Why did you bother to go?"

A bit shaken by his abruptness, I answer honestly: "In all my life, I've never been able to offer a sacrifice at the Temple—not even a dove. Now, I wouldn't even know how. But at least I can offer my services for the day."

"It was probably the better sacrifice, anyway. I always suspected that Yahweh just demanded the fat and the blood so that we wouldn't eat ourselves sick. But why should you give anything, Teoma? What do you owe to Yahweh?"

I begin to wonder about demons again. "Are you Yeshua the rabbi?" I demand bluntly.

"Or a demon, posing as Yeshua?" he responds. "No, I'm really Yeshua, posing as a demon. What do you owe to Yahweh, Teoma? He made you a slave. He took you from your family and raised you like a Greek. He'll take your life, eventually."

I think for a moment, and then answer carefully: "I don't know that I owe Yahweh anything. I don't know that

240

he did those things to me, or that he'll be responsible for my death. I just know that I'm from the tribe of Levi, and that Levites serve the Temple. I have to have *some* purpose."

Yeshua considers this. "A good answer. It will do, for now. But I think it's too late for you to become a Levite, Teoma."

"Do you have a better job for me?" I demand, peeved.

"I don't know," said Yeshua. "Would you still like to become the *Meshiha*?" He gives a half-hearted chuckle. But even in the moonlight, his face looks drawn.

"An old man gave up his life on the wall of the Temple today," I observe. "Maybe someone told him he was the Deliverer, and said to step off the wall and see."

Yeshua looks serious, and nods. "Maybe."

Now my mind is wandering back to the event, and wondering. In this place, the memory itself seems even more like a dream, an hallucination. The coincidences— the name of Yeshua's father, the same profession. . . .

"Tell me about your father," I demand, suddenly.

"What?" Yeshua looks startled.

"Yosef, your father. What happened to him?"

"Oh." He pauses. "I'll make a trade with you, Teoma. I'll tell you about my father Yosef. But first, you must tell me about your brother."

It is my turn to be taken aback. But I recover quickly, and plunge on. "My brother? His name is Eliya. He's a Levite. I think I saw him in the Temple once. He's my twin."

"Is he?"

"What?" Stunned by the question, I stare back at Yeshua's gaze. I have seen my reflection before, in water and in bright metal. In the moonlight, Yeshua could be one of those inexact reflections: the resemblance wavers from moment to moment.

"We don't look completely alike—that is, my brother and I. But he is my twin," I continue, uncertainly.

"Are you sure?"

"Why wouldn't I be sure?" I demand angrily. But suddenly, I'm not sure.

"Sometimes we need more significance than we have," says Yeshua. "Sometimes we need likenesses, patterns, meaning. Sometimes we may be so desperate for meaning that we have to create it for ourselves."

My mind explodes like a burst wineskin. *Could I be wrong about being my brother's twin? Why would I have invented such a story?* But as soon as the questions appear, their answers emerge like reflections: *If I am my brother's twin, I am like Ya'akob my ancestor, who emerged from the womb on the heels of his brother Esau, and who finally reclaimed his birthright by guile and perseverance. If I am so like my brother, I can resent him more for being a priest while I have been a slave. If I am a twin, I can feed my hate with injustice and irony.* Floundering, I claw my way through memories and possibilities, looking desperately for something sure, something substantial. . . .

Finally, I say, "Maybe I'm not his twin. Maybe I invented that. But if I did, it was so long ago that I don't remember it. I can't ever recall *not* being Eliya's twin."

"Then you're his twin," Yeshua assures me, "for at least as long as you'll need to be."

I feel worn out, full of the sullen exhaustion that follows a long rage. "Now it's your turn," I say, at last. "Tell me about your father Yosef."

"Yosef was a good man," replies Yeshua. "He died when I was twelve."

"That's all?"

"No. I loved him. I wanted him to live." Yeshua looks away; his shifting face seems luminous, almost transparent, like pale white fire in the moonlight. "When you lost your family, Teoma, you could hate them. All I had to hate was an absence."

I sit and absorb this: not Yahweh, not himself, but an absence. Yeshua has revealed far more than I had expected him to.

"Teoma," says Yeshua. "Teoma, I need to make some meaning for myself. I don't have much time left."

I take this for a cue. "I'll leave you to pray," I tell him. "Good-bye, Twin."

I walk on up the path, through the transformed dreamlike groves, and reach the Bet Aniya Road, and follow it to Lazaros' house. The moon is past its highest point when I reach the square. A half-dozen of Yeshua's followers sit, their hunched bodies full of tension, in the dust before Lazaros' door.

"What's wrong?" I ask.

"He's disappeared again," says Shimon the Rock.

"Ishkerioth and I were supposed to stay with him," says Shimon the Zealot. "He just slipped off in the moonlight. We don't even know where we lost him."

"It wasn't our fault," adds Yehuda Ishkerioth, plaintively, in a voice thick with wine.

"He's down in Gat Shemaneh, praying," I tell them.

"Is anyone with him?" demands the Zealot.

"No."

"Well, why didn't you stay, at least?" snaps the Zealot. "He should know better. He goes to the Temple every morning and baits the whole hierarchy of Yerushalayim, then goes off at night without anyone to protect him."

"He needs to be alone," I tell them.

"I thought they'd seized him already," the Zealot rants on. "I'm going down there to keep watch." He starts past me.

"He needs to be alone!" I shout. I grab Shimon the Zealot's shoulder as he charges past, and spin him around. He loses his balance and falls backward in the dust. Then he springs up again. His right hand slips inside his robe. I realize what's there.

"Use it," I tell him. "Kill a Jew."

"Are you a Jew?" he asks, glaring at me. But the hand comes out of his robe empty, and clenches the fabric's edge.

"He needs to be alone," I repeat. "He's praying. He's safe, so long as no one knows where he is."

"Ya'akob and I will talk to him tomorrow," intervenes Shimon the Rock. "If he wants to go out like this again, maybe some of us can wait for him at a distance."

"I'm going to bed," I tell them. I go inside, and find the house packed with sleeping bodies. So I take my cloak up to the roof and spread it there, although the night is rather chilly. I lie down, shaking with cold and fatigue and tension, and watch the moon until it sets. I am my brother's twin only in ancestry, and Yeshua's twin only in countenance and loss. Passover is two days away, and Yeshua is planning something terrible. Ashamed and afraid, I lie for a long time before sleep.

XLI.

A vision of the last days in Parthia:

Haban the merchant fingers his bleached, greasy beard. "You know, Yehuda," he tells me, "You're even madder than you were before. How many demons are you carrying around inside you now?"

"Only a couple, I think," I answer. "When they've left, then I'll be truly mad, maybe. Or maybe I'll just go *pffft*, and disappear."

"Interesting thought," says Haban. "Maybe we have no souls. Maybe our souls consist only of the devils we house." He leans against the ship's high prow, and chews the callous on his index finger.

"And how many demons do *you* have, friend," I ask him, "that you take on a batch of beggars and a former slave for free?"

"Not free," he corrects me. "We had a rough voyage over. We were blown off course, and the food got rotten. I lost five crewmen, including the carpenter. And the mainmast is cracked."

"We'll be glad to help." I respond. "I suppose you don't care to haul out and step a new mast here?"

"Of course not," he snorts. "Can you make the old one hold for another seven days' sail?"

"Let me look at it." Haban's ship is a small, plump merchantman with a single mast. I follow the shipmaster carefully down the half-planked deck, past the sailors keeping watch with spears and long oars over the crowds on the bank. The mast has a huge vertical crack that seems to run deep into the wood: apparently some hard gust has caught the sail at the wrong angle, twisting the mast and causing the wood to split along the grain.

"What kind of wood?" I ask him.

"Teak, from the east coast," he replies. "It cost a tenth of a cargo. I won't bother again."

"That wood is hard, but brittle. You're lucky it didn't shatter," I tell him. "Hmm. Haban, you don't need a carpenter; you need a smith. Iron bands would do the job, if they were heated up and slipped over the mast, then allowed to cool and shrink. But you'd really want to pull the mast before you tried that, too."

"You're right," says the merchant, dryly. "I'm not fond of making people shimmy up a bare pole with red-hot hoops in their teeth. Any other ideas?"

"You have rope? Lots of it? Extra thick?"

"Of course," snorts the merchant. "We buy jute rope along this coast, for cargo."

"We could splint the mast with wooden beams, and wrap it tightly with rope soaked in hot resin. But you'd have to anchor for a couple of days, while the resin sets."

"Anchor, or else use oars. Would your folk be willing to pull?"

246

"They'll try," I answer hesitantly. "They're not exactly able-bodied sailors."

"No, I suppose not," he says, eyeing our little knot of refugees on the shore. "But I suppose they could pull three to the oar, and I do need a carpenter. Anyway, it feels good to help someone once in a while."

"I thank Yahweh you were here."

"If Yahweh killed five of my men and split my mast just so I'd need a carpenter, then I have a quarrel to pick with Yahweh," observes the merchant, his face expressionless.

"Yeshua sold me to you for a purpose, all those years ago," I counter. "I can't prove that, but I see no use in believing otherwise. And if that's true, then it's only fitting that you should be the one to take me back."

"It was Ibrihim of Petra who sold you to me in Alexandria," he retorts, "and I don't think you want to go back."

"Why not?"

He hesitates, chewing his knuckle again. Then he says, "They'll be crucifying Jews all over the Empire before long. This new Emperor has some sort of grudge against Jews, and against you Yeshua-followers too."

"Oh," I say. What else can I say? "Oh . . . where else are you going?"

"Down the coast, to Malabar. I get good cinnamon there."

"Can you take us there?"

"Certainly. If you'll fix the mast, and they'll help row."

"We'll try." I wave to our party on shore. Our soldier, who calls himself Gund, starts barking directions, herding my little group of followers down to meet the ship's boat. Meanwhile, Haban himself starts giving orders. Several sailors are sent scurrying ashore to try and locate some resin among the chaos there. Others begin rearranging goods and stowing oars, or stand by to help our party aboard. Others still simply stand, waiting with oars and spears, in case someone uninvited tries swimming out to us.

The boat pulls alongside. None too gently, the sailors begin pulling our party up over the side. Mataya has tied the legs of her goat and brought it from shore with her; she erupts into a loud quarrel with a sailor who tries to take it from her arms.

When everyone is aboard, Gund joins me beside the mainmast. "Why do you bother with them?" he asks me.

"What?" I ask, alertly.

"These dregs. Why bother with them?"

"What dregs?"

"These people. These beggars. They should go ahead and die, and hope for a better existence next time."

"Maybe there isn't a next time. And they aren't all beggars, you know."

"Beggars, peasants. They're all beggars now. They're all living closer to the hells than the heavens."

"If they're all beggars now, then so are you," I observe.

"No, I'm not," he says. "I'm a *Kshatriya,* a warrior. It's my duty to defend the poor, if they're stupid enough to want to live."

I nearly remark that for the last few days, the poor have been defending *him.* But his eyes are open too wide, are too full of anger and reproach, are too vulnerable. He sees me looking into them, and looks away.

"I have to defend them," he continues. "That's my role, for as long as I'm in this body. But you don't. You're a holy man—or maybe a workman posing as a holy man. I don't know. But you're one of those. You should be in a monastery, preparing for heaven, or else you should be back in Takasilla, helping the Sakas rebuild their new capital. These people aren't your burden. They're worthless to you."

This man is like a field of swords, I think. *I must walk carefully.* "You're wrong," I tell him. "You're wrong several ways, though it's not your fault. You grew up in houses with high ceilings and fine carved doorways. You know the worth of buildings like that, and the worth of servants, and of horses, and money, because you could always pay for these things. But you don't know the worth of life when you can't pay for it.

"These people aren't Takasilla beggars. They're the village poor. They grew up in white-washed huts, and they survive by sharing. If one of them has an iron hoe, then all the others who don't have such a hoe come and borrow it. If a daughter loses her husband, or a brother-in-law loses his farm, then they can always go home, and live with their families, and play with their sister's children. They help each other and give to each other in a way no rich man could ever hope to." I pause to catch my breath. Mataya is trying to tuck the bleating goat between some coils of rope in the bow, where it will be out of danger from all the scrambling feet. "They're not perfect," I add. "They fight loudly and gossip viciously and cheat occasional strangers. But they aren't worthless."

"Well," says Gund, lounging against the cracked mast, "If they're so good, then what do they need you for?"

"I don't know," I said. "For hope, maybe."

249

XLII.

"For hope, maybe." How ironic that statement was, coming from me! I'd gone to help the poor, and ended up as poor and helpless as any of them; gone to bring them goodness and found that they had it to give me. This fine cotton paper, on which I write today, is the gift of one of them, who could not really afford it. It's only fitting that I would have believed that the only thing I had to offer them was what I had trained myself not to need.

Arul came to see me this afternoon. It was the first time we'd met since he took his leave of me on the plain of the Indus, in Parthia. This afternoon he stood in the doorway and said, "It really is you," until the guard asked him very politely if he would like to step inside my cell. I didn't recognize him at first; he was an old man with stained red teeth. (I'm an old man too, of course. But I haven't seen my face in a long time, and my hands were already gnarled when I was eighteen.)

"How did you come here?" I asked, after I'd recognized and hugged him. I asked that first, because it was the obvious thing to ask. But he looked at me, and burst out laughing. More puzzled than disgruntled, I waited for him to subside and explain himself. He laughed until he choked and coughed, and then spat a cud of red betel nut into my slop jar.

"I'm sorry, Revered One," he said. "I laughed because, first, you still don't pretend to be wise, but ask straightforward questions. Then I continued laughing because I realized I could spend three days answering your straightforward question, and still not tell the half of it. And then I laughed harder, because I knew that if I answered your question well enough, you wouldn't need to ask a single other question. And finally I choked on my own laughter, because I should have asked first, and because you're the whitest old man I've ever seen."

"I know where you've been, now," I countered. "You've been off learning how to chew your thoughts over and over, like a camel."

"You're right," he guffawed, and I joined in the laughter, and pictured a white old man in a prison cell, asking his revered guest, "How did you come here?" Then I nearly doubled over with mirth, and we both laughed until we wheezed.

When we'd finished laughing, he explained that he'd left his monastery in the mountains years ago, and had begun a long, slow pilgrimage to the south, searching out other followers of Gautama the Buddha. I told him that I'd heard of an island kingdom to the east, and that Buddhists were said to still rule there. But he said he'd already heard of them, and that he would go there next year, if he lived.

For now, though, he was living at the little Buddhist temple complex here in the city, and having long conversations with the local monks.

251

"They've developed some very different ideas from ours," he explained enthusiastically. "They think that peace comes from within, and can only be achieved by the efforts of the self. We think that peace comes from outside, and can only be achieved with help."

I found the issue intriguing, if a bit silly. "Have you ever achieved peace for yourself?" I asked.

He chuckled again; we both had to breathe deeply to avoid another fit of laughter. "Of course not," he replied. "Only an occasional few moment's illusion of it. And you?"

"No," I replied quickly, "although sometimes I think I'm getting closer. And the monks of the temple?"

"Not that any of them dare to admit."

"Then since none of you know what you're talking about, why are you arguing?"

His guffaw broke loose again. "I think we have the better of them, though," he continued, finally. "We say that since peace comes from without, then if anyone ever achieves peace, he becomes a *bodhisat,* and tells everyone else how to do it. They say that since it comes from within, the man who achieves it becomes an *arhat,* and doesn't need to bother with the world any more. So he goes off and never tells anyone, and then how do the rest of them know that peace comes from within?"

This sets us both off. Then, just as we are regaining control, I burst out, "Just think: two ancient 'Revered Ones' are sitting in a damp prison cell, laughing their lungs out!"

We clutched our aching bellies and howled and cackled. "Think of the guard!" he cried, then, and dragged me to the little peephole in the door, and we took turns looking out at the poor guard, who stood a little ways down the hall, looking alternately concerned and baffled and finally mortified, and we bellowed and hooted until finally he began to chuckle, too. At last we collapsed, gasping and exhausted, on the cool stones of the cell floor, and heard the guard still laughing outside.

"Revered One," I told Arul after a while, "I still don't know, but here's what I think. I think that peace comes from without, but only if you decide to let it in."

"It spreads like laughter," he maintained jovially. Then, after a moment, he took on another tone. "You know that they're going to kill you."

"Yes," I answered.

"When they release you, come to the *watt*," he said. "I'm in the first cell on the right side of the temple. I'll introduce you to the master there. I'm sure he'll give you sanctuary, and make you a teacher."

"No," I told him.

"You want to die?"

"No," I answered. "But I'm not your responsibility. I'm not a Buddhist."

"Of course you are," he answered. "Your Yahweh is just another incarnation of Peace."

"No, he's not," I told him. "If anything, Peace is another incarnation of Yahweh. But even if I could pretend to be a Buddhist, I wouldn't come to your *watt*. Your people are just as much a minority in this town as my own are. I've humiliated the king's brother by leading his wife from him, and I've made the King himself lose face by defying his order to lead her back. I'm not going to endanger my own people by staying with them, and I'm certainly not going to endanger *your* people."

"Where will you go, then?"

"There's a cave on a hill near town. There's a pool of water at the base of the hill, and a little brushwood for making fires. I'm used to stone floors; I'll wait there."

"Friend, you sound like a Jain. Are you going to starve yourself to death, if the king doesn't find someone to kill you immediately?"

"I'm sure he's found someone. My friends are ignoring the caste system. Yahweh is threatening local temple revenues."

"Then what are you going to do? Do you really expect heaven to come down to earth and save you?"

"Maybe," I told him.

Later, after he had hugged me and promised me he'd come again, I watched the guard close the door behind him, and sat down in my corner to think. There was very little now, I realized, that really mattered to me. If I died tomorrow, I might die not knowing if I would arise again or not. I didn't really care. It would not affect how I lived or what I did until then. Perhaps that was faith. Perhaps it was despair. What I called it didn't really matter, either.

I could think, then, of only one thing that might still matter. I had spent forty years, at least, since Yeshua's body was nailed up to die. Mattathias had written that the Temple was torn down to its foundations, and that nine thousand Jews had died on the walls and rocks of Gamla. I had become an old man, and Yeshua's kingdom had not come.

Perhaps Yeshua expected too much of us, I thought. *We are so poisoned with hate; there is so much suffering—so many hurt people lashing their hurt at others, so many greedy people forcing others into selfishness, so many Ro-*

mans and Jews and Greeks and Parthians and Sakas and Tamils and Hinds, so many priests and bureaucrats and soldiers. It has taken forty years to get the poison out of me alone. In forty years, people have died all around me, and I have made only one miracle, have raised only one young man from the dead.

Perhaps you trusted us too much, Yeshua. It was so easy for you that you didn't realize how hard it was for the rest of us.

No, that was foolish. Of course he'd known. When they drove those spikes into his wrists, each blow of the mallet must have told him how badly some people had wanted the world *not* to end.

Thinking these thoughts, I watched, almost abstractly, as one of Yeshua's paradoxes approached. At first it circled warily, like a small scavenger at the edge of my vision. Then it grew bolder. "Do you want life?" it whispered, creeping forward.

"Yes," I answered cautiously, not sure whether I saw an angel or a demon. Then I repeated "Yes," more loudly, making the word a shield.

"If you accept the world, you accept death," the paradox pointed out timidly.

"I want life more than the world," I replied.

"But death is the only way out of the world," said the paradox, greatly encouraged. "If you want your life, lose it."

Then I knew the creature's true nature. But that wasn't important, either.

"I could have left a long time ago, couldn't I?" I told it.

"Of course," it said. "Why didn't you?"

"Because I would never have really known if I'd escaped. If I'd have left the world, if I'd truly *believed,* then

I might really have gone to Heaven. Or I might have been only insane, and still bound to die."

The demon-angel chuckled. I laughed with it, and nearly sent it away laughing, but checked myself in time. Like everything else in the world, it contained both good and evil; its nature would rest in what I did with it, what I pulled out of it.

"I thought you didn't doubt anymore, Teoma," it remarked, conversationally.

"I don't," I replied. "I don't doubt what I need to do, and nothing else is important."

The paradox screwed up its beautifully hideous little face. "And what could you possibly need to do?" it asked wryly.

I hesitate only a moment. "I'll live until I die," I said, "without regretting either. I'll die without hating my killers. How much more faithful can I be than that?"

And at that moment I was both triumphant and desperate, elated and horrified, fulfilled and empty. I looked back at my answer, and saw how wonderfully perfect it was, and how terrifyingly hollow and smug. And then the angel demon and the stone cell and my ancient childish body were swallowed up into one terrible triumphant vision, and then another, and then another. . . .

XLIII.

Of the death of Yeshua:

Blackness. I lie in the Caves of Shelomoh, beneath the holy city, and weep. I don't know how I came here, or why—looking for a hiding place, perhaps, or a tomb. I have no lamp, and I think nothing of the dark, although I must be deep within the quarry chambers and utterly lost. I lie and weep on the cool stone floor, and my weeping changes into strange blurred whining sounds in the echoes of the cavern, until the unseen rooms light up with dreams.

The dreams begin with the one glimpse that I have had of Yeshua this day. It is on a narrow street that leads to the killing place. He is carrying the timber of the cross: a thick, splintery, poorly cut piece of wood, a carpenter's abomination, huge enough to stagger a healthy man. And Yeshua is not healthy; the blood soaks through his tunic in oddly bright little stains, little double scarlet patches to match the double iron balls that tipped each leather strand of the scourge. The street is lined with Greeks and

257

pilgrims and townsmen, some jeering. One of them, a young man, waits until the first of the Roman guards have passed, and then hurries into Yeshua's path and kicks his legs out from under him. Yeshua falls, and the timber lands on top of him, its end striking the pavement with a sickening clunk.

The Roman mercenaries spin around at the disturbance. For a brief moment, one of them seems to be staring straight at me. . . .

Lightning. Rain. Darkness running blindly through the alleys with me. It almost never rains in Yerushalayim. But today water falls like a wall of cold, drenching fires long before the Shabbat is supposed to have begun. I emerge from the alleys to find the Temple above me, blurred with the steam of rain, and the merchant's awnings shredded and flapping in the wind. The curtains of rain drive me back into the alleyway; they are like demons dancing before the Temple wall. A bolt of lightning suddenly reaches down to the Holy of Holies, the innermost sanctum, and dances white-hot across the golden roof. The bass blast of thunder deafens me, and the air is filled with the smell of burnt cloth and the terrible clean odor of the lightning itself. I plunge back into the alley. . . .

Darkness. No, not darkness, blackness. Shelomoh's quarry-caves lead down under the city itself, but the entrance is outside the walls. I must have passed the Hill of the Skull, on my way to the entrance. Why hadn't I looked? Or had I looked? Was I simply not allowing myself to remember? And then the memory comes: *The Ro-*

mans hang men on the cross naked. You won't look at Yeshua that way. The last act of refusal, the last petty defiance, the last excuse.... I sob in the blackness. I've failed. We've failed. Of course we would.

"You've failed, Yeshua!" I shout into the blackness.

Suddenly the blackness is no longer solid. It gapes for echoes: *you've you've failed failed Yeshua Yeshua you've Yeshua failed you've Yeshua failed Yeshua failed you've failed,* until all the words fill up the blackness with every meaning they can, and then fade into a mutter of syllables like a foreign crowd. I lie until the whole murmuring mob has died of old age, and wonder if real death sounds like that: all the meanings blending into fading foreign nonsense. In that blackness, I know what death looks like....

"You're going to die," Archimedes says, growing out of a new dream in the darkness, and I nod and note that he is a memory.

"Go away, old man," I tell him. "You're going to die, too."

And then I remember that he is probably already dead. His image fades into the deathly blackness, and only the voice remains. "Everyone dies," the voice says. "You have to accept that."

"No!" I cry.

"No. I won't ever accept that." We are standing before Hermione's tomb. Archimedes has spent all his money to put her here. He was content, when she was alive, to leave her in bondage; but now that she is dead, he has bought her body from his former master, rather than see it burnt with trash or buried in a common grave.

She won't be here, I tell myself bitterly. *Not even her body will be here. Her juices will run out through the little drain hole in the floor, and when the flesh has all rotted, they'll stick her bones into a little niche in the wall, and put Archimedes' body on the shelf where her bones were.*

But I don't tell Archimedes this. He has taught me to keep my mouth shut. Now, standing beside the open tomb, on the first piece of land he has owned since his capture decades ago, he rambles on with a sort of desperate, cheery pride. "Your master's guaranteed me that he'll take care of my own funeral arrangements, when my time comes. I'm giving him two month's wages for security. He tried to persuade me to get circumcised so he could bury me like a Jew, but I held out for a good Greek funeral, with mourners and singers, and a coin under my tongue for old Charon when I cross the River Styx."

"I could take care of all that for you!" I protest.

"You might, if you're here," says the old man, his voice suddenly flat and controlled.

"Why wouldn't I be here?"

"I'm training you too well," says Archimedes. "The master could sell you for a huge profit now." His voice is still flat, but his hand grips my shoulder fiercely.

That grip is the only thing that keeps me from lashing out at him, at this hypocrite with his gods and equations. I stand with his heavy arm against my shoulder blades, and his sweaty side against my right arm, and I shake with rage and fear. I have been forced to watch and listen while Hermione died for six weeks, screaming at the thing that grew in her belly in the place of a child. I have been like a son to this pot-bellied old Greek, who has made me help him feed the dying woman, and bathe

260

her, and change her fouled, bloody bedding; who has made me follow him to watch the emaciated, swollen-bellied body be placed in this hole to rot away. *He could have bought me out of slavery with the money he's spent here,* I think. *How could he love something as horrible as that whining, screaming, foul-smelling invalid, as that grotesque corpse?*

Then suddenly I've wrenched free from the embrace of that hairy arm, and am running, running from the corpse, from the claim of that arm that will someday die, from the fear of that black stony chamber, from the awful guilt of the hurt I've inflicted and the terrible certainty, sooner or later, of entering another such tomb. . . .

Pain shoots up my leg. I sit bolt upright in the chilly darkness.

"Yehuda Teoma?" comes a voice in the darkness. "Is that you?"

"Yes," I reply, awake but disoriented.

"I'm sorry I kicked into you." The voice is Yehuda Ishkerioth's. His silhouette looms against the starlight. Now I remember, groggily, that I am on the rooftop of Lazaros' house. Yehuda steps over me, and dumps his cloak, and drops his body on top of it, grunting with the impact of his landing. His feet scrabble in the palm thatch that covers the flat roof, as he kicks over on his side to arrange the cloak. "Yehuda Teoma," he mutters, then says loudly, "Huh, I'm your twin, too! Your name-twin." He cackles. I don't join in. He subsides.

"You know, Teoma, you shouldn't have left Yeshua alone like that," he says, after an uncomfortable silence. "He shouldn't go off like that. It could upset everything."

I'm still grumpy from having been kicked awake. "Let Ya'akob and Shimon the Rock handle it," I tell him.

"Why?" he retorts. "Because Ya'akob is an old man? Because the Rock's father owns two fishing boats?"

"Who are *you*, to tell Yeshua what he should do?" I erupt. "Are you his master, or is he yours?"

Suddenly, his voice is cold and flat. "My master is Adonai. I serve the nation of Israel. If Yeshua does the will of Adonai, I'll go along with him."

I recognize the edge under his carefully pronounced words. I've heard it before, in soldiers on duty. *You're dealing with a slightly drunken fanatic,* I tell myself. *Be careful.*

"Who decides the will of Adonai, Yehuda?" I ask, in as reasonable a tone as I can muster. "Can you? Or Shimon the Zealot?"

"Adonai does," he says. "Isn't that obvious? Look, they welcome him into the city with a parade, and put their cloaks under his donkey's hooves and treasure the stains afterward. They fill half the Court of Gentiles to hear him preach. He could have the whole town in his hands by Passover Day, if he'd just try!"

"Have you heard what he's been telling those crowds in the Temple?" I ask. "He isn't preaching armed revolt."

"He says the New Kingdom's at hand," Yehuda retorts. "He cleared the vendors out of the Temple. He could clear the Romans out of the Antonia as easily. We have to make him proclaim himself!"

"You can't make him do anything," I tell him. "He's tired. But he's still stronger than you'll ever be, in every way you can imagine."

"But he has to do it!" he almost shouts. "We have to make him do it!" Then he forces himself to sit back. For long moments, he lies there, perfectly still. Then he springs up and goes to the edge of the roof. Ignoring the stairway, he slips over the side and drops out of sight. I hear his feet strike the hard ground of the village square, and the little *woof!* of his breath as he lands, and the *scuff-scuff* of his feet as he trots away in the darkness.

Good riddance, I think, pulling the blanket up over my face. But then, as I drop off into sleep, something else occurs to me. *I've failed,* I think. *I could have prevented him, but I've failed.* The words follow me into my dreams, and fill the blackness of my slumber, not with images but with sounds: *I've failed Yeshua I've failed you failed Yeshua failed.* . . . This time, though, the words don't fade away, but continue to build, rising into a bellow, a scream.

Rabboni, is it I?

I crawl my way through the blackness, claw frantically toward wakefulness, waken into more blackness, more screaming and sobbing and bellowing voices. . . .

An eye opens in the blackness: a blind eye of blue-white light. I stumble toward the pain of its brightness, my own eyes reawakening into light as a baby wakes, screaming, into the pain of birth. Slowly my eyes adjust, and find that the light is not blue-white after all, but yellowish, reddish. I stumble through the eye of the quarry entrance, into evening.

I lean against the stone of the entrance, and wait for my breathing to slow. The limestone is still warm against my back; the air is warm, too, but starting to cool. The city smells of wood-smoke and cooking. *The Shabbat must be over,* a calm part of my brain thinks. *You've been underground for at least a whole day.*

Almost against my will, I turn and walk toward the Damascus Road—toward that other quarry, the open pit in the hillside, where the townspeople of Yerushalayim, lacking the skill of King Shelomoh's imported artisans to draw stones safely out of darkness, had grubbed out the blocks for the Second Temple after their return from Babylon. Holes were sunk in the living rock there, to cut a layer of blocks that were never needed. The holes make easy mounts for the butts of crosses.

A man can live on a cross for days. Perhaps he's still . . . perhaps I can. . . .

I scrabble my way through the shacks that hunch along the city wall, and emerge on a dirt path that circles the city, and run along it to the quarry.

The crosses are gone. No one at all is dying here today.

The Shabbat. They must have killed them before the Shabbat began. . . .

I turn away.

A batch of children rush by, rowdily beating each other with sticks. Two tasseled Pharisees pause in their argument as the children swarm around their legs. One Pharisee smiles; the other curses the children roundly. Near the Damascus Gate, a soldier of Herod Antipas' bodyguard chats calmly with a couple of Pilate's mercenaries. Northeast, across the ramparts of the gate, I glimpse the towers of the Antonia, where Yeshua was scourged. It stands there like a huge horned altar, as it did in my childhood.

They've killed an innocent man. Worse than that, they've killed him because he was innocent, and they aren't, not even the children. And I have run and hidden in a cave, and let them do it. . . .

There is no way to go on after such a thing, without life itself becoming an abomination. I start toward the mercenaries.

They ignore me, until I tap one of Pilate's men on the shoulder. Then he spins around, hand on sword hilt.

"Pardon me," I tell him. "I think you may be looking for me."

The soldier eyes me for a moment, then nudges his companion, who has already turned to see the problem.

"We speak no Aramaic," says the second soldier, in heavily accented Greek. "What do you want?"

"I said, 'I believe you may be looking for me,'" I tell him, switching to Greek. "My name is Yehuda Teoma, Yehuda the Twin."

"What would we want with you?" snorts the first guard.

"I'm a follower of. . . ."

"Move on, and don't make trouble," the second guard commands.

Flabbergasted, I back away.

"Well done," I hear the Herodian tell the two mercenaries, in Greek, when he thinks I am a safe distance away. "This whole town's pulled tighter than an old wineskin. 'Best to avoid incidents."

They don't even want you, I tell myself. *That's how important you are.*

Then, a moment later, a more startling thought comes: *They're afraid of you. They're afraid of incidents. . . .*

265

I glance feverishly about me for something to throw—a stone, a dead fish, a flaccid wineskin, anything. One blow, and Shimon the Zealot might get his rebellion. One blow, and Yerushalayim could burn, and Herod's Temple and the Antonia could be knocked to the ground.

But for the first time in the history of Yerushalayim, there seems to be nothing handy to throw. I run a few yards up the road. A woman passes, carrying a bale of woolen cloth: too bulky; they'd dodge it and laugh, and I'd have to fight the old woman for it to start with. A sandal-vendor has laid his wares out on the roadside. I eye the sandals. The sandal-vendor eyes me.

Then a string of donkeys scuffles by, on their way through the Damascus Gate. With a gleam in my eye, I wait for them to pass. When they've gone, I scoop up a double-handful of warm, wet dung, and turn back toward the soldiers.

They've already disappeared.

There are guards atop the gate, I think. I rush toward it, still carrying my twin handfuls of filth. The crowd that always mills about a major city gate parts around me as if I were a leper. Behind me, I hear muttering: "Manure. . . . " "Did you see. . . . " "Probably another. . . . "

I stop thirty yards from the huge double gate, and my hope sinks into my bowels. The parapet of the gate is topped by giant, evenly spaced limestone blocks: easy cover. The soldiers carry big, square Roman shields. They could dodge or block my damp missiles easily.

I no longer care. Holding my burden up like an offering before me, I stride up to the great gate itself.

The crowd at the gate sees or smells my burden and gives me space, jamming up the usual bottleneck even

266

further. I almost laugh at them: men who tread through manure everyday, who burn it, dried, in their fires, but can't stand the sight of it in a man's hands! Even the beggars scramble out of the way. I step up to the gate, step almost back to the center of the world, and cry out my first and only spoken prophecy:

"This is the people of Judaea and Galilaia! You see? This is Greece and Rome and Parthia!"

I raise both hands, still full of cooling dung, high over my head for the crowd to see, while the onlookers in front dam up a huger and huger mob behind them. Then, just as the dam is about to burst, I turn and fling a handful of dung with all my strength at each gatepost: first the left, then the right. The dung spatters and clings and falls to the earth in small bits.

For a moment, there is silence. Above me, on the parapet, I hear the melodic rasp of an iron sword sliding from its scabbard. I dance with hate and ecstasy.

The crowd begins to stir.

"It's just another prophet," says a beggar, "damn them all."

With a ripple of laughter, the crowd surges forward. I stand for a moment, stunned at how the beggar's stupid remark has made my great gesture so stupid as well. Even the guards are laughing! I rush forward to meet the crowd, to bury myself in it, smother in it, drown. . . .

Hours later, I find myself standing before the house of Lazaros in Bet Aniya. There is moonlight again, but no one is waiting outside. I stand looking at the closed door for a long time. Then I go up to it, and knock.

No one answers.

Through the loose-fitting door comes the smell of spices: sandalwood and myrrh and nard. I sit down by the doorpost, and stare at the waning moon until I sleep.

XLIV.

The songs of this land are diverse and full of faith. Since leaving Yerushalayim, I have seen men pipe tunes for serpents and march chanting over red-hot coals; singing, they have pierced their own cheeks with thorns and their ears with metal as I watched. Singing, too, milkless beggar-women have lulled hungry children to sleep, and beggars have drawn coins out of the purses of rich men. Outside the walls of my cell, I'm sure they still sing. There is no end to singing here, nor any scarcity of faith.

If anything, there is too much faith. Men believe anything, and worship everything. Once, in the north, I saw a temple dedicated to rats. Thousands of the creatures lived there, and ate the weight of several men in grain and milk each day. Not content with that, the rats gnawed the images of themselves on the tops of columns, and bit the feet and bodies of worshipers as they knelt. I have seen other temples dedicated to death, in the form of a many-armed woman with a necklace of skulls—I have never gone into one of those places. But they seem to be everywhere.

It's no wonder, then, that people have accepted my one small miracle so calmly. When he came to visit me this evening, though, I wondered again if he was an illusion that I still lived in—or if he was real, but my memory was false. I don't know even yet, and don't much care. You, my reader, will have to decide that, if you ever exist—just as you must decide if I am an honest man or a liar.

But the boy's face, this evening, was real and brown and radiant, and his teen-aged voice cracked realistically with excitement. "King Mahadevi has accepted our bribe!" he squeaked. "You'll be freed tomorrow! We're. . . ."

"Wait. What bribe?" I stopped him.

"We got word a month ago that he might free you in exchange for a fine. But the price he named was too high. Then yesterday Gund came to us, and said someone had given him the money anonymously. You'll be free tomorrow!"

Probably the priests of the temple of Shiva, I thought. *They've donated the bride-price of Migdonia, so that the King can release me without losing face, and I can be assassinated more safely.* But I smiled to reassure Anand. At least now my little congregation wouldn't have to pay for my death; that comforted me. I told him how pleased I was, and sent him back to help with the preparations for my homecoming.

Later, Arul came. "I just heard," he told me, as we hugged each other. "I've talked with the head of the monastery about you. My offer still stands."

"Thank you," I told him. "But my answer still stands, too. It's all right—I've had more than enough time to watch my stomach rise and fall, here in this place."

"So you'll walk out tomorrow, and your Yahweh will protect you." He chuckled to hide the strain in his voice. "I admire your strong belief, at least, Revered One."

"Don't!" I told him. "You wouldn't know what you were admiring. I'm not always sure, myself. But I think maybe faith sometimes has very little to do with belief. I think maybe it has to do with deciding."

We talked a little longer, and then we hugged again, and he left. Then I dampened the little cake of ink that Anand had left me, and mashed a piece of the cake in the little hollow in one flagstone that has been serving as my inkwell, and added some water from my drinking jar.

I will not sleep much tonight. What fear I have left would surely appear in my dreams. And besides, I still have three memories I must record.

Ponder these three visions, and decide.

XLV.

A vision of the dry lands between Kovei and Mylapore:

The boy's body lies in the road.

It is not a body at first: a half full rice sack, perhaps, or a fallen log. Then it becomes a pair of legs, sticking out in the dusty road beneath a tree full of white blossoms. Someone resting, perhaps? A drunk? A beggar? It's not until we are much closer, and the cloying scent of the blossoms fills our nostrils, that the legs finally become a body, and the body becomes a boy. We are much closer still, when he becomes obviously dead.

Then the dead boy becomes a terrible rictus of a face, twisted out of boyhood and beyond manhood by whatever agony that had preceded his death. He becomes grey-brown limbs twisted at unearthly angles, and the boy's white garment, wetted and torn off his loins and clotted several shades of grey by his final thrashing in the dust. He becomes a foul smell—not the sour musk of decay, but the sickbed smell, the odor of vomit and urine and feces,

272

and of pain and fear sweated out of the skin. The smell
mixes with the odor the white blossoms, which at this
nearness has itself become a whole range of smells: sweet
and slightly sour and giddy and heavy and delicate and
powerful. The flowers themselves have become thousands
of delicate individuals, hanging in massive clumps; their
long stamens are the color of slender sunlit bones. The
musks of death and flowers clash and harmonize and
overpower. The boy is recently, and very terribly, dead.

The boy's body lies in the road. What am I to do
about it?

"What happened?" I ask my little knot of followers.

Some stare at me uncertainly: *I'm* the holy man,
the wise man. I'm supposed to tell *them.* But Gund the
Kshatriya merely shrugs. "He looks poisoned," he says.
"Maybe a snake. Maybe from food. No concern of ours, Revered One."

But the boy's bulging eyes stare up at me accusingly.
Your god did this, they tell me. *If your God is all powerful,
then he must poison children, too.*

"No," I murmur. I stare about me: at the lush bone-
colored flowers and spiky leaves of the trees, and at the
thick-stemmed, barb-covered *kathara* plants that grow
all around us like nests of spears, and at the dry white
riverbed beyond the tree, and the crumbled pale hills of
the Eastern Ghats, that rise like ghosts from the plain
beyond the river. "Who did this?" I yell.

The old women who follow me stare at each other, as
if the murderer were among their number. "Who knows?"
says Gund, soothingly.

Then I hear a soft *plop,* as if something has dropped
from the tree. I swing around to face the tree again, but

my eyes, dazzled by the plain and the riverbed, cannot penetrate the shade. There is a soft rattling noise, like pebbles sliding.

"There it is!" cries Gund, pointing.

From behind a clump of *Kathara* next to the tree, a face appears: a tiny demon face, with glittery eyes and a blunt nose and no forehead. Then I realize that it isn't a face. It is a whole head, scaly; what I had taken for jowls and chin are really the neck, impossibly wide and flat, swaying.

"A snake," says Gund. "Be careful, Teacher. It's poisonous."

"He's called the killer!" an old woman half-whispers, half-shrieks. The whole group shuffles uneasily. Gund stoops to catch up a large stone.

"Who are you?" I demand of the creature.

"It's a snake, Honored One," repeats Gund. "A cobra. Please stand back."

"Reptile, son of Reptile," says the snake. "Harmer, son of Harmer."

The whole crowd, including Gund, fall back shrieking. At least I believe they have done so, though I note this only fleetingly. My whole attention is now on the thing that faces me.

"Since you want me to be more than a snake, I'll be so," it says. "Should I be the one who fed Eva the fruit?" It uncoils three more feet of body, and raises its head so that it is level with mine. "Why aren't you satisfied with a simple snake, Yehuda?"

A vision? I ask myself, amid my fear and exultation. I have the feeling that if something in my mind were only to twist itself a little bit, then this creature *would* be a mere snake again. I'm afraid of that, more than of the creature itself.

"Why are you bothering me, little twin?" it hisses gently "What do you want, that you have to interrupt my business?"

I find my tongue. "Why did you do this?" I ask, pointing to the boy.

The scaly lips look somehow peeved. "Because I'm a snake," it says.

"No, you're not!" I tell it, just in time. For a moment, it flickers, and nearly becomes a snake again. That is my most horrible fear, now: that this thing might really exist, and that I might be unable to see it. . . .

"I lie in the shade under the branches, and the boy's legs tramp up within a step of me, while he tears flowers down out of the tree. I have to defend myself, don't I?"

"That's a snake's reason, not yours. Why?" I demand again.

It swells up angrily, suddenly twice my height. "Why should I give *you* an explanation?"

"Because I'm a servant of Yahweh!" I hear that reply as though it has spewed from someone else's mouth—some fool, some proud fool who thinks he knows a god's will. But at the same time, I know where those words come from. I *am* a servant of Yahweh, whomever or whatever he is. I have no other identity left. The words are both foolish and true. The fool is talking to a snake, but the thing I am addressing is something else. . . .

"Really?" the thing is saying. "I didn't know that you were a *servant*." (In the language we speak, "servant" is the same as "slave") "I didn't know you slaved for anyone. I hadn't even realized that you were sure he existed."

"If you exist, then so must he!"

"Ah, but do I exist?" It begins to flicker again.

"You exist!" I shout. But it continues to slip forms like a fire in the night wind: *Snake* snake *Snake* snake. . . . "Why?" I cry a fourth time.

"To serve Yahweh!" The image steadies a little, towering over me. "I punish the wicked." It looks down at me thoughtfully, as if assessing the degree of wickedness in my body.

"Then why an innocent boy?" I demand. Fear is rising like vomit in my chest.

"*An innocent boy?*" The scaly mouth twists in an impossible smile. The sweet-sour smells of death and flowers roll over me in dizzying waves. "I was jealous," the thing explains softly. "Just down the riverbed is a lovely little green pool, emerald with algae, lined with white flower-trees. Last night, this innocent boy took a lovely innocent girl down there. First he made her bend down. . . . " It arches its back suggestively.

"So you changed him into *this*?"

"A snake has only one punishment to give," it answers. But it is no longer much like a snake at all. It has become a hideous swelling thing of scales and odor, of scent as much as flesh. The scales gleam like wet paint, black and red and yellow and white, patternless, oozing an oil like the scented fat of rich women, a smell of myrrh and carrion and crushed grass and ripe yellow melons. The flat shiny eyes stare down into mine. "We both serve Yahweh, little twin. But why aren't you doing your job? You go around building little shelters for people to die in. You get poor people killed. Why are you interfering with *me*?" it oozes.

276

I hesitate. It swells larger. *Can I die of a nightmare?* I wonder, as it rears above me. I couldn't dismiss this thing now if I wanted to; it is no more a snake than the boy was the boy's body. But somewhere, some other part of my mind tells me, *a snake is tensing to strike.*

In desperation I drop to my knees, and grope for the thing that is more terrible than my vision. I find the dead boy's fist, and clasp the cold knotted muscles of it against my palms.

It depends on what I do with it, I think. *It can serve Yahweh more than one way. . . .*

"Take back what you've done!" I bellow.

For a moment, it hesitates above me. Then the open mouth plunges downward. Behind me, I hear Gund yell.

The creature's jaws fasten onto the grinning rictus of the boy's face. The muscles of the scaly throat ripple unnaturally.

Then I look up, and find Gund beside me. In his hand is a heavy broken treebranch. But his hand is not moving. I follow his gaze down to the dust of the road before us, where the snake writhes in frantic curves and circles. After long moments, it seems to regain its balance a little, and twists rather drunkenly off among the *kathara* plants.

I remain kneeling, clasping the boy's clenched fist, feeling utterly empty. I hear my voice speaking, though it is not my voice. "One punishment," it says. "Only one punishment. Then only one reward."

Then I wait, knowing what will happen. After a little while, the boy's fist slowly unclenches in my hands.

277

XLVI.

A vision of Yerushalayim, after the death of Yeshua:

Foolishness, I think, through the red-and-black haze of my mood. If Shimon the Rock were going to call a meeting, why wouldn't he at least have called it in another town, in some place safer? But Shimon never was the brainiest among us. The meeting place had to be in Yerushalayim, in the same upper room. . . .

Not that it matters. If Rome wants us, Rome will find us. It certainly wouldn't be safer for us to go back to our homes—those of us who ever had homes. Perhaps the safest place would be in the hills, with Bar Abba and the Zealots—hardly a way of life likely to end in old age. And if I go to the outlaws, I will have to kill. After the way Yeshua has died, that would be the final betrayal, the final mockery. I will not give men the satisfaction of killing them, of killing like them.

Not that what I do matters.

Not that we matter. Pilate probably recognizes that. He wasn't that enthusiastic about the whole matter from the beginning, from what I've heard. He will probably just let us kick a little and die, like the headless body that we are.

Perhaps Shimon is right. Perhaps Yerushalayim is as good a place as any—perhaps better, because they would expect us to run away from here, as if we still had hope of something.

Not that it matters. Not that anything matters.

Still, some tiny part of me assumes that it does. Perhaps out of habit, I cautiously decide to circle the city and enter through the Dung Gate, which is more carelessly guarded than most. The path to that gate leads through the smoky valley of Ge-Hinnam, where the trash of the city is dumped. I enter the depression from its mouth in the Valley of Kidron, and pick my way carefully past heaps of rotten vegetables, animal bones and rags, as well as the browning heaps of flowers and palm fronds from the Passover festival. A few of the piles smolder half-heartedly, still damp at their cores from the rain. At one point, I step over a dog's corpse, bloated and grinning, and the part of me that still cares notes that I should be cautious about scavenging dogs and beggars in this place. That thought rouses me somewhat—enough to realize that people are nearby.

I hear their voices first, among the garbage piles:

"That's the last of it, Adonai curse it. Five loads!"

"I'm only glad it happens once a year."

"Twice. There's the Feast of Booths, too, and that's even worse to clean up after."

I stop, listening. They seem very close, but the confusion of trash heaps and boulders makes it difficult to pick out the direction.

"I don't know. It seems to me that the storm on the Shabbat evening left a bigger mess than usual at the Temple."

A short pause. . . . "That it did," the first voice agrees.

"Did you hear about the tomb?"

"Which rumor?"

"That something disappeared from it."

"I heard that somebody's guards got drunk and hacked something up for spite, and then hid it to keep people from getting even madder, if that's what you mean. Not a good subject. Important people don't like it discussed."

"Yes." The second man's voice has a strange quaver, like something wild choking on a leash.

The two are on my left, I realize; they must be resting behind a pile of trash.

Then they stand up, in full view.

Act unconcerned, I think, resuming my pace.

But the smaller of the two men is staring at me.

"Oh, Adonai," he says. "It's him. It's HIM!"

For a moment the three of us stand frozen. Then the larger man turns, stumbles on a cow-bone, recovers, and runs.

The second man still stands there. I get a long glance at his face—disbelieving, hysterical—before he falls forward, whimpering. "Adonai protect me," he grovels. "Save me. . . . "

"From what?" I ask brazenly, to mask my own confusion. But my voice squeaks.

"From . . . from . . . Adonai protect. . . . "

Suddenly the pieces lock together like a good carpentry joint: the frightened face I've just glimpsed; another face, a few days before . . . the same. This terrified servant is the man who'd tripped Yeshua on the path to Golgotha.

"Adonai . . . protect . . . this demon . . . Adonai forgive me. . . ." he babbles.

"For what?" I try to ask coldly. But my voice is wrong again—too soft.

He stops whimpering for a moment. "Are you a demon?" he asks, not looking at me.

"Hardly," I reply, but the sarcasm slips from my voice.

"Forgive me . . . they made me. . . . "

"They didn't make you."

"I had to. . . . "

"You didn't have to." I try to keep the sureness in my unruly vocal chords, as I back quietly away.

"But you said the Temple would fall! They said you were from Shaitan!"

Then I know. I've been mistaken for Yeshua again. I pause. "Am I from Shaitan?" I ask the poor slave before me. "Were they right?"

He is wearing a long-tasseled prayer shawl, I suddenly realize. He is a Pharisee. And from his other garments, he appears to be a servant of some wealthy priest's family—the slave of Sadducees, still wearing his wretched shawl, still hauling garbage for it.

"Were they right?" I repeat.

He shudders. Then, for a long moment, he seems to hang in stasis.

"No!" he explodes. "I didn't know. I didn't know. Forgive me. . . ."

I stare down at him: poor wretch, ugly slave, with nothing left but his proud fanaticism—and now, not even that.

281

"You're forgiven," I tell him.

I leave him sobbing, then, and pick my way toward the Dung Gate with renewed care. Now I have a purpose. . . .

XLVII.

There is only one figure in the room when I arrive. Twilight is fading rapidly into darkness, but the other man has not lighted a lamp. He sits hunched in a far corner, so that I don't even notice him until I'm well into the room with the lamp I've borrowed from downstairs.

"*Shalom,* Mattathias," I greet him.

He raises his head, but his body doesn't move. "Teoma," he says. "*Shalom.* I didn't think you'd come."

"Why not?" I answer. "What else can we do, now?"

"You've heard the stories?" he asks, unenthusiastically.

"Yes. I started some of them."

That reply should have provoked something. But he doesn't react. "I nearly didn't come, myself," he says, looking down again.

"Why not?" I ask politely.

"I'm not sure I could face Yeshua, even if he came back from the dead." Suddenly his voice is no longer dull. It quavers.

"Why?" I ask. "Because you ran away? We all did that. I heard that Shimon the Rock denied even knowing Yeshua."

But Mattathias shakes his head violently. "Ruth," he says.

"What happened to her?"

"Nothing. Everything. We ran out of the city together, the night it happened. We were trying to go back to Yericho. But Ruth fell over a stone and hurt her leg, so we spent the night in an olive orchard."

"So?"

"I had her, Teoma. We rutted on the ground like animals, with the whole night watching."

In the part of me that still feels, half a dozen emotions rattle noisily together: shock, disgust, pity, sympathy, perhaps even jealousy. But I am too worn out, too preoccupied, for either condemnations or comforting words. "Why?" I ask him.

"I don't know! Teoma, I have a wife. I left her with her parents and came with Yeshua. I never divorced her. She never looked at another man, so far as I know. She was prettier than Ruth! She may still be. . . . "

"It doesn't matter," I tell him.

"How in this holy city can you say that?" he snaps. "I betrayed my wife! I betrayed Ruth! How can you say that it doesn't matter?" He pauses. "You're right. That night, it didn't matter. Not after what happened. If Yahweh was going to let them do that to an innocent man, then it just didn't matter what we did. I just didn't care."

But the realization has not brought him any peace; he has just traded pain for despair. I stare down at his hunched body, jaundiced and flickering in the lamplight, and think, *maybe I could heal this man—at least cover his wounds for a while. But do I want to, when he'll die later, anyway?*

But I have fought this battle already. If I'm going to go on with my own crazy scheme, with my own temporary escape from the abyss, then I will need this man. I begin asking questions.

"Mattathias, did your wife love you?"

"She was as faithful as any woman could be," he replies, after a moment.

"Yes, but answer my question. Did she love you? Why did she marry you?"

"It was arranged with her parents," he answers, dully. "They were Hellenists; they didn't mind my job, and they liked my prospects. But she never objected. She liked me."

"So she married you from love, or out of obedience, or because she liked your prospects, too?"

"I don't know. Maybe all three. It doesn't matter. Does anything matter?"

No, Mattathias. Not that way. "Mattathias, did you abandon your wife, or did she abandon you? Did you order her to stay behind, or did she refuse to come with you?"

Mattathias pauses, then suddenly sobs. "She wouldn't come!"

"Then she divorced you. It was her hardness of heart, not yours. Send her her papers, and free her."

"But what about Ruth? She trusted me, Teoma!"

"Did you rape her?" I ask, relentlessly.

"No!" He half-rises, then sinks and shakes his head violently, then shakes it slowly. "No."

"Then at worst, you used each other."

285

"But I didn't love her!"

"Carry that through the Dung Gate! You've been looking after her ever since we left her village, and she's rewarded you however she could—mostly with companionship. That night, you two needed each other more than ever, and you didn't have anything to give each other but your bodies."

"But all we gave each other was guilt!" Mattathias stares up at me, his eyes large and wet in the lamplight. "It's not that simple, Teoma. My wife cried when I left her. Ruth cried in the olive grove. Teoma, I've lost my house, my family, my love—everything but guilt. . . . "

"So take your guilt to the Temple tomorrow and trade it for stones, if you want," I tell him. "I won't cast any, but I'm sure other people would. Just make sure you don't trade Ruth as well. She's skinny and wrinkled, but she's worth more than any guilt."

"You make everything too simple," mutters Mattathias. But he lapses into silence. I seat myself in another corner, and let him think.

One by one, the others drift in: Philippos, Nathan'el, Ya'akob, Yehuda bar Ya'akob, Shimon the Zealot. "Where's Ishkerioth?" Nathan'el asks the Zealot as he enters.

"He hanged himself," Shimon answers.

There is a long silence. "It's your fault," Nathan'el tells the Zealot.

"No, it's not. Yehuda deserved it," Shimon snaps back.

"And you don't?" bristles Nathan'el.

"Yehuda was a fool," returns the Zealot. "If he'd just told us in time, we could have packed the square with supporters, the way Bar Abba's men did. If he'd just told us. . . ."

286

"If he'd just not kissed Yeshua on the cheek to start with!" exclaims Ya'akob, entering the fray.

"If you hadn't fallen asleep on the job, old man," retorts the Zealot, "you could have warned him in time!"

"It wouldn't have mattered," interrupts Philippos. "None of it would have mattered. He knew there was a traitor, remember? He knew we'd fail him. He didn't want to save himself, and he wouldn't have let us save him. Don't you remember? All of those clues he left us, all those words. He wanted to die."

"No, he didn't," I nearly tell them. But the moment isn't quite right, yet, although I feel myself coiling. *How ironic,* I think, *that I may end up as the* Meshiha *after all.*

Yohan has come into the room, quietly, while the others were arguing. He seats himself in the corner by Mattathias; in the lamplight, his eyes still look feverish. "I have my mother back," he tells Mattathias. "I always wanted her to come back. But I never thought she would have grey hair, or arthritic hands. I didn't know she would be crying."

"But why would he want to die?" the Zealot is demanding, meanwhile. "We were winning! In another week. . . ."

"Maybe that was why he wanted to die," interrupts Ya'akob. "In another week, you and your friends might have had Yerushalayim in flames. He said the Temple was going to fall. Maybe he let them kill him, to prevent that."

"Careful, old man," says Shimon the Zealot.

"You be careful!" erupts Mattathias from his corner. I stare at him in surprise. "Some of us didn't come to him because we loved Israel," he rushes onward. "I never loved Israel. Just him."

287

There is a shocked pause. Little Mattathias, taking on the Zealot? Even Mattathias realizes what he has done, after a moment; he subsides into his corner and looks angrily away.

The Zealot ignores him. "You think we were a threat to Israel, then?" he asks Ya'akob. "You're siding with the Sadducees, with the Sanhedrin?"

"It's not that simple," replies Ya'akob, tiredly.

I feel a dull anger for poor Mattathias. *We aren't brethren,* I think. *Some of us have given up land and fishing boats—but the ones who owned them are still the ones who can talk.*

"Yosef the Arimathaean, who gave his family tomb for Yeshua, is on the Sanhedrin," continues Ya'akob. "Cleopas, who owns this house, is a Sadducee. It wasn't any one faction that night. It wasn't even the whole High Council. It was a rump court, a few powerful, frightened men. . . ."

"No!" interrupts his brother Yohan. "No! We're all to blame! Not just those men! Not Pilate! All of us! We made him die!"

Now, I think. *The center of the world is here.*

"Yohan's right," I tell them. My voice doesn't crack.

"Oh, really?" snorts the Zealot. "So how are you to blame?"

But I am not Mattathias, to be so easily crushed. I think, *the secret of winning an argument is to tell the truth, and smile at how deadly it is.*

"I could have stopped Yehuda Ishkerioth," I tell the Zealot. "I could have talked him out of it. But I let him go off to find the priests, and I went to sleep."

The Zealot is caught off balance by this. He hesitates. That is enough.

"I killed him by hating," I continue. "I hated Yehuda, I hated everyone—even Yeshua, sometimes. I am an expert at hate. So are you, Shimon. Listen to your own voice."

Silence. Shimon stands paralyzed, afraid to speak, afraid of what he will hear.

"We all failed him. No wonder he wanted to die," says Philippos, finally.

"No, he didn't," I reply.

"What?"

"He let them kill him, but he didn't want to die. He was trying to live." I pause, expecting a challenge. The Zealot glowers, but holds his silence; the rest are too flabbergasted or too despondent. I plunge onward. "He was breaking the rules again. He always broke the rules: loved when he was supposed to hate, ate when he was supposed to fast, forgave when he was supposed to get even. 'You want your life?' he said. 'Lose it.' He finally had to try that out. He just lost. . . . Don't you see? He was trying to strain the world until it broke open. But the world . . . maybe he almost succeeded . . . but the world just opened a crack, and swallowed him."

"Maybe he did succeed," says Philippos, hesitantly. "My father said he saw Yeshua on the road outside the city. He said Yeshua spoke to them, and said he'd come back."

"Had your father ever seen Yeshua before?" I ask him.

"Yes . . . no—yes, he had, from a distance. He said he didn't recognize Yeshua at first. That's why I didn't believe him then, but . . . but. . . ."

"He could have seen anyone, then," I answer. "He could have seen some country prophet. He could have seen me." Then I stand up in my corner. The lamplight plays dimly across my face: my long, straight nose, my heavy eyebrows.

Perhaps Mattathias glimpses what I have in mind. Perhaps he is just afraid for his friend. "Teoma, please don't," he whispers.

"He's dead," I tell them. "They stuck a spear in his lungs. He's dead. And we're going to die, too. One by one, by accident or murder, by fever or old age or crucifixion, we're going to die somehow. We can overthrow the Romans and we'll still die. We can live like hermits, like prophets, like Essenes or Pharisees, and we'll still die. I thought maybe Yeshua might have found a way out, a way through to Yahweh. But if he couldn't, we certainly aren't going to."

"He's alive!"

Shimon the Rock has finally arrived, along with his brother Andreas and Yehuda Thaddai and Ya'akob the son of Alphaos. Shimon's face looks drawn but smiling, and his eyes are wider open than they should be. "I saw him!" he says, rushing into the center of the room, tripping over Nathan'el in the process.

"Who did you see?" I ask.

Shimon glances toward my corner; then he stares. His eyes go even wider. Then I step out into the lamplight.

"Oh, it's you, Teoma," breathes the fisherman. "I saw Yeshua!"

"When?"

"Last night!"

"Did you recognize him when you first saw him?"

"No, but. . . ."

"He's dead, Shimon," I tell him, and start past him to shut the door.

"So why don't we all just die, too?" says Shimon the Zealot, grabbing my leg. "Why don't we just hang ourselves, and get it over with?"

"Because he doesn't have to be dead for everyone," I answer. "We may not have any hope left, but we can let others hope. We can *act* as if we had hope. I've already started rumors with my face. I could appear again, a few times, a few days. Then I could go away—go as far as I could, so no one would know when I died."

"But he's alive!" Shimon the Rock bursts out again. "I saw him! Miryam saw him!"

"Did Miryam recognize him when she saw him? Or did she decide it was him, afterwards? You *want* to believe, Shimon. You saw *someone,* and. . . . "

"He's alive," he repeats, stubbornly.

"If he's alive," I retort, "*then who raised him?* Wanting* just isn't enough. Maybe if one of us truly, completely believed, if he didn't doubt at all, then maybe he could raise Yeshua, the way Yeshua raised Lazaros. But is anyone here that strong? Are you, Shimon bar Yona? I heard what you did the night of the trial."

"He's alive," repeats Shimon, but there are tears in his eyes. "Maybe if you believed. . . . "

"No, Shimon," I tell him. "I'm sorry. I couldn't believe unless I touched the nail-wounds in his wrists. But maybe someday, if we keep the secret, someone will

291

believe enough. I don't know. I just know that we might as well act as if there's a way beyond death, whether there is or not."

But Shimon isn't looking at me. His eyes are fixed on the doorway behind me.

There is terror in his eyes, and wonder. . . .